MADE OF STEAM AND STARDUST

BIANCA BREEN

Stag Beetle Books

ONE

WElcomE tO mY world
chAotiC, isN'T It?
ThIs iS whAt I WaNt
THis is WHaT i dO
I waTCH theM sUFfer
I wATch TheM BuRN

A SCREAM TORE THROUGH THE FACTORY.

Gerdie flinched at the sound, but she didn't look up from the sheet of dull metal that was waiting to be cut to size on her workbench. She knew where the scream came from: one of the girls cleaning the Trunk machines as the end of the working day neared. The machines were never turned off: to do so would cost money, after all.

The girl's scream reduced to a whimper as an Action marched over, but every single worker in the Sweene & Sons factory – all one hundred of them – knew the girl would receive no sympathy.

From the corner of her eye, Gerdie watched an Action lean down to inspect the girl's hand.

'Who will finish cleaning the Trunks now?' The Action's voice was muffled slightly.

The question was rhetorical, and directed at the girl only, but Gerdie shot her hand into the air. 'I'll do it!'

The factory went silent. Even the machines seemed to dull their usual roar. Gerdie kept her eyes downcast as the heavy footsteps of a guard tread toward her in time to the ticking of the clock. His precise movements, along with the gleaming silver mask that marked the Actions as Conqueror Seki's personal guard, made him seem like an automaton, programmed to obey the conqueror's every whim.

She smelled the Action as he neared, a mixture of sweat and metal. How could they stand to wear those masks every day?

He stopped behind her. 'Go on then, girl.'

Gerdie swallowed as she left the workbench, scurrying past the Action.

As she made her way to the back of the room, she glanced upwards, as if pulled by Leo's gaze. He was there, of course, no doubt drawn by the scream, looking down at her from behind the soot-stained glass of the overseer's office. He shook his head at her. *No*, he mouthed. But she turned her head away and kept walking.

Attention was already off her as everyone turned back to their work. If they didn't produce daily quota, they wouldn't be paid, even if it was only a measly 4 ki each for adults, 2 ki for those under eighteen.

She was about to pass the injured girl, but she couldn't look at her. Out of the corner of her eye she knew the girl was clutching her hand to her chest, that it was shining with red. All of Gerdie's nerve was spent putting one foot in front of the other, because if it went wrong...

It wouldn't. It *couldn't.*

Slowly, carefully, she reached into her pocket, heart beating a bruising rhythm that she might be caught. The small metal cylinder tucked in there was smooth and cold against her palm. As she passed other workers at their benches, their rasping coughs made her cringe sympathetically, and she tightened her hold on the metal sphere. This had to work. There *had* to be a better way to keep these machines going while they were cleaned that didn't involve injury or death to those who worked them. She would invent a better way.

She curled her fingers around it as she pulled it out, careful to keep the metal hidden from sight. The cylinder was easily the brightest thing in the Sweene & Sons factory, the silver sparkly as diamonds.

Okay, Mechanical Obstruction Remover Tool version 2.0. Please work better than your predecessor. And reach a better fate. She shuddered as she remembered the sounds of last time, of metal grinding against metal, and the small explosion that had soon followed. It had taken days to collect the shattered remains of the original M.O.R.T., days of scurrying around the factory floor when the guards' backs were turned. The pieces of poor original M.O.R.T. were still shoved away in her satchel back at the orphanage, waiting to be used for another invention.

The machines growled and shook like angry dogs as they produced the metal sheets she worked on all day. Once the sheets were measured and cut by the workers, they were sent to another factory to be painted and textured to look like tree bark, then sent on again to cover the turbines that provided oxygen to the capital. The turbines were everywhere, drawing energy from the sun into an artificial photosynthesis beneath their blades to produce oxygen. Gerdie wished she could see the finished product; she had never seen a tree before – they had all been cut down before she was born to build factories and run machines – and the turbines around the old quarry she lived in weren't dressed up to resemble anything they weren't.

Once she reached one of the Trunks, the giant cogs inside turning ominously and rattling like there was something trying to get out, she crouched beside the belt and slipped the M.O.R.T. onto it.

'You know what to do!' she whispered.

The M.O.R.T. twitched, rolling from side to side. Two tiny, spindly arms emerged from its body, stretching like it had just awoken from a long nap. It must have felt as if it had: the M.O.R.T. had been tucked away in her pocket for days. Two stumpy legs poked out from the bottom – they'd keep the M.O.R.T.'s grip steady while its thin arms reached hard-to-get places within the machinery. The rounded top of the M.O.R.T. was connected to its cylindrical body by two screws that incidentally looked like eyes, though one was almost twice the size of the other.

Hey, beggars couldn't be choosers. She'd done her best with what she could find.

As it staggered down the belt and closer to the heart of the Trunk, the glowing fire reflected against the M.O.R.T.'s shiny surface so that it looked like it was burning too. But it wouldn't, not with the metal she'd used. Kolimant was one of the strongest materials mined on Treshane, and luckily, one of the most accessible. Heat resistance was the first lesson she'd received from her father when he started to teach her the invention trade. If Dad were alive to see the M.O.R.T., she knew he would be proud.

But if Dad were alive, you would not be stuck at the factory.

Gerdie tapped her fingers against her knee as she glanced anxiously around, but everyone was still hunched over their benches. Under the cavernous, smoke-stained ceiling, the big hanging clocked ticked to five. A whistle blared. She still had a few minutes of cover under the commotion of the hundred workers filing toward the door, eager to collect their money for the day.

'Come on, M.O.R.T.,' she muttered under her breath.

Whorls of black smoke billowed out from the Trunk, loosened from the cog-filled corners inside. She jumped to her feet with a triumphant cry, punching both hands in the air. Her invention worked! The M.O.R.T. was cleaning the machine so that she and the other children didn't have to. No more heat exhaustion, no more dehydration, no more crushed fingers. Gerdie beamed. She could create hundreds of Mechanical Obstruction Remover Tool version 2.0s, distribute them across the continent of Treshane, maybe even all of Bellona. She'd be world famous, known everywhere as a genius – the best inventor on the planet at only sixteen!

Then the usual rattling stopped. The machine fell deathly silent.

Oh no. Not again.

The machine roared into life again with such a noise that Gerdie covered her ears. Something small and silver shot from the machine and through the smoke with a high-pitched whistle that sounded like a metallic scream. The M.O.R.T. hit the opposite wall with a *clang* before disappearing behind a stack of shipping crates.

Gerdie made to run after it, but some of the adult workers were already making their way over to the spluttering Trunk and closing in around her fast. The machine shook violently, black smoke billowing from every gap. Gerdie ducked behind the closest workbench, hoping to make her way to the front of the factory before anyone realised she was the one responsible for damaging another machine. Two large hands grabbed her roughly under the armpits, hauling her off the ground until she was level with a silver mask, the dark eyes behind it narrowed.

Ah, cogs.

Gerdie fidgeted in the spindly seat opposite Bertram Peller's scuffed desk. She was alone in his office; he was conversing outside with the Action who had thwarted her escape, their rumbly voices making her stomach flutter with apprehension. If the incident with the Trunk machine was deemed as an accident, her pay would be docked for repairs, or she'd be forced to clean the Trunks – and they'd still be operating: to turn them off would cost money, after all. If they believed she'd done it on purpose, she'd be treated as all adversaries of the country were treated: the Core. She'd only ever heard rumours about the Core, the conqueror's exclusive punishment, but what she did know was that *if* those sent returned, it was with one limb less than they'd left with.

A portrait of Conqueror Seki hung above the overseer's desk, held in place by a thick gilded frame. The conqueror was a big man, bald, and his eyes were dark and hard. His likeness was painted in a red and gold military uniform, a long gun at his side, staring down at Gerdie like she was a bug beneath his shoe. He looked... inhuman. Now, she wasn't one to judge appearances – how could she be, with the pink-purple birthmark that covered the right half of her face from temple to chin? – but there was something alien about him that she could never quite put her finger on. He grew up in Trumble, apparently, an old city in the next state over, but no one who might have known him there was alive anymore to say.

The door of the overseer's office opened, and Bertram Peller entered. He didn't acknowledge her as he came around the desk and lowered himself into his chair, bony hands clutching a clipboard, spindly glasses slipping down his long nose.

'So, 4926,' he said, small eyes on his clipboard, his voice coarse like a hinge in need of oiling..

'My name is Gertrude,' she mumbled.

Peller ignored her. 'This is the second disturbance you've caused during your time here with us.' He finally looked up. 'Why do you hold such disrespect for Conqueror Seki?'

Because someone has to make a change around here, and he's done nothing for us.

'I don't, sir,' she said. 'It was an accident, and I'm very sorry.'

Peller peered at her for so long she started fidgeting again. Finally, he said, 'I'm withholding your pay for three days to assist in paying for damages.'

Gerdie loosened the breath she'd been holding, her heart sinking. The punishment could have been much worse, but three days with no pay meant she'd have no spare money to buy parts for her next invention. She didn't have time to waste as it was.

'And if you cause such a disturbance again, you will be removed from the company,' Peller continued. 'Is that clear? Good. You're dismissed.' He made a salute with his right hand, five fingers to signify giving the conqueror your all, thumb bouncing off forehead. 'Hail Seki.'

Gerdie returned the gesture, but with little enthusiasm. 'Hail Seki,' she repeated glumly.

She left Peller's office, head hung, and nearly bumped into Leo, who was peering around the corner, listening in.

'I tried to tell you,' he said. Then, more sympathetically, 'It didn't work, then?'

'I blame the Trunk,' she said. 'The M.O.R.T. *was* working, I swear it.'

The corners of Leo's mouth turned down with disappointment. His skin was a shade of brown that always made Gerdie think of a sheet of hammered bronze, and his dark hair was thick and wavy. His right eye was brown, but his left eye was a light grey green. This fascinated Gerdie, like someone had run out of parts as they made his eyes and grabbed the nearest thing they could find. They were so lovely, but Leo was always looking down, hiding them.

'We'll find a way,' he said as they made for the stairs. His right leg, a metal prosthetic, squeaked as they walked. The prosthetic was stamped with a black *T* for traitor. He had never told her where the prosthetic came from, but her theory was that his parents had been part of the rebellion, the Cats, killed for their actions, and that Leo was guilty by association. 'Do you need any more parts?'

'I'm not sure yet. I didn't have a chance to retrieve the M.O.R.T. For all I know, the Actions found it and threw it out.' Her heart sunk at the thought.

'I'll look for it,' Leo said kindly.

She gave him a grateful smile. There were many advantages to being friends with the ward of the factory's overseer, and his after-hours access to the factory to collect her misplaced inventions was just one of them. Leo was only a year older than Gerdie, and they'd met on her second day in the factory, when he'd caught her tinkering with a Trunk; she was trying to find a way to isolate certain parts in the machine to clean them, but without turning off the machine entirely. Instead of reporting her to Peller, Leo had handed her the tools from her bag and asked what else he could do to help.

They stepped out of Sweene & Sons and into the narrow street. The oppressive heat of the day, lingering in pavement and brick, had beads of sweat sprouting on Gerdie's upper lip. The wind offered no respite: when it blew, it felt like standing in front of an oven and opening the door. Red brick buildings rose tall and close on either side, topped only by several cranes and a blanket of smoke. Rising even further above was a turbine, its enormous rusty silver blades lazily revolving horizontally. If only they worked to reduce air pollution. Maybe if she...

Gerdie shook her head. One step at a time.

She and Leo turned left, toward the train station. Leo lived close to the factory, apparently, but usually walked her to the station; sometimes it was their only chance to talk. The narrow main street of Balthasar was crowded as people tried to get home. Old cars rattled past, beeping impatiently, and streetlights flickered on, dropping a murky yellow light onto it all.

Leo cleared his throat and handed her a handkerchief. Taking the hint, she caught sight of her reflection in the darkened window of a closed teashop. Her red hair had come loose from its braid and spiraled around her head, her glasses nearly lost in it, her face so smudged black with smoke and sweat that her port wine stain birthmark was barely visible. Well, small mercies.

'Thanks,' Gerdie said, and rubbed the handkerchief across her face. It smelled of lemon and paper. She held it back toward him, now covered in black.

He eyed it warily. 'Keep it.'

Gerdie shrugged, shoving it into her pocket. She turned to ask him if he was going to the Trumble Day celebrations this year when she noticed the corners of his mouth were more turned down than usual.

'What's wrong?'

'Do you...' He sighed, shaking his head.

'What?' she prompted.

He hesitated only for a moment before saying brightly, 'I started reading a new book the other day. It was really popular on Earth, apparently. It's called Harry -'

'Leo,' she interrupted with exasperation. 'You know that if you want to distract me you don't do it with books, you do it with something I actually care about. Now what's the matter?'

They stopped at a red light. His eyes darted away. 'Do you ever think that maybe the robots aren't going to work?'

'I just need a bit more time,' she said. 'Tiny Spiny Bot and both versions of the M.O.R.T. have not gone to plan, I'll admit, but –'

'That's not what I meant,' he said quietly.

Not this again. Gerdie stared at him. 'Are you giving up?' she demanded. 'You can't give up. Why would you say something like that?'

He shrugged helplessly, still avoiding her gaze.

Anger flared inside her, hot and irrational. This was just like Leo. Though his offers of help were sincere, they were shadowed by doubt and uncertainty, like something was pulling him back no matter how hard he fought against it. Well... he had a right to be afraid, of course. Sometimes she was, too. She just wished he would make up his mind about being in or out instead of the one leg in, one leg out dance he frequently practised.

'You wouldn't give up if you knew what it was like to work in those factories or feel the fear of cleaning a machine while it's still running.'

It was a low blow, and Leo's gaze dropped even further, but right now she didn't care, and what she said was true, anyway. He'd never had to work in the factory. *His* job was paperwork, and though he might find it tedious, at least there was no risk of smoke inhalation or broken fingers. Gerdie bit the inside of her cheek, hand reaching inside her pocket. Her fingers found the warm, rough face of her father's coin. She sighed. 'If you could just get me the M.O.R.T. from the factory, I'll sort out the rest.'

The pedestrian light turned green, and they crossed the street. The sun was sinking behind the skyline of factories, and Bellona's two moons, Maylow and Oriana, were brightening with every passing minute: one yellow, one white, like two mismatched eyes that were always watching the goings on of their mother planet.

Leo stumbled without warning, grabbing hold of Gerdie's arm so tightly she nearly fell with him. Had his prosthetic caught on something? In the boiling heat of the day, his skin inside the prosthetic tended to swell, making his steps rigid. She'd offered to adjust it or make him a new one. They weren't her favourite things to make –those were little domestic-kind robots – but she would do it for Leo. He refused every time.

Leo straightened, and she was about to ask whether he was alright when a familiar voice leered, 'Watch where you're going, hoppy. You're on your last leg, after all.'

The sneering faces of Bryan and Carter Musgrave, brothers with only eleven months between them, blocked Gerdie and Leo's path, forcing the people behind them to steer suddenly with disapproving clucks of their tongues. Gerdie had spent a few years at school with the boys, but just like she had when Dad died, the Musgrave brothers had been forced into a factory when their dad lost an arm in a machinery accident. Their mother had been bedridden for months now with a brain disease.

But that was no excuse for bullying others.

'Get out of our way,' Gerdie tried to growl, but it sounded more like a sigh of inevitability.

The boys had the same mop of brown hair, same long sharp nose and the same bad attitude. Bryan, the older, slightly taller one, held up his middle finger at Leo – the nail was black and spotted with red, but Gerdie didn't think this was entirely the reason for showing him this particular finger.

'Got this on a faulty Trunk,' said Bryan, and Gerdie heard the taunt that coated his words like rust.

'Do you want him to kiss it better?' she asked sweetly.

Bryan narrowed his eyes at her. '*No.* I want him to see

what a *real* job looks like. We don't all get to hide behind the overseer's skirts.'

'It's a tiny boo-boo on your finger, Bryan.'

Leo's eyes were fixed on his shoes, ears darkening red. Gerdie felt guilty for snapping at him earlier now. Things were bad enough for him without his only friend being disappointed in him. Well, she was pretty sure she was his only friend, anyway. She remembered seeing him with a skinny blond boy a few times, but she hadn't seen that boy for a couple of years now. Leo's parents had died when he was younger and someone – foster system, relative, or demon – had thought old, unfeeling Bertram Peller would be perfect for fatherhood.

Where Gerdie's past ordeals fueled her forward, Leo's made him retreat further into his shell.

'You're right,' said Bryan. 'It's just a finger. At least I'm not a cripple like Smeller Junior here.' He elbowed Carter, who dutifully guffawed.

'Alright, that's enough,' snapped Gerdie.

Their nastiness quota met for the day, the brothers turned and ran towards the train station, their laughter quickly lost in the sounds of the street. She'd have to make sure she avoided being in the same carriage as them, though she usually avoided them as much as possible anyway.

'Those guys are rusted parts,' she said to Leo. 'You okay?'

He shrugged her off. 'You'll miss your train,' he mumbled.

Balthasar's train station was a large red-brick building, lined with arched windows and graffitied columns. The giant face of the clock in the centre read 5:45.

Leo stopped by the entrance and the automatic glass doors slid open. 'See you tomorrow?'

Gerdie let her tongue loll out of her mouth as she gave him the conqueror's salute. Leo gasped and grabbed her hand, pulling it down.

'Are you crazy?' he hissed. 'If an Action saw you...'

'Well, good thing they didn't. See you later, comet crater.'

He grimaced in response, but at her meaningful stare he sighed and dutifully responded, 'In a while, engine dial.'

Satisfied, Gerdie ducked into the station. The curved metal-framework ceiling was lined with skylights smoke-blackened on the outside, and electronic boards displayed platform numbers and departure times in flickering orange light. Cafes, luggage shops, and ticket machines stood firm while hundreds of end-of-day commuters swarmed around them. Gerdie walked past all this; she didn't even need to check the number of the platform: the train to Rendip Quarry Station always departed from platform sixteen. She was jostled as she went by people staring at their phone screens, unaware of their surroundings. Gerdie couldn't afford a phone anymore, and even if she could, the reception in the quarry was too bad. She often thought about how much easier life might be if she could post about her inventions on social media.

She continued walking further still, into the oldest part of the station where a single dingy platform was teeming with commuters – most of the factory workers lived in the old quarry. No one spoke; the only sounds were the occasional faint *whoosh* from the trains on other platforms, and the constant coughing that came from days spent at the factories.

In a few minutes, the train's dim yellow light illuminated the tunnel. It slowed as it approached, rattling so violently it was as if it were about to break away and disintegrate. But it didn't; it wheezed to a halt along the platform and sank a little into the tracks, eventually creaking open its doors. The set of carriage doors Gerdie stood in front of stopped halfway open, and she was forced to wrench them the rest of the way and squeeze inside.

She found a seat and slumped against the scratchy torn material, pulling her satchel around to rest on her lap, feeling the loose pieces shift around inside, clattering and tinkling amongst themselves.

One time, when the train broke down just as it began its descent into the quarry, it was five hours before anyone from Balthasar Station knew about it. Gerdie and the other passengers had waited, acting on the instructions that crackled barely audibly through the train speakers. But after over an hour with no development, some passengers got out and began to walk, and Gerdie had wondered whether she should too, but fell asleep instead. When they finally got the train moving again, weaving down the sides of the quarry, the sun was beginning to lighten the horizon, and Gerdie barely had time to run to the orphanage and brush her teeth before she was back on the same train and returning to the factory.

Thankfully, the train ran smoothly that night. Well, as smooth as it could over uneven tracks and squeaky, shuddering wheels. Again, she wished she still had her phone. After Dad died, she couldn't afford the data plan, so she sold the mobile phone for a bit of money. She missed playing *Fantasy Park 2* and hoped her dragons were doing well.

Gerdie let her chin drop to her chest and closed her eyes, but the train rattled too violently for her to doze. And someone in the next carriage was coughing and coughing and coughing. Gerdie winced in sympathy. *Just hold on*, she thought. *Things will get better.*

Not for the first time, she thought of Earth. It must have had super clean air. She'd have to look over some books on Earth for ideas on how to clean the air of pollution.

When the train shuddered to a halt at the bottom of the quarry, an automated voice announced over the speakers in a static voice that they'd reached Rendip.

As Gerdie followed the crowd out of the station, she thought of the girl in the factory, her hand glistening red. Life-changing injuries happened so quickly. *Death* happened so quickly. One day Dad had been there, pouring too much maple-flavoured syrup on his pancakes and making her laugh until her stomach hurt, and the next day he was gone.

The lump in her throat squeezed its way into her chest, and she sniffed, blinking back tears.

Gerdie let her legs carry her up the broken escalator and into the sticky evening, let them take the familiar path down narrow Slate Street to Miss Wyatt's House for Waifs that had been her home for almost a year. The rocky quarry walls encircled her, tall and steep, and just visible above them were the pointed black chimneys of Balthasar's outer factories, spewing their steady stream of smoke. She passed a few houses and an old crumbling corner shop until she reached the orphanage. The wonky old building had once been a row of miners' houses, but the walls inside had been knocked down to make one building. The exterior walls were still painted four different colours, though, which Gerdie loved. She let herself in and into the kitchen, grabbing whatever she could find, which ended up being a small bowl of dry rice and dehydrated chicken. She gagged as it made its way down, but her body needed it. Then she climbed the cramped creaky stairs to the room she shared with five other orphans, eyes itching with tiredness.

As she climbed into bed, muscles aching, she let the tears come, sliding down her face in a steady stream.

She would not end up like the girl in the factory. She would become not only an inventor recognised by the Inventor's Guild, but a world-famous one at that. She was *not* going to die like a factory worker, coughing up years of smoke and hard labour, surrounded by strangers. And though she missed her dad, she was *not* going to join him with the Angels so soon.

Her life was going to count for something, and her name would be among the stars.

Two

Gerdie lay in bed, staring up at the dark ceiling and listening to the rasping sounds of five children with pollution-induced respiratory problems. Her tears had either run out of momentum or run out altogether. Whichever came first, she supposed. She tossed left, rolled right, then sighed, accepting that sleep wasn't going to come so easily. She turned to face the bed left of hers. It was empty and cold, not yet filled after Henry's death. He'd been gone two months now, killed in a boiler explosion two factories down from Sweene & Sons.

Set just beyond the empty bed was a small, uncurtained window, and the only view was the looming side of the quarry, topped by the darkened silhouettes of the Balthasar factories. Even here she couldn't get away from them. They surrounded her, and felt as though they were closing in, limiting any chance of escape. *This is your life*, they seemed to say. *We are your life. We will always be here.*

Gerdie flopped over onto her back, releasing a frustrated huff of air. She flung out an arm toward the bedside table, feeling for her coin. It was the last thing Dad had given her before he died. It wasn't much: it fit comfortably in the palm of her hand, a dull bronze with five bumpy edges, and both faces etched with markings Gerdie couldn't read, but it was still better than the large bald profile of Conqueror Seki stamped on both sides of each ki coin.

This coin was everything to her; it was all that was left of Dad and the life she'd had before he died. Actions had come and taken everything else when she hadn't been able to pay the rent on their house.

Every time she'd asked Dad about the coin, he told her a different story about its origins and how it had come to be in his possession, so that even she didn't know the true story. Maybe it was none of them. Maybe it was all of them.

'This is a coin from the Angels,' went one of the stories, and she could hear his gentle voice as if he were right beside her, picture his callous, grease-stained hands and thick greying hair. *'They say once in a thousand years an Angel comes down to Bellona. They make sure everything runs smoothly down here. But they secretly enjoy human comforts. They would drink and gamble, and have – well, I'll tell you the rest when you're older. Or, on the second thought, never. Anyway... some of the Angels can be tricky.'*

'Like Bian and Brone!' Gerdie had exclaimed, excited to remember something she learnt in school, even though her class had already moved on from Angels to the first colonies of Bellona.

'The very same. Bian and Brone came down one night, seeking mischief-'

'As usual,' Gerdie giggled.

'And just like you.' Her father tickled her, and she rolled around in her bed. *'Don't think I've forgotten to talk to you about the trick you played on poor Mr. Tulk last week. Anyway, Bian and Brone had come down to gamble and brought with them huge bags of gold coins. But the coins weren't real, they would disappear after a few hours, once the Angels had long left*

*Bellona. So, Bian and Brone gambled all night, and they
cheated, of course, but so the cards favoured the humans. And the
humans laughed and cheered with joy at the riches they believed
they were winning, with no idea that in the morning the gold in
their pockets would be gone. But a real Angel coin had accidentally made its way into the bag of fake riches, and a man named
Jay Hendersen won it in a game of poker. I met Hendersen at
the Balthasar Sunday market, where he was betting that no one
could solve the Wooden Goliath Puzzle faster than he could.'*

'And?' Gerdie asked eagerly, enraptured by the story.

Dad grinned. 'And I bet I could.'

A small, delicate noise brought her out of her reverie, and
she listened hard, heart skipping a beat. It was coming from
the window. She ripped off the covers and sprang to the
window, where something was tapping at the glass with two
thin metal legs.

'M.O.R.T.!' she exclaimed joyfully. 'You're alive!'

'Shut up, Gerdie,' someone mumbled from the other side
of the room.

She lifted the window as high as she could, which wasn't
much: the pane was stuck shut with years of soot and grit that
wafted down the quarry walls from the factories. But it was
enough for the M.O.R.T. to slip through and fall into her
outstretched hands. It must have escaped before Leo could
find it. She felt it relax against her palm, folding its stumpy legs
beneath it and releasing a soft whistle that sounded like a
relieved sigh. She'd placed a GPS tracker in the robot, but since
she'd taken the device from an old Apple mesSENDer bot
she'd found in the junkyard, she hadn't been sure until now
that it was actually going to work. She examined the M.O.R.T.
in the dim light. A bit scuffed and black in places, but it had
survived the pressure within the Trunk machine. Her heart
soared. With a bit of tweaking, the M.O.R.T. would be
perfect. She retrieved her shoes from under her bed, already

making a mental list of materials and equipment. She'd need polyrekovene first, a soft plastic with a suction cup effect, which would prevent the M.O.R.T. being fired out of the machine again. She knew exactly where to find it. She grabbed her satchel, gently placing the M.O.R.T. inside, where it was nestled amid pieces of scrap metal and her few inventing tools and notebooks. She hoped it wouldn't notice it was among parts of dead ancestors.

Gerdie crept down the rickety stairs to the ground floor of the orphanage, trying to keep quiet but never quite remembering which stairs creaked. Not that it really mattered; Miss Wyatt, the matron, snored so loudly she could sleep through a factory explosion, and once she actually had.

The front door was locked, but Gerdie had already pulled a thin, curved piece of wire a little longer than a bobby pin from her satchel and slotted it into the keyhole.

A stair groaned behind her, and she whipped around. Pat was on the last step, a glass of water in his hand. In the weak light from the streetlamp outside, she could just make out his striped dressing gown.

'What are you doing?' he whispered.

'Leaving,' Gerdie replied, turning back to the door and wiggling the hook, listening for the sweet *click* of success.

'What about curfew?' he hissed.

Gerdie rolled her eyes. 'Pooh-pooh the curfew. This is Rendip, not New Londinium. Conqueror Seki probably doesn't even know we exist down here.'

'I'm going back to bed,' Pat grumbled. She didn't miss the quick salute he'd made at Seki's name. 'I don't fancy being locked in the Core for aiding and abetting.'

Gerdie relaxed her grip on the pick to glance at Pat over her shoulder. His rat-like face was screwed up, making his pointed nose look so much more pronounced that she could almost see whiskers twitching at the end of it.

'But if it makes your arm fall off, think about the mechanical arm you could get instead. That would be so cool. Imagine all the nose-picking you could do because your arm would never get tired.'

Pat let out a disgusted groan. 'You are so weird. I never saw you, okay? Enjoy your mechanical arm.'

'I will,' she chirped, and whipped back around to continue fiddling.

Pat disappeared up the stairs, and after a few seconds the lock clunked, the door handle loosening. She slipped out into the warm night.

Even this late, Rendip was never quiet. The sleeping machines of the factories above the quarry still purred softly despite no one being there to man them. Tall, iron lamp posts glowed dully along the street, and grit and smog floated in their light like swarms of midges. Though it wasn't visible during the day, you could taste the dirty air like iron in your mouth. Feel it on your skin, in your hair, gritty and greasy and gross. She followed the cracked footpath along Slate Street, jumping and weaving through its jagged path lined with other old miners' houses. Even by the dim glow of the streetlamps, Gerdie knew her way. She had travelled this path so many times before.

The concrete footpath was soft where it was plastered with leaflets. The official proclamations were often distributed around Rendip, the most unfairly treated town in all Treshane, maybe even in all of Bellona.

The most recent leaflets – still white, not yet ground into the concrete – read:

With the expansion of Treshane's northern districts, Olvic and Jumper Top, the production rate of Trunks has now been doubled. Every able-bodied man, woman and child, must report to your closest factory for work. Those who are not able-bodied must report to factories for tasks such as reception, management, and marketing.

The leaflets were spongy underfoot as she walked on them. Coloured television pictures flashed through the thinly curtained windows of the flat, semi-detached houses she passed. Sometimes she watched the programs through the windows, out of sight of the inhabitants within, but there was no time for that tonight.

The dim lights of Ada's house were on, as Gerdie knew they would be. She wasn't entirely sure that Ada ever slept at all. In the days when Dad was alive, and he'd worked late into the night at Seki's fortress in New Londinium, or the Inventors Guild in Balthasar, she would stay the night at Ada's. Gerdie wasn't even sure how her father and Ada knew each other; Ada had always just been there, a constant presence in Gerdie's life. She was the genius behind Lucerna's Six-in-One Alarm Clock and several of the big tech brand's other products. A great inventor.

Well, she used to be, anyway.

Last year, Ada and Dad had been working on 'their most important project yet', but whenever Gerdie asked about it now, Ada's eyes would fill with tears and she would turn away, so Gerdie stopped asking. And, during those times Gerdie stayed the night, no matter what time during the dawn hours she wandered into the kitchen to get a glass of water or a dry biscuit, Ada would be in the armchair by the window, staring up at the stars like she was waiting for something.

Gerdie climbed the first two steps of the townhouse when her foot kicked something, sending it flying and then crashing into the front door. The tinkling of broken china was followed by the splashing of liquid, and when a pleasant, herbal smell reached Gerdie's nose, she realised what she'd stumbled on: a cup of tea. There were at least three or four of the steaming porcelain cups and saucers set among the steps. All mismatched, now that Gerdie looked closer – she noted sadly that the meteorite cup was paired with the dinosaur saucer.

The lock clicked, and Ada's long, thin face appeared on the other side of the door. A sliver of yellow light cast a beam over the crime scene. 'Who's there?' she barked.

'It's only me, Ada.' Gerdie gestured to the mess. 'I'm sorry, I broke one of your teacups.'

Ada clucked her tongue. 'They're for the Angels.'

Gerdie climbed the last stair, wary of where she stepped lest tea soak through the thin soles of her shoes. 'Don't let Conqueror Seki hear you say that.'

'Pah.' Ada waved a hand. 'Seki is too far away from the quarry to hear anything little old me says. Whether he worships them or not, the Angels are still up there, watching and deciding our destinies. Now, what are you doing here so late?'

Gerdie reached into her bag and held out the crumpled, scratched remains of the M.O.R.T. 'I really thought I had it this time.'

Ada regarded the battered M.O.R.T. with a raised grey eyebrow, then opened the door wider. 'In you come.'

Gerdie followed Ada into the cramped sitting room, squeezing between two mismatched plush chairs and breathed in the familiar scent of cinnamon and mould. 'I think if I replaced the light bolt with a number four, the M.O.R.T. will be capable of cleaning the Trunk machines. One to a machine. Could you imagine? Also, do you have any polyrekovene? I want to attach some to the feet for balance.'

Ada hummed in reply; her pale blue eyes narrowed as she concentrated on the robot.

Gerdie perched on the end of a ripped blue armchair, wringing her hands as she watched Ada. 'What do you think?'

'Tea?'

'Yes, please.'

Ada waved a flippant hand. 'Well, you know where everything is.'

Gerdie hopped off the armchair and tottered into the tiny kitchen. The space was a complete mess, and that was coming from someone with a floordrobe. Multiple packets of the same tea were opened, teacups and saucers scattered across the counter. Gerdie managed to find a clean cup and spooned two teaspoons of sugar into it. She located the kettle among pots, colanders, and rolls of paper towel, and flicked it on.

While she waited for the water to boil, Gerdie poked her head into the next room. Ada had her back turned, head bent and muttering to herself as she fiddled with the M.O.R.T. Gerdie chewed her bottom lip as a thought occurred to her. She shouldn't. It was rude to sneak through people's houses without their knowing about it... But she didn't have parental guidance anymore, so she left the kitchen to creep down the hallway, passing closed door after closed door. Bathroom, study, and Ada's bedroom she knew and had been into multiple times, but there was one room that remained locked, that she had never seen the inside of. It had belonged to Ada's son, who Gerdie only met once, briefly. He'd barely spent time at home and was angry *all the time*. Gerdie remembered ripped books and multiple pairs of boxing gloves. He ran away two years ago and was never heard of again, and Ada went a little bit mad with grief when he left. That's what Dad thought, anyway, but Ada had always been eccentric to Gerdie.

'You would never run away from me like that, would you, Gerdie?' Dad had said, after telling her about Ada's son.

'No way. And you'll never run away from me, right?'

Dad chucked. *'No, never. But, my darling...'* and here his voice became uncharacteristically sombre. *'If something* were *to happen to me -'*

'I would live with Ada?' she had asked, though she didn't want to bear thinking about a life without Dad.

Dad's mouth had tightened. *'No, Gerdie. After her son ran away... well, I don't think she's quite up to taking on another child. Ah,'* he said, flapping a hand and smiling again. *'Why am I talking of grim things? Good thing nothing will happen to me, hey?'*

Gerdie pushed the memory away, but she couldn't help thinking how much she would love to live with Ada if she could.

She reached the last door on the left. It opened soundlessly, as she knew it would.

One wall had a tiny window that looked out onto part of next-door's house, the other a rickety bookcase defying physics by staying upright while supporting dozens of tomes. But the other two adjacent walls... they were Gerdie's favourites. Every inch of the walls was covered in paintings of plants and flowers. The paintings were all shapes and sizes, arranged in a straight formation that Ada's late partner must have established, because Gerdie didn't believe Ada could be capable of such neatness. The two of them had fit together like a jigsaw puzzle, much like the paintings. Gerdie's chest tightened as she remembered Lexell. He had been such a kind man, so in love with Ada, he'd had one of those laughs that compelled you to laugh with him, no matter what your mood was, his eyes the greenest and kindest she'd ever seen.

She saw them in these paintings, and she stared with an amazement they never failed to draw from her. These green things had existed once, and there had been so many of them on the old planet of Earth that it had been *covered* in them. She had seen those pictures of Earth from afar, green and blue with wisps of white. Bellona's trees had been cut down to build cities and burned to run factories. And then, after Seki overthrew the royal family all those years ago, he ordered what little nature remained to be destroyed. Food was now carefully grown and distributed under the watchful eyes of the capital.

'They'll be back, you know.'

Gerdie jumped, hand flying to her stuttering heart as she turned guiltily to Ada, who had appeared beside her.

'Sorry, I didn't mean to come in here. Well, I did, but...'

Ada regarded the wall of paintings and didn't reply.

Gerdie took this as permission to remain. 'The plants will be back, you mean?'

Ada nodded. 'Some things come back. But not all things.'

Was Ada thinking about her son? Gerdie touched the closest painting with a fingertip. It was of a... fern, maybe? She couldn't remember, but the green painted leaves were thick and sloped downward. They must have been so soft in real life. 'Will I ever see them?'

'Yes,' Ada said seriously. 'Machines cannot keep nature back, no matter how hard old Seki tries. And there is a change coming, Gertrude. Something big is about to happen.' She turned abruptly and swept from the room. Gerdie followed, curious.

'It has already begun,' Ada said, and pointed a bony finger toward the window.

Gerdie followed the finger, and that's when she heard it, the commotion outside of excited chatter, sounding like the drones from the capital that hovered about the factory once a month, checking in on their progress. Dozens of people were flowing from their houses and out onto the street. Everyone's faces raised to the sky. Gerdie tried to throw the window open, but it was too stuck, so she bolted for the door and out into the street, knocking over another cup of tea.

'It's a comet!' people were shouting. 'A comet! It's headed straight for us! We're all going to die!'

Gerdie tilted her head back. There, between Maylow and Oriana in the navy sky, was a bright, twinkling light, bigger than any star Gerdie had ever seen. It was quite pretty, sparkling and colourful.

'It ain't!' another called. 'It's just a planet. Nolava, probably. It's always close this time of year.'

'It's the Death Comet!' someone else screeched, which set off the screaming like a line of dominoes.

Gerdie squinted at it. She'd studied comets at school, since so many had hit Bellona, and it was thanks to one of the first collisions that tore open the ground to reveal the planet's wealth of minerals. Everyone learnt about the Death Comet that had destroyed Earth two-hundred years ago, and Mars seventy years ago. If this comet hit, it would cause an unthinkable amount of destruction. But how could something so magnificent be so dangerous? Even as she watched, it seemed to be growing bigger and brighter. She couldn't see a tail, so maybe it was just a planet. Still, her heart beat hard and fast, as if it knew something she didn't.

THREE

The sky's newest addition – be it star, planet or comet – was all anyone was talking about.

Gerdie woke early the next morning to the excited whispers of the other orphans. They saw the light the night before when they had stuck their heads out of the windows, woken by the commotion outside. Like the adults, not all of them were convinced it was a comet.

'Reckon it's just a dying star,' Donny was saying.

Gerdie rose and stretched, listening with interest as the five of them huddled around Pat's bed, already dressed.

'No,' Pat sniffed. 'It's obviously a comet; I could see its tail. Are you blind as well as stupid?'

'Pat,' Donny said in exasperation, 'you're the one who put salt instead of sugar on your porridge yesterday.'

When Gerdie and the others left for the factories, they were met with a crowd of people on the street, surrounding a lamp post outside the orphanage. Gerdie darted forward, pushing her way through to see what made this particular lamp post so special. A leaflet had been stuck to the post overnight, made of better-quality paper than the ones that scattered the damp ground. This paper was thick and shiny. It was signed with Conqueror Seki's seal, a ten-pointed star with a crown above its top point. She shoved her glasses on to read.

Residents of Rendip Quarry, your supreme ruler is aware of the situation that faces Treshane. A comet has set its course for our country, but I will be doing everything within my power to stop it. This is not a sign from the Angels. This is a serious threat that will be dealt with immediately. Please remain calm, continue your normal business, and remain vigilant of future notices. Know that your ruler will take care of you.

Signed,

Conqueror Seki, Ruler of Treshane, Emperor of the Skies, King of the Stars.

Gerdie squeezed back through the crowd, letting herself be jostled as others made their way forward to read. She was too lightheaded over what she'd just read to care.

Seki was going to stop the comet, but how would one even stop a comet? Was it possible? She pushed her hair back from her face as the realisation occurred to her. If Seki had plans to stop it, that meant there *had* to be a way. Who knew what kinds of machines inventors could create with materials from the capital?

What if *she* was the one to stop it?

What if she invented something so large and powerful that it could stop a comet in its tracks? If she could do that, then she would be a hero, famous for her invention; the saviour of Treshane. Her smile built, giddy with excitement. She could do this, she *knew* she could do this. And if Dad were with her, he would agree with her. He would probably even help her build something, give advice as he used to. She could already imagine it: being escorted to the palace in New Londinium, meeting Conqueror Seki himself, being congratulated personally by him. How he would grant her anything she wanted, and she would bring the conditions of the factories to light. She would save everyone.

She pulled her battered little notebook from her pocket, adjusted her glasses and, hardly noticing the number of mumbling adults she bumped into with her head bent, began to scribble.

Once the factory whistle blew, signaling the end of another long, hard day, Gerdie walked to the station on her own because Leo had been forced to stay behind; some end of month papers needed doing or something. She boarded the train for Rendip, but as it entered the quarry, she jumped off the train a stop early. It wasn't technically a stop, and the train didn't technically... stop. As it weaved down the sides of the quarry, the train slowed to a crawl to make each bend, and Gerdie used this momentary reduction in speed to force the doors open and hop out of the carriage. The east side of the quarry held a large open area of scrap metal, known as Odds and Ends, the local junkyard. Despite its chaos, its overwhelming smell of metal and burned rubber, the occasional unsavoury individual who had nowhere else to go, it was her favourite place to be. That wouldn't change even if her wage allowed her to peruse for parts in actual scrap metal dealers. When Rendip had been a working quarry, the junkyard had been the blacksmith's, where the miners' tools and equipment were made and repaired. Now, it was a dumping ground and a treasure trove. It was on the opposite side of the station and the orphanage, and she'd have to make the thirty-minute walk back in the dark, but it was worth it. It was a safe walk, anyway. Everyone in Rendip knew each other; no one locked doors, they all knew one another's business. In fact, one of the myths of the quarries was that if you did something bad to your neighbour, something worse would happen to you. Gerdie believed it: just last month, Daniel Riggin stole little old Doris Steffey's watch after she'd accidentally dropped it in her driveway, and a few days later Daniel lost his eye in a factory explosion.

Had anything bad happened to her mum yet?

Mountains of scrap metal rose, bits and bobs and baubles lit orange by the sunset. Flies made lazy circles around the piles, and the occasional *bang!* or *crash!* echoed across the site as other rummagers searched for the parts they needed for whatever project. The heat was intense, each metal piece radiating like a miniature sun.

It was so easy to become lost here, and she often did. She rubbed her hands together as she surveyed the junk, loving that feeling of possibility, of never knowing what she might find. Would it be a working phone? The voice box of a discarded toy, for prank-pulling purposes? As long as it wasn't an angry family of Skunk lizards again—that was something you only wanted to experience once.

But back to the task at hand.

She needed to build some kind of rocket, something to meet the comet halfway and knock it off course or break it up entirely – and she had to do it before Seki did. She'd built a miniature rocket with her dad before, and it had worked perfectly. Of course, it would have worked better if she hadn't set it off *inside* the Inventor's Guild and blown a hole through the roof, right as a tremendously wet winter started. Live and learn, that's what Dad always said.

Oh, but first she needed to look for what she needed for the M.O.R.T., since Ada didn't have any polyrekovene lying around. Heading for the closest metal mound with eagerness, she could already picture the (hopefully) final part she needed to keep the M.O.R.T. steady while it worked. She shifted through the smaller pieces scattered at the base of a mound of rusty pipes. There were a few rubber suction cups connected to a knot of old Christmas lights, but they would be no good against the extreme heat of the factory machines. She needed ones made of silicone, which was what Ada had eventually suggested last night to make the M.O.R.T. stand against the pressure of the Trunks.

Nothing here. She rocked back on her heels, blowing out a breath as she surveyed the next mound. It was made of much the same as the one in front of her; piles of Ame and Starbist slats and pipes, the most common metals found beneath Treshane's surface. There was also a wheel larger than Gerdie, a giant remote, an old water tank, a pair of feet—

She froze.

There was a body lying between two piles of scrap metal. It wasn't moving. Rising on shaky legs, Gerdie slowly approached the body, moving quietly as if she was scared to wake them. *Please, Angels, let them just be sleeping.* She crouched behind an old metal drum and peeked over the top.

It was a boy. He didn't look very old or very tall, his hair so light a yellow it was almost white, cut short. His feet were bare, poking out of brown trousers, a white shirt tucked in and supported by brown suspenders. His clothes were pressed, skin white and smooth. He looked brand new, like one of the dolls in the toy shop at Balthasar Station, the ones other girls had begged their parents for, then teased Gerdie when all she wanted to play with was a spanner. Two small moths settled on his chest.

She cleared her throat. When there was still no movement, she came around the drum and crouched beside him, placing her glasses on her nose and raising a hand with the intention of pressing it to his chest to feel for a heartbeat.

His eyes opened.

Gerdie let out a shriek. She lost her balance and toppled backward into a pile of metal, which promptly came crashing down around her. She raised her arms above her head to shield herself, but most of what made up the metal mountain was metal sheet cut-offs, only feeling like a light rain when it bonked her on her head.

The boy squeezed his eyes shut. 'The noise…' he moaned. His voice was soft and ethereal: more like a girl's voice than a boy's.

Gerdie rubbed her head where a cog had bounced off it. 'I'm so sorry! You frightened me.'

He furrowed his light eyebrows. 'Fear…?'

'Yes, fear. Because I thought you might have been dead and then I'd have to call the Actions, and they already don't like me much, and they would probably put me in the Core for killing you even though I didn't.' She pushed herself to her feet, wincing at her scraped hands as she adjusted her glasses. 'Are you okay? What are you doing out here, lying on the ground like that?'

The boy stared up at her. His eyes were the bluest Gerdie had ever seen, surrounded by long pale lashes. He slowly pulled himself upright, and Gerdie helped him to sitting with a hand on his arm and a supportive 'alley-oop.' She nearly snatched her hand away as soon as she came into contact: he was cold as ice. With his back held as straight as a drainpipe, he lowered his head and stared at his hands in his lap like he'd never seen them before. Gerdie glanced over her shoulder, wondering if he belonged to anyone, if there was anyone who knew what to do with him because she certainly didn't. But this section of Odds and Ends was deserted but for the two of them.

Gerdie turned back to the boy, studying him again. He was lying in a dip in the rocky ground, shaped around his body, like he'd made a snow Angel in the dirt.

'You look like you just fell from the sky. What's your name?'

He frowned, and she could practically see the cogs of his brain turning. 'I... fell.'

'You're Fell? That's your name?'

'Fell,' he repeated, though he didn't look too sure about it.

'Yes.' Gerdie regarded him with a quirked eyebrow. 'Are you going to repeat everything I say? It's very strange, you know. My dad used to tell me off about that sort of thing. Said it was annoying.'

He smiled. It was a sweet smile, a sweet smile on a baby-face.

'My name's Gertrude Sailor, but you can call me Gerdie.' She glanced at her watch. 'Curfew's about to start. We should be getting back. Where are you from?'

The boy glanced up at her again. 'The Merten Cloud.'

'The what?' Gerdie frowned. She'd never heard of it before. 'Is that, like, another planet?'

He looked around the junkyard and didn't reply. Odds and Ends seemed like a strange place for a holiday.

'Okay, well...' Gerdie propped her hands on her hips. 'Want to come back to the orphanage with me? Miss Wyatt will let you stay, I'm sure. She doesn't much pay attention to anything we do, anyway, unless you touch her chocolate stash. I'm sure she won't notice an extra person.'

Fell dipped his chin in a nod but made no move to get up.

'Well?' Gerdie prompted.

Seeming to realise what she wanted, he raised one knee. Then the other. He pressed his knuckles to the ground and tried to push off them, but struggled under his own weight, which couldn't have been very much, small as he was.

She grabbed his icy upper arm and hoisted him to his feet. When she went to brush his back free of the red dust, she froze. His back was clean: the shirt as crisp and white as if it had just been made. She slowly lowered her hand, staring at him. He stared back – but not at her birthmark, she noticed with surprise – wide eyes full of curiosity, as if *she* was the strange one. There, that was the other thing that made him seem so odd. The faces of the other people her age were tired and lifeless, even the youngest among them. But this boy's face showed nothing but innocence and interest.

Gerdie ushered him around the scrap metal piles, tugging on one of his suspenders every now and then to keep him moving in the same direction, as he was so busy looking around him that he veered this way and that. He was walking slow and stiff as if he had not used his legs for some time. How long had he been lying in Odds and Ends? This boy must be ill. It would explain why he was acting so strangely, why he was so pale and cold. Her hand went to her pocket for her coin when it wasn't keeping Fell in line.

As they walked along the railway tracks, the quarry train chugged toward them, heading back to Balthasar Station. She watched as the train grumbled past, and Fell covered his ears and groaned.

Gerdie turned to him in alarm, grabbing his arms. They were hard with tension. 'What is it? Fell, what's the matter?'

His eyes squeezed shut. 'So... loud.'

'It's just a train.'

Once it had passed, and all was silent once more, he calmed down a bit, but Gerdie followed his movements with a watchful eye as they continued forward. Was there something wrong with his ears? With his head, maybe? What kind of illness did he have? She couldn't leave him like this. Her dad was always one for helping those less fortunate, whether it was gifting prototypes of inventions to schools or donating money to organisations working to solve the air pollution crisis. Gerdie rarely thought of herself as fortunate these days, but at least she remembered her own name.

She kept watch out of the corner of her eye as they continued. There was something... *different* about him, and not just in the way he was acting. It was as if his edges were slightly blurred, always shifting, like the way light caught on a polished stone.

He followed her dutifully, and as they turned onto Slate Street, the lamps glowed and a light rain started to fall, bringing an unpleasant smell rising from the hot, dirty pavement. She hurried Fell along, wanting to be out of sight before the inevitable happened. They made it through the orphanage gates just in time: doors along the street swung open and buckets appeared on doorsteps. The more water that was caught instead of hitting the streets, the less the town would flood. Ah, the joys of living in a giant bowl. The pumps that drained water from the quarry had been broken for a month now. During the summer it wasn't a problem, but when winter came...

Despite Gerdie's assurances that Miss Wyatt wouldn't care about Fell's arrival, she still ordered Fell to wait outside while she poked her head into the entryway of the orphanage. There wasn't a waif in sight, but there was a murmuring coming from down the hall. Dinner time. Her stomach grumbled at the thought, even though the food would be the same bland corned beef, bread, and potatoes as it always was. Fresh fruits and vegetables were grown by Orchard & Co. in New Londinium, with no seeds available for purchase. A huge facility, she'd heard, and the only crop production on Treshane, which meant the company had ultimate control over the pricing and distribution, and most of the time it was just too much for Miss Wyatt to afford.

She gestured to Fell. 'Come on, let's go.'

It took more suspender-tugging once they were inside to get Fell to climb the stairs. He was enamoured with everything in the orphanage's tiny entryway. The tiny, dusty picture of Miss Wyatt's great-grandmother. The broken hat stand with no hats on it. The row of frayed shoes. Why did the most mundane things make him so curious? It was almost as if he'd never seen any of it before. Maybe he'd come from Goliath, the only other (and much bigger) continent on Bellona. They did things differently there across the One Sea, she'd heard. Goliath still had a royal family; no conqueror had thrown a coup over there and killed them all. She'd seen paintings of Goliath's royal family, when she was small and Dad had taken her to Colborough, to the art gallery there. The king, queen, two princesses and a prince were dressed in fur-lined cloaks and mounds of glittering jewellery. Even then, they had not looked as intimidating as Conqueror Seki's official portrait. No pictures existed anymore of Treshane's ex-royalty, and sometimes Gerdie wondered what they had looked like.

The bedroom was empty, of course, the orphans downstairs at dinner. She ushered Fell inside, running a hand over her damp hair and pulling her glasses free. Fell immediately circled the room, stopping at Lewis' bedside table and picking up a battered copy of *Tales from the Galaxy*. Gerdie stared at it in surprise. Dad used to read to her every night from those tales; she hadn't realised Lewis owned a copy.

'So, what brings you to Rendip?' she asked as she pulled off her boots. One of her toes was wet through her sock. Great, another hole in her shoe.

Fell didn't seem affected by the rain at all; no drops on his hair or shoulders. 'I have something to do.'

'What is it?'

No reply. Was he hard of hearing, or just ignoring her?

Gerdie huffed. 'Well, if it's such a big secret...'

He didn't seem to notice her attempt at information gathering. She perched on the edge of her bed as she watched him, the rain drumming steadily on the orphanage roof. He was picking up other objects at random now, studying them with the same marvel he'd shown things downstairs. A hairbrush, a teddy bear with an arm missing and one of its eyes hanging on by a thread, a little metal flower Gerdie had made, modelled after one of the paintings hanging in Ada's house. It was this last one he lingered on. Gerdie had taken a large, thin cog and bent the teeth inward to form petals, and pieces of broken glass had been melted together to make a stem. *It was very pretty*, she thought modestly.

'Do you have family?' she asked.

He placed the metal flower gently back in its place. 'Family?' He had to think about that for a minute. 'Yes.'

'Where are they? Are they... still around?'

Fell shook his head.

'Oh. I'm sorry. Me neither. Not anymore, anyway. My father passed away last year, consumption, you know. It took him fast; I never even knew he was sick until Mr. Tulk from the Inventor's Guild told me he was d--' Her voice grew tight, and she closed her mouth. She'd never even gotten the chance to say goodbye.

Fell turned to her, the weight of his gaze heavy on her skin. She pulled her glasses from her pocket and onto her nose to hide her misty eyes, and when she felt comfortable enough to look up again, Fell was staring out of the window.

Maybe he was an automaton. She'd heard of such machines, how technology in New Londinium was more advanced than Rendip Quarry. How their machines moved without sound, were sleek and smooth, didn't even require steam. She'd heard stories of machines that fly, lifting people about as if they were Angels. Fell moved with a fluid grace she didn't think capable of a human, and he seemed to repel dirt and water, if the bottom of his pants were anything to go by. She doubted the theory as soon as it sprang to mind. The depth behind his eyes wasn't machine, but it didn't seem human to her either. It was something so much more than both.

She recalled the stories her father told her about Angels coming down to Treshane. Was Fell one of them?

'You can have this bed, if you want.' She gestured to the bed beside hers, the one that used to be Henry's.

Fell stared at it for a few seconds, then slowly lowered himself onto the faded grey quilt. He bounced a little bit, looking delighted at the give of the mattress. She supposed it must be nice after lying on the hard dirt ground of Odds and Ends.

'Do you want something to eat? Drink?'

He shook his head.

'Okay, well, we can sort you out in the morning. Get you to wherever you need to be.' She waved her notebook. 'Do you mind if I...?'

Fell shook his head again, and Gerdie flipped open to a new page.

He lay down and turned his head to the window again but looked as stiff on the bed as he had on the uneven ground of the junkyard. He was staring up into the sky as if looking for something. His long pale eyelashes fluttered.

'You don't have to worry about the comet,' she told him. 'I'm going to stop it from hitting Bellona. I'm an inventor, you see, and I plan to build a machine that will intercept the comet before it can make contact.'

Fell didn't say anything, and she deflated. He didn't look the least bit impressed by her genius. So she left him to his staring, and she scribbled until the other orphans drifted in – they didn't even notice Fell, tired as they were from the day's work – and she scribbled until hers was the only light left burning, and the last thing Gerdie saw before she eventually lay down and closed her eyes was Fell's small mouth moving like he was talking to the stars.

I knOW you ARe thErE, liTtle onE

I sEe YOU
I hear yOu
I FEEl You
thErE is NO HIding frOm mE
I aM cOMIng fOR You
i HAve DEFEAted tHoSe whO cAMe BEfore
And yOU WiLl be no DiFFerEnt

Four

Leo lifted his hand and shook out the cramp that was forming in his fingers. He leaned back in his small creaky chair and glanced at the digital clock on the desk. Nearly eight. The windows of the tiny office were dark, rain lashing at them.

The stack of paper in front of him was giving him a headache, and it didn't help that he hadn't slept much last night. He'd had the dream again. Dark endless tunnels and a whispering voice so haunting he sometimes heard it in waking, like it was trying to reach him no matter where he was.

Peller appeared at the door and with a single jerk of the head on his thin neck, freed Leo from the desk.

They didn't speak on their way back to the apartment. Sometimes, it was as if Peller forgot Leo was there at all. He raised his head to where the comet was a bright, twinkling light in the orange sky.

When Seki killed his parents seven years ago, he'd been shoved into Peller's stiff unwelcoming arms at only ten years old. Though Peller was elderly—much older than the twenty to thirty-year-old Actions Seki usually kept by his side—he was one of Seki's closest acquaintances (Seki didn't have *friends*.) Leo thought it was a pretty poor *thank-you for your services* to be sent to live and work at the factories.

But his loyalty meant that Peller could be trusted to keep an eye on such a prisoner as Leo. And Leo was meant to be grateful that he was just a prisoner, content that he had lost a leg and not his head, content that he wore a black *T* and not a noose.

The townhouse he shared with Peller was tall and rickety, like most of the buildings in Balthasar. After the Death Comet destroyed Mars, a flurry of refugees had come to Bellona, and the then royal family had to house as many people as possible. Peller's townhouse had heating and indoor plumbing, which a lot of the other houses lacked. Peller climbed the crumbling stone stairs, groaning slightly as he lifted each of his old knobby legs, and unlocked the chipped front door. Leo's own leg where his knee met the prosthetic was aching, growing tighter and more painful with every step. He gritted his teeth and followed in silence.

As soon as the door was opened, Peller dropped the keys onto the entryway table and disappeared into the next room. The sound of the television blared, casting flickering light onto the wall. Leo went into the kitchen and took two meals out of the freezer. Though at times it might seem as if Peller forgot Leo's existence, he never did, especially if Leo forgot one of his chores. Leo leaned against the counter as he watched the microwave count down, the back of his neck prickling. Behind him was an oil painting of Seki in a gilded frame. It was stuck to the wall; Leo had tried to take it down once, shortly after arriving at Peller's and when he still had some fight in him. He'd paid for it dearly, never tried again. So, it loomed there, watching him always. It seemed to say, *I am always here. Do not forget who holds the power now.*

Seki's symbol, a ten-pointed star, was painted in the bottom right corner. Each point of the star represented a planet in the Hector-Nero system, and that Seki ruled them all. He didn't, though. Not really. Only four of the ten planets in the system were inhabited by humans, two others destroyed by the Death Comet hundreds of years ago, and to Leo's knowledge Seki hadn't even left Treshane in years. But Seki didn't seem to care about those details, ignored the fact that the only other continent on Bellona had its own monarchy—for now, Leo thought bitterly. It was all or nothing when it came to their conqueror.

The microwave beeped. Leo handed the meal to Peller, who accepted it without a word, his eyes glued to the television screen. The state news was on, the presenter broadcasting information on the Cats, an underground group who resisted Seki's rule. The picture showed a smoking factory with the headline: *Cat Attack*.

'*We're crossing now to Alfie Jones who is in Toodany Park…*' the presenter was saying.

The scene flicked to a reporter standing outside one of the newer factories. Wide windows set into sleek white walls, and its slanted roof sharp as a shard of glass but for one end that was nothing but a smoking gape. Officials in reflective vests gathered around the entrance, flanked by vehicles flashing blue. '*Thanks, Margaret. About two hours ago, an unknown number of Cats broke into Botsworth Factory and reprogrammed the settings of the laser cutters here to a highly dangerous level. Once switched on, the machines cut into the very ground and struck a gas pipe.*

The machine malfunctioned, creating the havoc you see behind me now. Botsworth Factory produced signs and other advertising products for businesses in New Londinium. Conqueror Seki will no doubt see this as a great loss…'

The Cats—named after the Catells, the royal family that Seki had overthrown seventy-five years ago—used to be public, protesting in the streets and in front of Seki's palace, demanding environmental policies and improved workplace conditions be put back in place. The punishment for their protests grew too harsh for them to continue. If anyone was caught, they were taken to the Core. They didn't return without injury, the visible ones replaced with a crude metal prosthetic stamped with a large black *T*.

Traitor.

When the news began sharing the results of the latest soccer match, Leo took his own dinner into his room. Placing the meal onto his tiny desk, he eased himself down onto his bed. He lifted his pant leg to reveal the raw and angry skin that surrounded the prosthetic. Some of the scabs had rubbed off and were bleeding. He picked at them but didn't remove the prosthetic. He couldn't bear to see the ugly twisted stump of his missing leg.

Faintly, he caught a knock at the front door. His stomach clenched. What now?

He heard the mumble of voices as Peller answered whoever was outside. After a moment, the door shut, and Peller's footsteps grew closer until he finally opened Leo's door. Peller never knocked, just in case Leo was up to something and didn't want to give him the chance to hide. In Peller's bony hand was a sheet of paper.

'Two Actions at the door,' he grunted. 'They're looking for a boy. Seki's orders.'

Leo's stomach flipped even though he wasn't the one in trouble this time. The Actions were nothing but thugs, chosen by Seki because they were strong and dominating and good at doing what they were told without asking questions. Peller handed him the paper. Leo glanced down at it, at the stamp of the official seal, then frowned. There was no picture of the wanted boy. All the paper said was: *Young boy of unknown description. Highly dangerous... do not engage... behaviour is unusual.*

Among his confusion, he felt sick. But it was more out of fear *for* this young boy, who would soon feel Seki's wrath. There was no doubt about it, because no one ever escaped Conqueror Seki. Leo scanned the poster again.

Whoever, and wherever the poor boy was, Leo hoped he was a fast runner.

FIVE

'I THINK IT'S HIM.'

'Reckon it might be. 'E's a bit weird lookin', ain't he?'

'Could be one of them locals from Goliath, eh? The ones who came from Earth first? My da used to tell me stories about them...'

Gerdie opened her eyes. The five other kids surrounded Henry's bed, where Fell was still lying. He was staring up at them with a curiosity that matched theirs, not at all alarmed by the press of faces. He looked like a newborn baby surrounded by cooing aunts and uncles. But instead of adoring, they wore expressions of suspicion.

Gerdie sat up, rubbing her eyes, and asked, 'What are you doing?'

'Conqueror Seki released another announcement on the radio this morning' Pat explained. 'He's sent out a warrant for a boy, no description or nothin', but doesn't seem like a coincidence that this guy turns up out of nowhere.'

'Where else could a kid hide but in an orphanage?' Alicia added.

Gerdie threw the covers back. 'Looking for Fell? Why? What did he do?'

Pat shrugged. 'No idea. But I suggest he clears out quick smart before someone hands him in. Or someone comes looking,' he added, with a pointed look.

Her stomach turned at the thought of the Actions turning up at the orphanage. She realised now how stupid it must have been for her to bring him to the orphanage without knowing who he was or where he came from. Was he a thief? A murderer? What if he really was an Angel, but one of the tricky ones?

As she watched Fell rub his eyes, seeming unfazed by the dozen faces trained on him, she relaxed. He didn't look dangerous, and he'd needed her help. If he was a bad Angel, he'd had plenty of opportunities to cause harm already.

Peller's words drifted to the forefront of her mind. *And if you cause such a disturbance again, you will be removed from the company.* Fell couldn't stay. Harbouring a wanted boy most likely fell under under the category of 'disturbance.' Besides, she had a comet-stopping machine to invent and build.

She shook her hands in their direction. 'Alright, that's enough everyone. Leave him alone. Shoo!'

Grumbling under their breath, the children dispersed, and she took their place standing over Fell. His hair was rumpled where it had been against the pillow, and it finally made him look like a normal teenager, like he was just as susceptible to the laws of sleep as a human. Not a robot, or an Angel. She couldn't imagine the Angels having messy hair.

She poked Fell's shoulder, urging him to sit up. 'We've got to hide you before Miss Wyatt finds you. Or Actions.'

He eased himself up off the bed. 'Where?'

Gerdie tapped her bottom lip. 'You said you're here

because you have something to do. If you won't tell me what it is, will you at least tell me where you need to go?'

Fell thought about it, a crease forming between his thin eyebrows.

'Back to Odds and Ends?' she prompted.

Fell shook his head.

'Where then?' She wanted to help, she really did, but even she had limited patience. That comet wasn't going to stop itself. The faster she built the machine and sent it into the sky, the less of a danger it would be to Treshane when it blew apart.

'I'll take you to the train station,' she said. 'You can find your own way from there.'

He shuddered at the mention of trains but didn't object.

Before they left, Gerdie grabbed a tattered round hat from the peg by the door and jammed it on Fell's head. It was two sizes too big, but if Seki really was after him, it covered his distinctive hair and fell over his eyes so that half of his face was hidden. Hopefully it would be enough to hide him long enough for him to get to... wherever he needed to get to.

The early morning rush of the station was over. As they stood beneath the digital timetable, there were still a few people milling about, some reading the thin newspaper as they waited for a train, but most just staring glumly at the board.

Fell looked around, then glanced back at her expectantly.

Gerdie shook her head, sending her pigtails bouncing. 'I'm sorry, I can't help you. I can't get into any more trouble, and I have something to do, anyway.' Even though her curiosity burned with wanting to know who he really was and what he needed to do.

She bought him a ticket. It was a bit painful to hand over the ki, considering she was down a week's wage.

She took Fell to platform three, the train going to the city with the most stops in between, in case one jogged his memory. He kept looking at her expectantly, blue eyes so intent she had to force her hand from reaching up to cover her birthmark. She gently touched his shoulder. 'I hope you remember what you need to do.'

Leaving him on the platform, she climbed the road to Odds and Ends. She searched through the piles of scrap metal, and checked her notes, but couldn't find what she was looking for. Frustration bubbled inside her. What if she couldn't do this? Was it useless after all? She glumly kicked at an old paint can. Well, if she let the comet hit Treshane, then their problems *would* be solved because then they would all be dead.

She plopped down onto the gravelly ground, leaning back against an old fridge. *Think, think, think.*

Unbidden, Dad's voice came to mind. *My dear girl, you don't need to invent something to be special. You are worth more than what you create.*

She squeezed her eyes shut. *You're wrong, Dad.*

It was easy for him to say things like that—and he said them often—with his amazing opportunities and position within the Inventors Guild. Well, what did she have? Nothing. Only what she could invent.

She wouldn't give up this easily. Even if the comet came to nothing, she couldn't live her life in the factory, even as short a life as it would undoubtedly be. She pushed off from the fridge and marched out of Odds and Ends. She would go to the Inventors Guild, ask for their help. Surely this was an invention they would support.

The Inventors Guild was in Balthasar, about twenty minutes from the top of the quarry. She chose to walk to save money on the train ticket and would have to avoid passing Sweene & Sons. She wouldn't have been paid for work today, anyway, and if all went well with her invention, she'd never have to go into the factory again except to replace the machines.

The incline of the quarry was steady but steep, and her legs were burning by the time she reached the road at the top, then it was a flat walk past little houses crammed together like staples in a box, and into the city. As she came up to the statue outside a pub of the Angel Cameron, with his big round helmet tucked under his arm, she saw two Actions ahead, coming her way, easily discernible even from this distance by their metal masks. She ducked behind a parked car; if they saw her, they would wonder why she wasn't at work.

She held her breath as they approached, pressing close to the car as other vehicles passed by her on the road.

'...sure, then?' one was saying.

'Well, no,' the other replied. 'How can he be sure when there's nothing to go on? That kid could be any of the little brats in the factories.'

Gerdie's blood turned cold. They were talking about Fell, she was sure. She inched toward the back of the car to stay hidden.

'All Conqueror Seki said,' the second Action continued, 'was that the boy's different. He'd be acting strange, or something.'

'Hm,' the first grunted. 'He from the Goliath or something? The Isles of Furrow?'

'No idea. Guess we'll find out, though, if he really was spotted at Farnleigh Bridge...'

Their voices faded as they disappeared from view, and Gerdie shot to her feet. Why hadn't he gotten on the bloody train?

Farnleigh Bridge wasn't far from where she was. She had to find Fell before the Actions did.

It looked like the Actions were taking Little Byron Street to get there, but Gerdie knew a quicker way to the bridge. She hit the footpath the Actions had just taken and sprinted in the opposite direction. She went by the east way, where the pedestrian underpass would provide a faster way there than the Actions. It meant she would have to climb the sides of the underpass to reach the top of the bridge, but she knew there were small ladders there for emergencies.

Luckily for her, Fell was in the pedestrian bypass, in the shadow of the bridge. His pale hair glowed as if it were in direct sunlight.

He was crouched on the ground, watching a fat grey moth feebly flutter its wings on the concrete. He was slowly reaching a finger toward the moth like he wanted to pat it. She skidded to a stop beside him, startling him into looking up. His blue eyes brightened when he saw her.

'What are you doing up here?' she panted. 'Why didn't you get on a train?'

Fell's eyes darkened at the very thought. She pressed a hand to her side, stabbing with a stitch. 'Come on, then. Your ticket should still be good to—'

'Hey!'

Gerdie whirled around – the two Actions were at the top of the bridge, their masked faces looking down on them.

'Stay where you are!' one yelled.

Yeah, right.

The nearest emergency ladder to the underpass was on the other side of the bridge, and the Actions were already running toward it, dodging cars as they ran. Gerdie got to her feet and pulled Fell upright. He made a small noise and glanced down at their clasped hands. One was bloody.

'Oh, Fell. You're hurt!'

The area was covered in broken glass and sharp stones, no doubt he had encountered something like that. He was staring at his hand, mouth slightly open like he'd only just realised he was hurt. Then his breathing quickened, and he swayed slightly. Gerdie was sympathetic, but they didn't have time for his panic attack right now.

'It will be okay. But we need to go, we need to hide. Now come on, move!'

They ran through the underpass, feet slapping against the concrete. The ceiling rumbled as a car passed overhead. Gerdie threw a look over her shoulder: the Actions had reached the ladder and were quickly climbing into the underpass.

The pass opened between a narrow street, and Gerdie dragged Fell up the short causeway and between buildings.

'Through here,' she panted, veering left.

Another left, then a right, and Gerdie finally slowed. She pressed her hands to her knees to catch her breath, listening for sounds of pursuit. When none came, she straightened.

Fell didn't even look winded. Pale cheeks a little flushed maybe, but he was breathing through his nose, unlike Gerdie's ragged mouth breathing. Wow, she was unfit.

'Come on,' she grumbled. 'Inventors Guild is this way.'

The Inventors Guildhall, though large and clean, was simple and plain on the outside; there was nothing to suggest that it was the home of geniuses and builders and thinkers and dreamers. The only colour came from an arch of stained glass above the front door depicting a rocket flying past three planets, and the welcome mat was scuffed and stained a dusty grey from the minerals around Rendip and Balthasar and once said *Put a ding in the universe* – a quote from some famous Earth inventor – but had now faded to just *ding in th*.

Gerdie seized the owl-shaped knocker then let it fall. The resounding thunk echoed through the long hallway she knew lay behind the door, audible even from the outside. After a few seconds, the two locks clicked.

An elderly man with more white hair sprouting out of his ears than his head peered through the crack in the door. 'Yes? Who calls—oh, Miss Sailor. It's you.' His voice turned flat.

'Hello, Mr. Lee,' Gerdie said with a small wave. 'I'm afraid

I'm in a bit of a pickle with my friend here. Mind if we seek shelter?'

Mr. Lee heaved a sigh like they were *quite* the inconvenience, when she knew he'd only been interrupted from having a cup of tea and a shortbread – the crumbs were still on his shirt. He finally opened the door and allowed them to pass, narrowing his eyes as he took in Fell. Mr. Lee might have heard the radio announcement that Fell was wanted by Seki, and Gerdie's stomach fluttered with nerves, but he said nothing, shutting the door behind them. The inventor behind the Text Satellite that allowed for fast messages between inhabited planets, Mr. Lee was a stocky man with a long face ending in a salt-and-pepper beard. Gerdie slipped past him and dragged Fell down the passageway and down to the kitchen.

The cook, Mrs. Welch, wasn't there. The little old lady was always nice to Gerdie, sneaking her cookies and small cakes when Dad wasn't looking.

Gerdie told Fell to sit and rummaged through one of the cupboards for the first aid kit. She was good with cuts and broken bones – she'd had a lot of practice in the factories and orphanage. Human bodies were a bit like machines. They all had the same components, and some even needed spare parts, like Leo's leg and the other unlucky protesters stamped with a black *T*.

She grabbed a clean cloth and a band-aid. 'All right,' she said, going back over to Fell, who was perched on the counter. 'Hold out your hand, let's have a look.'

Fell held out his hand and Gerdie stared at it in shock. It was perfectly fine.

'The... other hand?' she said faintly.

Fell did as she asked, but it was clean as well, not a scratch or mark in sight. Just impossibly smooth white skin. Had she imagined the injury? No – there was still dried blood on her own hand.

'Um...What?' If she looked carefully, there was a faint pink line on his palm.

Fell met her eyes, the cobalt of his own glittering with innocence. He glanced down at his outstretched hands as well. 'I healed,' he said.

'You... certainly did.' She sounded breathless. 'But how?'

Fell ran the thumb of his other hand over his palm. 'It's just something I can do.'

They were built differently in the capital. Or Goliath. Or wherever he was from.

Gerdie's heart pounded. She washed her own hands, then, with nothing left to do for Fell, led him back down the passageway and into the third room on the left. She couldn't help glancing at him out of the corner of her eye all the while.

It was a casual sitting room, where the inventors would take tea and brainstorm ideas. The walls were lined with portraits of past members, and all of them had achieved great things. One day, Gerdie's portrait would be up on that wall; the first girl inventor to ever be immortalised in the Inventors Guild, idolised for her magnificent inventions, an inspiration for all inventing girls. She remembered staring up at this wall with Dad when she was nine or so, asking when his portrait would be up there, and he had only smiled sadly and said he didn't know if he wanted it to be. Thinking back on that memory made her frown. Dad had always been humble about his inventions; had only visited the other inventors at the guild when it was necessary, and she felt a sudden prickling at the back of her neck, like maybe she shouldn't have come here at all.

It was too late for that, and she still didn't know what to do with Fell. Four of the inventors were milling in the room, and Gerdie sat herself down on the velvet lounge, dragging Fell down beside her. She smiled enthusiastically at the stern faces. Mr. Groz, with long grey hair he kept tied back and a sharp nose, invented the quad-wing, tweaking the hundreds of years old helicopter designs from Earth so that the transport was faster and more maneuverable in tight places like between streets and buildings. Mr. Jameson, the youngest among them at thirty, was the sculptor behind the First Aid automatons that could respond to any medical emergency in a short space of time, and as he turned at Gerdie's appearance, the massive glasses he wore magnifying his eyes to a comical size. And then there was Mr. Tulk, the man who had designed the turbines to look like the trees they pretended to be, skinny as a twig himself.

Mr. Lee perched on the seat opposite her and looked down on her with his large nostrils flaring. It made his moustache quiver. Gerdie squirmed in her chair, smile fading; she knew how the inventors felt about her. Though her father had been a member of the guild, the other members had not liked her much. They didn't approve of a girl inventing, of course, but there was also the small problem of Gerdie constantly wreaking havoc in their workshops. When she was four, she brandished her new screwdriver and unhooked the fan from a working, spinning quad-wing rotor prototype, sending it flying into the next room and knocking poor Mr. McJetts' cup of tea from his hand. When she was seven, she invented a tiny vacuum to clean surfaces. It worked so well that it sucked the varnish from the tables and most of the fabric from the sofas, leaving only the springs sticking out.

Gerdie's hand went into her pocket and fiddled with her coin. 'Thank you for letting us stay, Mr. Lee,' she said.

'Not at all,' Mr. Lee replied, but his voice sounded strained. 'I'll just go and get some tea.' He stood abruptly and walked stiffly from the room.

That left Mr. Tulk and Mr. Jameson sitting opposite in an uncomfortable silence, and Mr. Groz was staring out of the window as if looking for something. Gerdie couldn't wait for tea. The inventors were always adding things to their plain black leaves, herbs and spices and the like, to create a unique blend, the ingredients ordered in specially from the capital, and not for cheap, she knew from Ada. The inventors' brew *was* delicious, but it took a long time to brew. She bounced in her seat. 'How's the new turbines coming along, Mr. Tulk?'

'Oh, fine, yes, fine.' He turned away, adjusting the cuffs of his grey cardigan.

The inventors were usually standoffish toward her, but there was something that made it seem as if they knew something she didn't, like they were waiting for... what? Mr. Lee returned with a tray, balancing cups and a teapot, his lips pressed tightly together. He had been too fast making the tea, and it made Gerdie's stomach flip unpleasantly. Something was wrong. She pulled the coin from her pocket and into her lap.

The effect was immediate.

Mr. Tulk and Mr. Jameson leapt to their feet, Mr. Groz took several purposeful steps forward, and Mr. Lee dropped the tea tray onto the table with a *crash*. All had their eyes on the coin in Gerdie's hands. The inventors moved with a speed she might have expected from Mr. Jameson, but not from the creaky old limbs on the other three. Mr. Lee and Mr. Tulk restrained her arms, and the other two inventors had grabbed Fell, forcing them from the couch.

Mr. Lee's and Mr. Tulk's grips were painfully tight, and she struggled. Fell, on the other hand, looked as calm as ever, if a bit curious and confused.

'What's going on? What are you doing?'

'I'm sorry, Gertrude.' Mr. Lee wrested the coin from her fist.

Gerdie gave a cry as it slipped from her hand, and she struggled harder. 'No, please, no! That's *mine*!'

'I don't think you understand how important this disk is,'

Mr. Lee said, holding the coin up to the light with one hand while the other tightened its grip on Gerdie's arm. 'How long we've been searching. I should have known Stefan stole it.'

'I don't think *you* understand,' she said, tears pooling in her eyes at the loss of her coin. 'That is the last thing I have of my dad's. Please, give it back, I'm sure he didn't steal it. It's worthless to you.'

'That's where you're wrong, my dear.' Mr. Lee turned to Mr. Groz and murmured, 'Call the Actions. This is our chance to get Gertrude out of the way for good.'

She knew they didn't like her, but to hear it voiced in this way right in front of her.... Mr. Groz and Mr. Jameson, who had been holding Fell, gave sudden yelps and jumped away from him. They rubbed their hands together, looking at Fell with twin expressions of puzzlement and alarm.

'He went cold,' Mr. Jameson said. 'Like holding an ice cube.'

'Let her go,' said Fell. His voice was soft, making the command sound more like a suggestion.

'Stay where you are, boy,' Mr. Lee warned, but he looked nervous. 'This doesn't concern you. Wait...' Comprehension dawned on his face. 'Is *this* the boy Seki wants? Didn't Captain Walton say to look out for funny business?'

Fell closed his eyes. He began to glow.

His already pale skin brightened as if backlit by dozens of light bulbs. His hair floated from his forehead like it was caught in a gentle wind, but the air in the room was still. As he inhaled, tilting his head up and raising his arms, he looked for all the world as if he were meditating.

Mr. Groz and Mr. Jameson relaxed their shoulders, faces slackening, the indignation surrounding their mouths turned to soft, satisfied smiles. Hands slipped away from Gerdie's arms, and when she turned, she saw that Mr. Lee and Mr.

Tulk had the same expressions of pleasure, as if they were daydreaming of happy things.

Gerdie did not feel relaxed or pleased. She swiveled her head from Fell to each inventor then back again until her neck ached. Fell was causing this; he had to be. But how? She was staring so hard at Mr. Lee that she jumped when something cold touched her shoulder. Fell.

'Get your coin,' he said gently.

Gerdie nodded, and forced her limbs to move, grabbing the coin from where it was just barely enclosed in Mr. Lee's slack hand.

'It won't last long,' Fell said. 'Let's go.'

They ran from the Inventors Guild, Gerdie throwing one last look over her shoulder at the four slack faces, and didn't stop until the guild had been out of sight for a few minutes. Then she ducked into an alley between a row of townhouses. Hopefully it was far enough away for it to be considered a head start; as soon as the inventors came around, they would call the Actions, and Actions were fast when they were on the hunt. Gerdie stopped by the first of a row of townhouses, bending to rest her hands on her knees as she tried to catch her breath.

'What are you?' she demanded between breaths. 'Are you an Angel? Tell me right now!'

'I'm not an Angel.'

Gerdie straightened. 'Well, did they send you or something? Do you work for them?'

He shook his head. Gerdie tilted her head back against the brick and released a sigh, rubbing a shaking hand over her eyes.

'Is that why Seki wants you? Are you a robot or something? Did you escape from him? Is that it?'

'Seki wants me...' he began slowly, 'because of what I can do.'

'I'll say,' Gerdie replied. 'What *was* that in there? Like a—a spell? Magic? Can you do magic?'

He took a step back, blue eyes widening. 'It's not magic,' he said hastily.

She put her hands on her hips. He obviously wasn't going to be forthcoming with the explanations. 'Okay, well... Whatever it is you can do, I'm not surprised Seki wants you for it. He probably wants to experiment on you, huh? I've heard of that happening, you know. People who go to the capital and never come back.' She pushed off from the brick wall. 'We should get moving. You said... whatever you did to them wouldn't last long, and trust me, we don't want them to find us. Although...' she added, 'that is a *very* pretty price on your head.'

Fell narrowed his eyes.

'I'm only joking,' she said with a grin. 'Come on.'

Gerdie poked her head out from the alleyway, looking up and down the street. No sign of Actions. Yet.

She ushered Fell out, and they walked quickly, away from the guild.

'Gerdie, wait!'

She whirled at the familiar voice, shielding her eyes against the early afternoon sun. 'Leo?' she called incredulously.

He was hurrying toward them, limping heavily. His leg always looked like it pained him so much, and she grimaced in sympathy as she watched him.

'What are you doing here?' Gerdie asked.

'I saw you... walk past my window,' he said between breaths.

Gerdie glanced around at the tired-looking townhouses. 'So, *here's* where you live. Hey, why aren't you at work?'

'Why aren't *you?*'

She pursed her lips. 'Touché, sir.'

But Leo wasn't paying attention to her anymore, he was staring at Fell with an expression of disbelief. 'Who is this?'

'This is my new friend. I'm helping him.'

'Is this...is this the boy Seki wants? There's a warrant out for his arrest.'

'Yes, I know,' she said. 'We've just dodged some Actions.'

'Then what are you doing with him, Gerdie?' he said, finally turning to her.

'I found him,' she said proudly.

A small furrow appeared between Leo's brows. 'What's your name?' he asked Fell.

'It's Fell,' Gerdie replied.

He gave her an exasperated look. 'Can't he speak?'

'He can,' she said. 'But I don't think he likes to.'

Fell shrugged.

The furrow between Leo's brows deepened. 'Gerdie...' he sighed. 'You can't afford to get into any more trouble. If you're caught with him, you'll be labelled as a traitor. You'll be sent to the Core.'

Gerdie made a *tsk* noise. 'Well, I don't care about that anymore, Leo. I'm sick of doing everything Seki says—no, don't salute,' she said as Leo raised his hand. 'All his strict and crazy laws? Come on, Leo, what has he ever done for us except increase workloads? He doesn't care about us, and something must change.' She flung out her arm, pointing to the sky where the comet was just visible. Leo flinched at the sudden movement, like he thought she was going to hit him.

Oh, Leo.

'I'm going to stop that comet from hitting us before Seki does, then he'll have no choice but to reward me, to *notice* me, and I'll have his ear, I'll make things better for us, Leo, I promise. You won't have to live with Peller. But please don't tell the Actions where we are. Come with us. Pooh-

pooh the conqueror.' She held out her hand, inviting him to take it.

Leo stared at her open palm with the same longing she felt when she thought of Dad, and she saw him swallow before taking a step back.

'I...I can't,' he said, so quietly she barely caught it.

Gerdie let her hand fall. 'What are you afraid of?'

His eyelids lowered so much it was as if they were closed, and she knew she had already lost. 'You don't understand.'

'Oh, I do,' she said. 'You're a rusted part. You're acting weak.'

He looked up then, hurt filled both his brown eye and the green.

She sighed, instantly chagrined. 'Sorry, Leo. But I don't understand why you're so reluctant to make change happen sometimes. We could do this, you know, and *I* will, even if you won't. I guess I'll see you...well, when everything is different.'

When he didn't reply, she slowly, tentatively, raised her arms and gently wrapped them around him.

'Bye, then,' she whispered.

Slowly, tentatively, his own folded around her in turn. They'd never done this before. Leo didn't like physical contact, she knew, and she usually respected that, but who knew when she would see him again? They hadn't gone as long as a few days at a time without seeing one another, and she realised just how much she loved having Leo as a friend.

It always took a separation to realise just how much you loved something.

'Remember,' she said, recalling Dad's words as she breathed in Leo's faint lemon scent, 'if you tell yourself something enough, eventually it becomes true.' She gave a final squeeze, then let him go. His eyes were full of pain, upset with her, or maybe with himself. He turned and left; shoulders drooped.

'Do you think I was mean?' she asked Fell as they both watched Leo limp back down the street.

'His heart is heavy,' Fell said. 'No matter what your words are, nothing you say isn't something he has already thought.'

Gerdie blinked. 'Wow, Fell. That was deep.' And sounded too wise and adult-y in his high voice. It also sounded sad. She spared one last look at Leo before she and Fell took the other direction.

They kept walking until they were in the north end of Balthasar, where the shops were more run down and quieter, and the mountainous east side of Rendip Quarry loomed. She'd never been to this part of the city before; there had never been any need. This time, she had a need: there was no other direction to go but north.

Forward.

'I think we just need to go far enough until things calm down. Stay out of the way, you know?' she said, thinking out loud. 'Then we can decide our next move. Sound good?'

Fell nodded.

'Good.'

And they marched on.

YOu Do not beLONg hErE
IT iS MIne
It is ChaOs
SUFfer in iT
I wiLL FinD yoU

Six

WHAT ARE YOU AFRAID OF? GERDIE'S WORDS thumped in his ears like a second heartbeat as Leo trudged down Balthasar's streets without really knowing where he was going. Tears built behind his eyes.

What are you afraid of?

He was afraid of so many things, but especially of Conqueror Seki. He had good reason to be. He wondered if he should have told Gerdie the truth from the beginning, when they first met. Wondered if he should have told Hadrian, whether that would have stopped him from leaving two years ago. Wondered if it would have made any difference.

It was too late now. She was gone, so was Hadrian, and Leo had stayed behind.

When Leo blinked his surroundings into awareness, he realised he was on Govert Road, heading home. He must have truly given up, if even his subconscious had directed him here.

There was a man on the front steps. Though he was shorter than Leo, his broad shoulders and dull metal Action mask tucked under his arm made the familiar man look much taller.

Leo sniffed and quickly wiped at his eyes as Austin Grue rose to his feet.

'Peller should be home soon,' he said, optimistically, as he reached the front steps. Grue was the Action often sent to Balthasar with information and requests from New Londinium. Was he here about the wanted boy? Had he and Gerdie been found already?

'I'm here for you,' Grue said. 'You've been summoned.'

Leo's stomach turned. 'What for?'

Grue inspected his fingernails. 'I don't ask the questions, little man. You have been summoned, so a-summoning you will go.'

Leo's palms grew sweaty as he wracked his brains for what he might have done recently to warrant a summon to the palace. Had Seki seen Leo with Fell, even for the brief minute that it was? In the past, Leo had often been watched, but with behaviour good enough to satisfy Seki, he was left alone the past few years. Had the surveillance started up again without him knowing?

He followed Grue around the corner, to where a quad-wing—a small helicopter with four rotors—was parked on the street, its sides emblazoned with the conqueror's seal; meaning that cars swerved around it without complaint.

Leo got in, took his usual seat at the very back. The trip was a short one: the quad-wings moved fast. He watched the smoky blanket over Balthasar fall away beneath them as they climbed higher and higher. Then the old quarry, the tiny houses clustered together in their crater-like hole. The ground became a blur of barren landscape and blocks of factories, dotted with towns here and there, as well as the all-important oxygen turbines.

Leo desperately wanted to ask Grue again why Conqueror Seki had asked for him, but he knew there was no point. Grue wouldn't tell him, loved to watch others squirm.

He clenched his hands in his lap, keeping his gaze fixed on the window.

Grue was chewing something as he stared, looking amused at Leo's discomfort. Leo fidgeted, not meeting his gaze.

'Trumble Day,' Grue grunted.

Leo glanced up, waiting for Grue to elaborate.

'Balthasar and Rendip ready for it?'

Leo shifted in his seat. 'Peller has been seeing to all of the preparations.'

Trumble Day was an annual event held on the anniversary of a comet crashing on Treshane, obliterating the distant city of Trumble. It was where Seki was from – apparently – and only Seki survived the collision that left hundreds of thousands dead. Seki was not really from Treshane, or anywhere on Bellona; he was a giant, his voice accented to an extent that no one had been able to pinpoint its origin. Trumble Day was full of games and food and worshipping of Conqueror Seki's name.

It wasn't a day to remember the dead—it was a day to celebrate Seki's survival.

'*All of the preparations,*' Grue mimicked in a baby voice. 'Still talking like a little princeling.'

Leo clenched his jaw and went back to staring out of the window. After twenty minutes, the quad-wing slowed and descended as it neared the capital city. Hundreds of turbines were scattered around the outskirts, their blades spinning slowly and powerfully in artificial photosynthesis. Then they were flying over New Londinium, the golden splendour of the city laid out for Leo to see. It glittered in the setting sun and still took Leo's breath away, even with what was about to happen once he landed.

It had been four months since his last visit to New Londinium. He sometimes forgot that there was life outside the factories—nearly a whole other world—where there was light and advanced technology and clear, clean air.

And in the centre of it all, the palace emerged beneath them, a sprawling red and white brick structure with a black sloping roof. Protected from the rest of the city by a large wall.

The quad-wing touched down in the large open area just behind the palace—Leo had seen photos of when the area had been green and lush. Now, it was covered in a layer of concrete.

The back entrance to the palace wasn't quite as grand as the front. Though it was made of the same brick, it lacked the golden statues and fixtures that the official entrance boasted. The interior, however, was worse. When the palace had been under the care of the Catells, in the photographs Leo's mother had shown him, every room was decorated with tapestries, furniture, and books, the windows thrown open to let in light and air. And though the rooms were spacious, they still looked homey and comfortable. Under Seki's control, however, the rooms were cluttered, dirty and dark.

Grue ushered him into the throne room; a cavernous room lined with arches that supported a domed ceiling, the sprawling murals of stars and planets and clouds painted on it now faded. Crystal chandeliers hung low, and as they caught the last of the sun's rays, they sent rainbows dancing along the cracked marble floor, creating a twinkling kaleidoscope. Leo wondered if that was what it was like to be among the Angels.

No. The Angels would never treat him as he was about to be treated.

The room was filled with people shifting from foot to foot nervously, though some looked excited. A handful of Actions in their patterned metal masks were scattered before them, watching the crowd intently. Leo was placed to one side, and he let out a small breath of relief. So he wasn't in the direct firing line of the conqueror after all. No one had seen him let the wanted boy leave with Gerdie, which meant they hadn't been caught. He hoped it stayed that way.

There were numerous painted portraits of the conqueror around the city, but none of them could accurately capture the way the presence of the real thing shifted the very air around him.

Conqueror Seki was a hulking mass of man. He sat on a grand chair like a king on his throne. Leo supposed he was. Though there had been no official coronation or stealing of the title, he had taken the place of a king. A long line of kings and queens gone in a click of Seki's thick fingers. The old throne, the *real* throne, had been cast aside. It was still discarded in one corner, lying on its side, collecting dust. Seki was too big for it, but instead of removing it completely, he kept it there, in plain sight, as a reminder.

Seki's face was lost in shadow, but the parts of him covered in gold and shining metals—which was most of him—glittered and tinkled. But it was his voice, his harsh, gravelly voice, that burned into Leo's mind.

Rebels to the north destroyed one of Burton's generators, cutting off power to half the city. Lash.

Hagen's canning factory fell behind their quota due to two broken machines. Lash.

Lash.

LASH.

A hush settled over the crowd as a rickety man shuffled forward to stand in front of Seki, visibly shaking, hand a blur as it touched his forehead in a salute. Leo watched a bead of sweat run from the man's temple and onto the floor. Finneran, one of the senior Actions, announced him as Earnest Mills. Seki leaned forward. He raised his hands until they were level with his shoulders, and it was here he began the dance. That was how Leo thought of it, this habit of Seki's. Seki was never still. His hands moved and twirled as he stared at the trembling man before him, fingers twisting and twitching.

'So, *you* are Earnest Mills,' Seki said.

'Y-y-yes, supreme one,' the man stammered.

'And it is you who has asked to leave your job at…?'

'The siding warehouse in Burton. And I-I'm sorry, my lord, but I hurt my shoulder and -'

'Are there no doctors in Burton?'

'Of course, my lord, but –'

Seki leapt from his throne. 'THEN *WHY* WOULD YOU ASK TO LEAVE?' he thundered.

The very walls seemed to shake, the sky darkening beyond the trembling window panes as if even the sun hid in terror behind the clouds.

Leo flinched, lowering his gaze. His breath came short and sharp through his nose, his body fearing the wrath even when it was not directed at him.

With Seki's enormous size towering over him, Earnest buckled completely. Seki lowered himself onto the lush cushion, his face a mask of calm as if his outburst had never happened.

'Three months in the Core, third division. Let's see how your shoulder fares after that.'

Earnest paled, so shocked that he didn't even protest as an Action pulled him away. His mouth opened and closed like a fish out of water.

'Finneran, bring the next one in,' Seki said through a yawn.

'Yes, sir.'

Finneran disappeared into the next room, returning shortly with a middle-aged man in a pressed suit.

'Frank Pankerk,' Finneran announced. 'A supervisor at Neddie Invention Industries.'

The corner of Seki's mouth curled up. 'Yes. And where is Leo?'

Leo's heart sank, but he stepped forward. He knew there'd been a reason for his presence today; he was never just called to watch the proceedings, life wasn't that kind to him. Seki blinked hard, squeezing his eyes together as if trying to encourage something stuck in them to move. It was another unsettling habit. It made him look mad, unpredictable. He was both, after all.

After a last cruel smile in Leo's direction, Seki turned back to the man in front of him. 'Speak your news of Newburn.'

Pankerk inclined his head, then licked his lips. 'Rebels blew up our stores and escaped. We believe they were members of the Cats.'

'How many rebels?'

'A-about twenty of them.'

'And the supplies?'

'The shed held about ten tonnes of Kolimant sheets, sir. They were important to the project, sir. This sets us back a week or two.'

Leo raised his head. *Project?*

Seki was quiet a moment, fingers still dancing in the air as he considered. 'Leo gets five lashes. And you, Pankerk, get two years in the Core. Second division.'

'No, please!' Pankerk howled, as two Actions came forward to seize him by both arms and drag him from the throne room, and his screaming continued to echo long after he had disappeared. A third Action snaked a hand around Leo's wrist and tugged him toward the post, using no excessive force. They knew him by now. He never resisted.

He caught the eye of Thomas Badbey, the governor of New Londinium, standing offside to Seki. His wrinkled tie reflected the lines of his face, the skin under his eyes as grey as his hair. Their first and last conversation, a few years ago, rose unbidden to Leo's mind.

'I'm sorry about your parents,' he said, taking Leo to one side before he entered the throne room for Seki's third issued punishment. 'Have you...' He glanced around, but they were alone in the dim corridor. 'Have you given any thought to finding the sceptre?'

'What difference would it make?' Leo asked bitterly.

'I and the other governors of this country are not simple thugs like the Actions,' Badbey said. 'We know more than anyone what he is doing to Treshane. Everyone is scared, but until the sceptre is found and returned, there is nothing we can do. If you find the sceptre, Leo, Seki won't be recognised as our leader anymore. It will give everyone hope, give them a reason to stand up and protest his cruelty.'

Leo lowered his head and turned away. 'I can't.'

At the post, he obediently removed his shirt and placed it to one side (too many had been unnecessarily ripped). Then he raised his arms, the Action securing them to the ropes that hung from the post. Would the Cats continue to rebel if they knew what it meant for Leo? These events were out of his control, yet he was punished for them.

Leo was silent, bracing his forehead on the smooth wood of the post. He closed his eyes, hearing the heavy footsteps of Adam Walton, the captain of the Actions, and the sound of the whip being dragged across the marble floor.

There was a beat of silence. Then he heard the shifting as Seki leaned forward in his throne.

'Lash.'

The quad-wing didn't take Leo back.

Once his five lashes were up, an Action released his hands from the ropes. Seki had already moved on to the next item on the agenda. Slowly, Leo bent his knees and lowered himself enough to grab his shirt with the tips of his shaking fingers. He couldn't bear the material on his back, but he gingerly pulled it on anyway. He was thankful he'd worn a dark shirt; it hid the blood that was already seeping through as he limped out of the palace.

Though the train had seats free, he stood by the doors, eager to avoid the stares and questions of the other passengers. He didn't think he could handle sitting down, anyway.

When the train stopped at Balthasar, he hobbled down the platform and into the warm evening. He glanced upward to where the comet was visible as a large, twinkling light. It gave him a peculiar feeling, a cold prickling at the back of his neck. That could just be the aftereffects of being whipped, of course, but he wasn't sure. Something about the comet felt different. Would it be stopped before it hit Bellona? Did he care?

When Leo finally returned home, it was nearing eight. Peller was at the kitchen table, a bottle of red wine opened beside him.

Peller opened his mouth as if to ask why Leo was so late, when his eyes fell to the blood smeared on Leo's arms. Peller pressed his lips together, put his empty glass in the sink, then retreated back into his bedroom. He'd left the bottle on the table, something he would never do on purpose, even if the wine was cheap, made from the grapes artificially made near New Londinium.

Leo didn't even like the taste of wine, or most kinds of alcohol, but it was good at taking some of the pain away. That's what he needed right now. After forcing a few gulps down, he walked stiffly to the bathroom, back burning with every step. He opened the cabinet and pulled down a cloth and a small bottle of antiseptic.

In his bedroom, he soaked the cloth and wrapped it around a plastic back scratcher he kept in his wardrobe.

Slowly, he eased an arm up and dabbed at his wounds with the back scratcher, eyes filling with tears as the antiseptic stung.

Hadrian had done this for him in the past, more than once.

'When will you stand up for yourself?' he would say, his anger making him press hard against the cuts on Leo's back until Leo hissed in pain.

'Sorry.' Hadrian's voice softened and he relaxed his touch. 'But Conqueror Seki shouldn't be allowed to get away with this. To get away with any of it.'

Leo blew out a breath. Though it wouldn't change anything, having Hadrian angry on his behalf made him feel a little bit better. Especially as, after Hadrian finished seeing to Leo's back, they would quietly watch a movie and eat the snacks Hadrian had brought back from his recent visit to the capital.

But Hadrian wasn't there anymore.

Leo switched arms to try and reach the other side of his back with the antiseptic, but the movement pulled at a sore spot on his shoulder, and he quickly dropped the back scratcher.

He gritted his teeth. It would have to do. Leaving his shirt on the floor, he made his way stiffly down the stairs and into the living room to perch on the edge of the couch. He turned the television on and flicked through the channels, keeping the volume down so he didn't wake Peller.

He settled on *Earth Ever After*, a new fictional drama series about survivors on Earth after the Death Comet. Bellona *loved* Earth, its inhabitants eating up any reference, any glimpse, of what life had been like there. Worshipped Earth, almost, as the place it all began. In this episode, one of the main characters, Micah, was leading the ragtag group of survivors across a raging river.

Micah's voice was strong and steady as he eased the others' fears and doubts, and it made their eyes light up with hope that they might make it across safely. Micah was a true leader. Someone brave, optimistic and confident. Someone who rallied his people together to lead them to victory.

Leo could never be like that. He hadn't even been enough to stop his best friends from leaving, one after the other.

As he watched, his eyelids started to droop. He leaned back in the chair, but immediately shot upright again with a wince. For a few blissful minutes, he'd forgotten about his back. He flicked the television off—but not before seeing that Micah had succeeded in getting everyone across the river and was now kissing a girl—and rubbed his eyes. He stared at a spot on the floor, trying and failing to find the energy to climb the stairs to his bed, when his mind drifted back to Conqueror Seki's palace.

What had Pankerk meant by the 'project'? The sheets of Kolimant were used for high temperatures, he knew from Gerdie. And with such a vast amount, had Seki ordered a new type of machine? Was it just something to do with the factories? Leo sighed. He shouldn't dwell on it, not even bother trying to find out. What could he do about it, anyway?

Nothing. Just how Seki liked it.

What are you afraid of?

Everything.

Leo had the nightmare.

He walked through a narrow black tunnel, and it seemed to go on and on and on. All he knew was darkness and cold, his lonely footsteps echoing feebly against stone. A voice whispered to him in the darkness, never quite speaking clear enough for understanding. Something felt different about the dream this time, and as he continued to walk and walk and walk into nothingness, he realised what it was.

Tonight, he could hear the voice clearly.

'*It is time. It is time.*'

Leo picked up his pace, peering through the dark as he tried to see where the voice was coming from, even though his skin tingled at what he might find. The voice didn't sound entirely...human.

He opened his mouth but every time he tried to speak, his own voice was lost, throat tight with the words he couldn't say.

'*It is time.*'

He woke up, shooting upright and hissing as the sudden movement sent a bolt of pain through his back. He'd fallen asleep on the couch, the television murmuring its late-night jewellery shopping program. He gritted his teeth, breathing through the pain. As it slowly subsided, he realised his right leg tingled. He both welcomed and hated the sensation. For a brief moment, he could pretend the leg was still there. He could pretend it would be nothing to just jump off the couch and walk wherever he wanted with no hurt or trouble. As the tingling faded, so too did his dreaming, and pain was his companion once again.

He'd finally heard the voice. Who had it belonged to? What was it time for? As soon as he thought it, he knew. Someone was telling him to find the sceptre. Had it been his brain bringing back the conversation with Governor Badbey? Or had it been...?

No, it couldn't have been his father. Father was dead. He and Mother were gone. Shot during the night seven years ago by Actions who discovered their home, stole Leo from his bed and took him to the Core to teach him subservience.

He hobbled to his bedroom, finding it illuminated in faint yellow light; he'd forgotten to close the curtain. As he slowly lowered himself stomach-side onto his bed, he could see the comet through the window. A smudge of white against the sky, streaming above the staggered skyline of factory chimneys.

He closed his eyes, but it was still there, a burning impression against his eyelids.

Sleep would not come, not with the pain in his back and the feeling that he was being watched by the comet, and the mysterious voice in his head. He thought of Gerdie, of her plea for him to go with her, of her promise to make things better. Would his parents be ashamed of him if they could see him now? Should he have gone with Gerdie? He squeezed his eyes tight, but the tiny thought grew in momentum, and the more he tried to push it away, the more it consumed everything else in his mind.

Go with her go with her go with her –

He pushed up from the bed and reached for his shoe.

SEVEN

As Balthasar disappeared below the steady climb out, the landscape became rugged and bleak, and hills rose like goosebumps on skin, an unmarked road weaving between them. Gerdie had seen what Ada had called 'rolling green hills' in her paintings, but these ones were dull and rocky. She wondered if they'd once had grass growing on them. Apart from the occasional car whooshing past—and the humming of the nearby turbine—the unmarked road was quiet; the highway and other main roads were connected to the north side of Balthasar. Though it might be quiet and forgotten, this part of the land wasn't exactly empty.

Old factories and steel plants sat abandoned, sunk among the hills. They had been in use when Rendip was a working quarry, but the area had been rendered ineffective with the quarry's closure. More than half the residents had moved to find jobs elsewhere, like Osman, the new neighbouring quarry where the metal sheets measured to size in Balthasar's factories came from.

Gerdie glanced back to check their progress up the hill. As evening set in, Balthasar's lights were barely visible beneath the chimneys and smoke. She turned her face to the horizon, where the sun was quickly slipping away. They wouldn't get far in the dark.

'Let's rest in here for the night,' Gerdie said, gesturing to the nearest structure. Old blast furnaces were left to rust, and three giant metal drums stood like forgotten sentinels, striped in red and grey. A network of pipes made an orderly but useless web. It would be dirty, but safe from prying eyes.

Fell looked at it curiously. He didn't look like he needed rest, his blue eyes bright. He nodded anyway and followed her inside. Fell's skin still had that eerie glow, but it provided just enough light for Gerdie to find the light switch, after she grabbed his wrist and directed his hand around like a torch. *So weird.* She had a brief flare of panic that he might be radioactive, but she quickly shook the thought away. Something else was at work here.

The electricity still worked; the lights flickered on, if a little reluctantly. Fell winced as if in pain.

The factory's ceiling was too high for the light to reach, leaving a murkiness above them, and the place smelled of metal and dust. She found a nearby lantern and slowly made her way around the cramped space. Steel beams crisscrossed under the ceiling, where a few of the slats had fallen off, leaving big square holes for the stars to peer through.

Though the crumpled factory was large, it was so full of old machinery and dusty boxes, and the floor peppered with glass and slats from the roof, that they were forced to perform contortionist-worthy moves to get through. Excitement bubbled in Gerdie at the parts she could salvage here. Toward the middle of the room, Fell plopped onto an overturned crate stamped with the light bulb logo of the Neddie Invention Industries, where he rested his chin in his hands. He finally looked tired. The day must have finally caught up with him.

Gerdie's hands had a mind of their own, fluttering here

and there to touch everything she could. She came across a desk with abandoned blueprints stretched across its surface. The blueprints were covered in so much dust they were nearly impossible to read, but she found a rag nearby and wiped them down, leaving streaks that eventually cleared to show... what? Gerdie frowned; her glasses were no help in the dim lighting. The blueprints were complicated, but she recognised a few things, and they were enough to make her stomach turn. One section was a plan for something that looked like a weapon—the cylindrical design was like that in a gun, and there...that looked like a large blow torch, and there were plans for a cannon. She shuffled along the desk, scanning the rest of the blueprints. A shape to one side caught her eye. Circular, but with bumpy edges. It was made bigger for the diagram, but pointed to where the shape would live on the automaton's chest, like it was a button or a key. A question mark was scrawled beside it, like whatever it was was missing or not yet acquired. The irregular circle shape looked so famil-iar. Where had she seen it before? She couldn't put her finger on it.

Seki's official seal was stamped on the corner of the blue-prints: a ten-pointed star with a crown on the star's top point.

A familiar name beside the seal made her freeze.

Stefan Sailor.

Dad.

Why was her dad's name on dangerous blueprints, approved by the conqueror? She'd known nothing about him working for Seki, and Dad had always been so gentle and kind—she couldn't imagine him designing weapons like this. Her eye caught the date at the top of the page. 2nd May-Partial, 2320. Just a few days before her father died. Is that why she hadn't known about these drawings? Or had he never planned to tell her at all?

Gerdie stepped back on shaky legs and bumped into something hard and cold. She turned, expecting an old machine or something, an early Trunk, or maybe one of the quarry drills.

But it wasn't a machine.

It was an automaton.

'Whoa.'

Gerdie took a few steps back to take it in. The automaton was humanoid in shape and at least fifty feet tall; she'd thought it was the back of the factory wall at first. It sat, slumped, with its legs stretched out, the bottoms of its feet the same height as Gerdie, and she realised she'd weaved between its legs without noticing. The metal had a dull surface, but when she rubbed at a spot on its foot with her sleeve, the grime cleared to reveal a shiny bronze. She tilted her head back to see the top of the automaton. It was more skeleton than robot. Its bottom half looked close to completion, but this progress slowly dwindled further up the automaton's body until there was only a brief outline of what would be: the shape of a chest, shoulders, and head, and a bit of scaffolding that was still standing. What was it for, and why did its production stop? She turned to Fell, about to ask him what he thought the automaton's purpose might be, then quickly shut her mouth.

He didn't look well – not just tired, but sick – even in the dim light she could see that. It wasn't possible for him to be any paler, but he was looking a little green around the edges. He stared at his shoes, a tiny frown wrinkling his otherwise smooth forehead. A moth had settled on his shoulder. She glanced at it curiously – it must have been in the factory, but her first thought was that it was the same one from the under-pass and had followed them all this way.

She asked, 'Are you okay?'

His head fell into his hands. 'The noise.'

His voice was strained like he was trying to hold back

vomit. She would know; she had a fear of vomiting and thought if she could talk through the feeling then it wouldn't happen. She was wrong every time.

Gerdie paused, listening. She couldn't hear anything except for her own heartbeat in her ears and the creaking of the wooden roof as the wind battered against it. Something – a hanging chain, perhaps – tinkled above; it made her think of loose nails. Were there any parts in here she could salvage? This had once been an official factory; the parts she could find here would be more useful than anything dumped in Odds and Ends. She spotted what looked like an engine of perfect size higher up, perhaps it was once to be used to power the automaton, so she started to climb.

Dust loosened under her hands. She peered through the rings of metal—they formed a kind of ribcage, and held a number of parts that looked intact. What had halted production if everything appeared to still be working fine? At about halfway, she paused in her climbing to examine something jutting out to one side. It looked like the barrel of a gun, but as she squinted harder at it, she saw the long nozzle and connecting gas container of a fire torch, so large it made her stomach squirm.

This automaton reflected the blueprints, a structure for all those weapons...what Dad had been building before he died.

She continued to climb until she was level with the engine and poked an arm through, stretching her fingers to reach for it. These types of engines had thick outer layers, so if she sent it falling to the floor there should be some shock absorption. There was a clang and a shudder beneath her, she whipped her arm back as the automaton vibrated as if hit with something. She tightened her grip and peered down, ready to shout at Fell to be more careful, but something creaked above her. She turned back to the automaton. Its skeletal head had moved, tilted now, and seemed to be peering at her in curiousity, though it had no face, as if wondering why she was hanging from its chest. She swallowed. It didn't really move, though, did it? Its head had always been in that position. Another shudder vibrated the metal beneath her with such intensity that one hand slipped, and then she was dangling. Terror gripped her throat; she couldn't scream, couldn't react. Something moved out of the corner of her eye. One of the automaton's giant, skeletal hands careened toward her. She ducked just in time, feeling her hair ruffle in its wake. She wasn't so lucky with its other hand: it hit her full in the chest and sent her flying back and then down, down, and she finally found her voice to scream. She was going to die, it was too big of a fall, too much to land on, and she was going to break her back, at least she would see her father again –

But it wasn't something hard or cold or sharp that she landed on. It was something warm and alive. She felt two arms, one at her back and another under knees. It let out an *oof* as she landed on it.

She rolled away with a groan. She barely had time to register who had caught her – and that they *weren't* Fell – before she was knocked back again. The automaton's hand came down with a crash against the concrete floor right where she'd been seconds before. She rolled over with a groan, too many points in her body throbbing with pain to count. She raised her head.

And there was Leo.

He was on his back, face grimacing in pain. Her heart surged with happiness at his appearance. His eyes were scrunched closed, completely unaware of the robotic hand diving toward him.

'Leo, watch out!' Gerdie tried to scream, but winded as she was, it came out as more of a gasp, with none of the urgency she felt.

He heard her, though, and opened his eyes in time to

dodge the metal hand. He wasn't quite fast enough though, and the fist came down on his metal leg, pinning him in place. Leo screamed, trying to drag himself away. The hand came up again, releasing him, and was about to come down again when Fell darted forward and took Leo under the armpits, dragging him away from the blow. Seconds later, it landed where he'd been.

'Run!' Fell ordered Gerdie.

Gerdie scrambled to her feet, adrenaline numbing her throbbing body. She rushed forward to take Leo's other side, supporting him against her. She and Fell dragged Leo toward the factory door as the automaton emitted a series of creaks and squeals. Gerdie didn't need to turn around to know it was moving again, possibly getting to its feet, coming straight for them.

'Go, go!' she shrieked, but Fell didn't need encouragement. Together, they ran as fast as they could with Leo moaning between them and burst through the door of the factory and out into the warm, windy evening.

They kept moving, even though the noises of the automaton had stopped as they left the factory. It hadn't followed them, though the wall of the old plant shuddered. Gerdie was relieved, but she still wanted to put as much distance between themselves and the crazy machine as she could. Finally, when the factory's roof had disappeared behind a hill, Leo groaned and pitched sideways, making Gerdie stagger.

'Fell, we have to stop,' Gerdie panted.

'This way,' Fell said, not sounding at all out of breath. 'Just a little further.'

Gerdie bit her bottom lip. Did Fell know this area? She had no other ideas, and Leo was growing heavier and heavier against her shoulder, emitting soft moans. She hoisted him up against her again, and Fell did the same.

They came to a winding maze of rocks. The Angel's Marbles, she thought the formation was called. It was a man-made formation—like so many structures on Treshane—formed when the quarry was first dug and the larger boulders dumped in one spot, which the students from Balthasar Art School had promptly played with. She supposed Fell was leading them in so they'd be hidden from passers-by.

Just as it was getting too hard to weave the three of them through the closely packed rocks, Fell stopped.

'We're here,' he said.

Gerdie peered around him.

A single tree in the gap. Smaller plants huddled around its base, like nuts and bolts pulled against a magnet. It was *green,* and soft-looking and so strange in this habitat of hard and rough drab things.

They lowered Leo onto the ground beside it. Gerdie couldn't stop staring at the tree. She'd seen one just like it in Ada's painting, but it had been surrounded by many others. She wasn't sure they even grew individually like this. But paintings didn't capture the *smell*: something a bit like the inventors' tea, and something a bit like cleanliness.

Fell knelt by the base and plucked one of the smaller plants from the ground.

'Don't!' Gerdie blurted.

Fell gave her a quizzical look.

'You'll hurt it,' she said. 'Won't you? Aren't they alive? Isn't it like pulling a strand of hair from your head? Because sometimes my hair gets caught on my glasses and I end up tearing out a few strands of hair and—'

'It won't hurt,' Fell said. 'It will help Leo.'

'Oh.' Gerdie lowered herself onto the ground beside Leo. Her fingers drummed against her thigh. 'Can I touch it?'

He extended a hand toward the tree as if to say *go ahead*. Gerdie stretched out her hand and brushed her fingertips against one of the leaves. It was smooth, but coarser than she'd been expecting, and cool, too. She stroked another leaf, and then another, and then the bark, hard and scratchy. When she finally pulled her hand away, her palm had little flecks of brown on it. She wiped it on her pants.

The only thing more astonishing than the tree was Fell. He had recovered from whatever was making him look so ill in the old factory, and now that mysterious glow was back, softly illuminating his skin. His gaze was lowered as he rolled pieces of the plucked plant between his fingers, and she took advantage of his distraction to watch him. Star made boy, everything about him was made brilliant under the green of the tree. From his fuzzy-looking light blond hair, the slightly rounded tip of his nose, to his thin deft fingers.

She thought she felt that same brightness inside her, thought she understood the effect this small piece of nature was having.

Subtly, she glanced at her own arm. Sighed. No glow.

Who – *what* – was he?

'Do you need any help?' she asked. 'Is there anything I can do?'

Fell shook his head, eyes on his work. Gerdie shifted closer and gently removed what remained of Leo's prosthetic, placing it to one side to make things easier for Fell. She tipped her head back, drinking in the orange-purple of the sky. It seemed to stretch on forever. No quarry walls blocking it, no tall buildings, no long chimneys pouring columns of black smoke.

And the *stars*.

Already they were visible and numerous. She felt like she hadn't seen them in such a long time. Even if they were visible above the ceiling of smoke over Rendip, she couldn't remember the last time she'd taken a moment to look up. She loosed a contented breath as she gazed, tipping her head so far back her neck started to ache, but even then, she couldn't stop. She picked out the *Emily's Arrow* constellation, which she hadn't seen since she was a child. It wasn't until Leo moaned, stirring, that she finally brought her head back down and to the reality before her.

Fell had finished with the plant and was now crouched beside Leo, rolling his pant leg up, exposing the extent of Leo's injury. Gerdie winced – the automaton had all but crushed his leg; he was lucky his prosthetic had taken most of the brunt. The dark blood mingled with the brown of his skin, but it was glinting in the moonlight enough for Gerdie to see that there was a lot of it. His pant leg was soaked.

'Will he be okay?' she asked.

Fell was too concentrated on his work to answer. Gerdie felt useless, *hated* to feel useless, so she went to cushion Leo's head, provide some comfort from the hard rocky ground. As she went to maneuver him, he resisted, whole body stiffening.

'No,' he moaned quietly. 'My back...'

Leo twitched, trying to move. Gerdie helped to roll him over onto his left side, where he quietened again. Curious, she lifted the hem of his shirt, revealing angry red marks striping his skin. Her mouth went dry. These weren't an accident, she would have heard. Who could have wanted to hurt him like this? Because she couldn't imagine quiet, kind Leo doing anything to deserve such a punishment. Finally tearing her eyes away from the sight, she glanced at Leo's face, left side smooshed against the ground. The one eye visible was moving back and forth under his eyelid. What horrors haunted his sleep? She realised just how little she knew this boy, whom she'd called a friend for over a year. She lowered his shirt, covering up the marks once again.

Fell was at Leo's right leg, rubbing green mush over the skin there. He pushed Leo's pant leg up further, exposing the network of scars beneath it.

'Oh, Leo,' she whispered.

Somehow, this was worse than the welts on his back. Self-inflicted pain had sharper edges and left deeper scars.

She left Fell to work on Leo's leg while she examined the mangled prosthetic. It was the wrong size, for a start. She couldn't understand why he'd never fixed this simple problem. But she could do it; the socket was made with thin leather, which was an easily moldable material. It wouldn't be perfect, but it would do until he could get another one. She'd heard from other people that their prosthetics were modelled especially for them, so why hadn't Leo had that? As for the rest... She put her glasses back on, pulled her headtorch from her bag, and examined the parts. It was a simple design, the smashed parts were so basic and accessible that Gerdie always carried them on her. The rest just needed some wiggling back into their rightful places, and she would remove the slats around the socket to make the prosthetic lighter. The slats gave the leg a solid appearance, but they were made with heavy iron. Besides, the black *T* of traitors was on the slats.

She pulled her satchel onto her lap and started rifling through it, eager to get to work. The world narrowed to pliers, nails, bolts, and the oiliness of grease on her fingers, until Leo moaned and broke her concentration. The yellow moon Maylow had crept higher into the sky; she hadn't realized how much time had passed. She gently placed everything aside and crawled over to the boys.

'Leo?' She glanced at Fell. 'Is he all right?'

Fell gestured; the end of Leo's missing leg no longer looked angry. Though still scarred and stained with green the skin looked smooth, the scabs gone.

Gerdie gasped. 'How did you do that?'

Fell tipped his silvery head back to stare up the tree and she followed his gaze. It stood like a sentinel over them, and was making a quiet, soothing *whoosh* noise.

'What's it saying?' she whispered.

Fell looked at her, head tilted in question.

'That noise,' she elaborated. 'The tree is talking to us, isn't it? I don't know the language.'

'That's the wind,' Fell said, smiling softly, like the way Dad used to when she was a kid and would question materials in his workshop. 'It moves the leaves, and they brush together. But,' he added, as Gerdie sat back with a disappointed sigh, '*I* think it's speaking.'

Gerdie straightened. 'And what do you think it's saying? Do you think it's lonely out here? Do you think it misses its friends?'

Fell's only answer was a gentle sigh. She thought he was a little bit like the tree, in that he also seemed out of place, something strange and bright in a bleak landscape. Was he on his own here, too? Or did he have family and friends somewhere? Did he miss them?

Leo had gone back to sleep. Gerdie made the final adjustments to his prosthetic, then laid it beside him. As she placed the tools back in her bag, her hand brushed the automaton blueprints, and she pulled them free. She couldn't stop staring at Dad's name. *Stefan Sailor*. It didn't sound like her dad to work on something so potentially dangerous and harmful. Dad told her *everything*. They shared every idea and every prototype and every failure. So why not this one? What had Dad been thinking? What was the purpose of these automatons, and why had the ones in the old factory been abandoned? What if...

Her stomach flipped with apprehension. What if these

blueprints had something to do with his death? She'd never seen him sick, despite his cause of death being consumption. Gerdie had never seen the body or had a chance to say goodbye. She only knew what she'd been told and had been too upset to ask questions. Some part of her hadn't really wanted to know. Well, with her father dead, and her quieted grief—she'd never be rid of it, after all—she had questions. Scanning the blueprints again, she caught a stamp in the bottom left corner of the production company: Cadschel.

'I think we should go to this company,' she said to Fell, pointing to the name on the blueprint. 'I think my father had a connection here, and I want to find out what it is. And anyway, they're clearly professional inventors, whoever they are, I mean, they work for the conqueror! If anyone can give me advice on inventing my comet-stopping machine, it will be them. It won't be a wasted journey.'

Fell nodded, but didn't quite look as if he understood.

'And maybe,' she added, 'we'll pass something that looks familiar to you.'

Fell brightened at that.

A wave of tiredness hit her then. It must have been past curfew, not that there was anyone around to notice. She didn't even really know why curfew had been implemented in the first place. Three years ago, Conqueror Seki had sanctioned it, with dire consequences promised to those found breaking it. Was it to keep Balthasar and Rendip Quarry safe from the night? So that he knew where everyone should be? It was anyone's guess.

Her public sleep time announcement went ignored. Fell seemed content to simply sit beneath the tree, staring up at its branches and the sea of stars beyond. Gerdie inched closer to the base of the tree as if she were afraid it would snap at her if she got closer. It did nothing but continue to whisper, and she laid her head on the grass at its base. It was cold, but soft, and smelled like nothing she'd ever smelled before. It made her think of how she felt with a pencil in her hand and her notebook in her lap, when an idea flowed from her brain and onto the page like an oil spill.

EIGHT

'This is a coin from one of the states of Goliath,' said Dad. 'It was left to me by a dear old friend before he passed. You see, his great-great-great grandfather was an explorer, and he and a small group of men and women mapped a part of Goliath by foot when the Kaufman first landed.'

Ten-year-old Gerdie sighed. 'I'd like to be an explorer.'

'You can be whatever you want to be, my dear girl. Now, the explorers came across a small crater, from a comet that hit long ago, and right in the middle was this coin.'

Gerdie's eyes widened. 'Who left it there?'

'Well, they don't know,' Dad said conspiratorially. 'But it's not made of natural materials, which means someone put it there, which means we were not the first to land on Bellona.'

'Wow,' said Gerdie. 'There might have been aliens here once!'

Dad winked. 'Wouldn't it be something?'

Gerdie slowly came to, the dream disappearing like smoke through her fingers. She was bid *good morning* by a stiff neck and a sore back. Someone was whispering. She opened her eyes.

The tree swayed above her, leaves brushing together in conversation. Sunlight flickered over her face. She watched the tree for a moment, its movement peaceful, so different to the rhythmic, calculated movements of a machine. Then she stretched, feeling knots down her back in intervals so regular she was almost impressed. *Congratulations, orphanage beds, you're officially not the most uncomfortable place to sleep..* She sat up, wincing as something twinged in her side. Lifting her shirt, she saw an angry bruise had formed against her ribs where the automaton made contact yesterday. Her stomach grumbled, but unless it knew where breakfast would be coming from, it was unhelpful.

The boys were already awake. Fell was crouched beside Leo's leg, applying more of the plant mixture to it. Leo's gaze fixed on the tree with a wistful expression.

'How are you feeling, Leo?' she asked, coming to sit beside him, just as Fell leaned back and brushed his hands free of mixture, scattering tiny balls of green to the ground.

'I'm okay,' he replied. 'Whatever Fell's been using is working. I'll have to get some of it.' His smile faded as he started shifting, looking uncomfortable. His hands fluttered around the end of his missing leg.

'I fixed it for you,' Gerdie said. She reached for the prosthetic and made to put it on for him, but Leo snatched it from her.

'No, please,' he mumbled. 'I'll do it.'

He shuffled away slightly, turning his back as he attached the prosthetic. Gerdie wanted to watch, eager to see if it fit, but he clearly didn't want an audience, so she turned her back as well, offering a small shrug to Fell.

'Leo,' she began hesitantly, her eyes on the tree again. 'About those marks on your back...'

She didn't know what she wanted to ask, so she hoped he would pick up the question for her. He was silent, though.

She glanced over her shoulder. Leo dipped his head down so far that only the tip of his nose was visible. She turned all the way around to face him and hugged her knees to her chest.

'Who did that to you, Leo?'

'Conqueror Seki,' he said. She barely caught the name.

A small gasp escaped her. 'But why? What did you do? What could *you* have possibly done to deserve something like that?'

He met her eyes briefly before glancing away again. While curiosity smoldered in her chest, she was hurt that he didn't trust her with things, even after a year of friendship. She was an open book; he knew everything about her, even how Mum left her and Dad for another man when Gerdie was eight, and how she never had the chance to say goodbye to Dad. Leo had a dark past: he didn't need to reveal anything for her to understand *that*. He was, after all, under the care of a man Seki trusted, and his black *T* prosthetic labelled him a traitor to the conqueror.

He clearly wasn't going to answer her, so she said, 'You saved my life back there in the factory. Thank you. What made you change your mind, by the way?'

'You did. I thought about what you said, and I realised you were right. I've been living in fear for too long.'

'I'm usually right. And I'm proud of you, Leo.'

'Pooh-pooh the conqueror, right?' He gave her a small smile before his expression sobered. 'What was that thing yesterday?'

'I don't know. Well, I do know, I found the blueprints. It's some kind of weapon.'

Leo's eyes widened. 'A weapon? What for?'

'Seeing as they were commissioned by Conqueror Seki, could be anything,' Gerdie said grimly. 'Anything bad, that is.'

Leo turned thoughtful. 'I've heard tensions are high between Treshane and Goliath lately, but surely nothing that requires border protection like that. It's the beginnings of a trade war, I think.'

A shiver pushed its way up her spine. Things were scary enough in this country without thinking about fighting with another.

'I can't tell how far along the automaton development is,' Gerdie said, 'but according to the blueprints, it's missing some kind of key.'

'Small mercies,' Leo said. 'But I recently heard Conqueror Seki mention some kind of project. It needed a lot of Kolimant sheets.'

Okay, now she *really* wanted to know what kind of connection Leo had with Seki for him to hear about projects like this.

She tapped a finger against her lips. 'There was no Kolimant in that factory that I could see. Putting Kolimant on automatons like that would make them nearly indestructible, though.'

It was a very scary thought.

She pushed to her feet before offering Leo a hand.

'Well?' she asked, as he stamped the prosthetic, testing its weight. 'How does it feel?'

Leo took a few steps, eyebrows rising in surprise. 'Much... better. Thanks, Gerdie.'

'You're welcome. It was just a simple stretching of the band and also I adjusted the—' She broke off. She heard voices and they all froze, straining to listen. It sounded like at least two men, but they were too far away to make out what they were saying.

'Actions,' Leo whispered.

'How do you know?' Gerdie whispered back.

'I don't. But best to be prepared for the worst-case scenario, right?'

'I'm going to have a look,' she said, moving around a boulder.

'Be careful!' Leo hissed.

She weaved her way through the Angel's Marbles until she reached the edge, then peered around a rock. There were two men walking in her direction. She recognised the gleam of their uniforms. Actions.

'We've been walking for ages,' one was saying. 'They're probably long gone by now.'

'I told you,' the other replied, 'one of 'em's injured. It must be them, no one else comes this way. Look—there's another drop of blood, see?'

Gerdie glanced down. There was a drop of blood by her foot, as well. It must have come from Leo the night before. They'd led the Actions right to them.

She ran back to where Fell and Leo were waiting by the tree. 'It's Actions,' she panted. 'They'll find us soon because Leo bled everywhere.'

Leo's mismatched eyes widened. 'I-I'm sorry, I didn't mean to—'

'It's okay,' Gerdie said, 'Of course I don't blame you, but we need to move, *now*.'

'Hey!'

The three of them whirled around. The Actions had found them already. One was squeezing through a gap between two rocks, but he was much bigger than Gerdie, Leo, and Fell, and weighed down by a thick coat as well as a weapons belt. One of the buttons on his coat scraped across the rock until it popped off and fell to the ground. Seeing their chance in his struggle, Gerdie turned to run, only to find the second Action appearing from behind another boulder. The man, with dark red hair and a handlebar moustache, took a moment to gawk at the tree, and it might have been just enough for her, Leo, and

Fell to escape through another way, but they had nowhere to run. The big guy and Handlebar blocked the only gaps large enough in the formation for them to get through, and Big Guy was already free and advancing on them.

Gerdie yelled, 'Fell, do your thing!'

Fell closed his eyes, but Handlebar struck him across the face before anything happened, sending him reeling backwards. Gerdie lunged forward, so focused on Fell and Handlebar that she didn't smell the smoke until it was too late.

Big Guy had set the tree on fire, and flames consumed the trunk, licking up toward the branches.

'No!' Gerdie screamed. 'No! You're killing it!'

So fast, too fast, the tree disappeared beneath the blaze, reduced to flakes of ash, swept up by the wind, dancing erratically in the air as if they didn't know where to go, looking as panicked as Gerdie felt.

Fell recovered enough to perform the same spell over the Actions as he had to the inventors. He looked dazed from the hit to his face, and his act didn't have as complete an effect: the Actions took a step forward, looked as though they had forgotten what they were supposed to be doing, before looks of determination returned to their faces. It went on a few times, with the Actions breaking through Fell's weak efforts, but it was enough for Gerdie and the boys to inch past toward a gap in the rocks. They ran from the formation. Adrenaline pushed her forward, hurling her through gaps in the rocks, feeling the pain moments later.

They ran aimlessly, just wanting to put distance between them and the Actions. When Gerdie glanced back, black smoke furled from the Angel's Marbles, and there was no sign of the Actions. Rocky formations – natural, this time – rose from the orange ground, and after weaving through them for a few minutes, Gerdie, Leo, and Fell finally slowed. The formations were tall enough to keep them hidden. As they paused to catch their breath, Gerdie couldn't stop the tears from rolling down her cheeks. The poor tree. Fell had said it didn't feel pain when he plucked the leaves, but she knew it had felt pain beneath the flames. She couldn't stop thinking about it, hardly paying attention to their surroundings. There wasn't much to see anyway; there was a strange rippling haze around them. It limited visibility, which made Leo nervous, which then made Gerdie nervous, but as they walked on and on with nothing new appearing – not Actions or any other living soul - they began to relax.

But Gerdie worried about Fell. A bruise was blossoming on his cheek where Handlebar had struck him. And while it didn't look as bad as what she would have expected such a blow to have done, it still wasn't fading as fast as the wound on his hand had. His eyes looked sunken, the bags beneath them darker than the bruise on his cheek, as if he hadn't slept for days. As if the Actions had burned more than just the tree.

As they walked, funny brown rocks started to dot the landscape. They had flat, circular tops with a ringed pattern and what looked like thick legs digging into the ground.

'What are these?' Gerdie asked. The rock-things quickly surrounded them.

'I think they're tree stumps,' Leo replied. 'This used to be a forest, I'm guessing. Many trees grew here, until they were cut down.'

Gerdie tried to imagine being surrounded by more of the tree she'd seen in the Angel's Marbles, and found she couldn't. Fell also glanced around them at the field of tree stumps, looking a bit ill at the sight.

After some time, through the haze she could make out buildings, stretching out along the blurred horizon.

'Is that a town?' she asked.

Leo squinted. 'Looks like. It must be Mallincroft; we've been travelling west.'

'Can we stop there? I don't know about you two, but I'm tired and hungry.'

'I suppose we could... Fell, what do you think?'

Fell looked as sick as he had in the old factory with the automaton. Gerdie gently touched his arm, skin still deathly cold.

'Are you okay?' she asked him.

He didn't answer. Gerdie shared a worried glance with Leo.

'He's probably just hungry,' she declared, then she swallowed as she added, 'And sad about the tree. I am, too.'

Leo said, 'And me.'

The haze began to clear the closer they got to the town, but the landscape remained bumpy as they walked between two formations like a wobbly miniature canyon. Gerdie made out a rectangular hole set into the side of one as it loomed to their left. Miniature train tracks emerged from the darkness and ran across their path to weave through the rocks. The tracks were run down and rusty, obviously hadn't been used in years.

'What's that?' Gerdie asked, pointing to this particular mound.

'An underground mine,' Leo replied. 'They were originally used for mining before quarries started to be used. We're definitely heading toward Mallincroft, then. We can follow the tracks.'

'Does anything live in there? Can we have a look?'

'No and no. Fell's sick and you're hungry, remember?'

Her stomach grumbled as if in agreement, and she trudged along behind Leo, but she couldn't help glancing back at the black rectangular doorway with longing.

They followed the tracks as they led around the mounds, and the town came into sight. What had looked larger from a distance, but as they entered and passed the short rickety buildings along dirt roads, seemed tiny beneath the looming turbine a short distance away. Leo's eyes were darting this way and that, but not to take everything in. His chin was tucked into his chest, one hand worrying at the fingernails on the other. His anxiety was enough to make Gerdie's own stomach flip-flop, and she scanned the tops of the buildings for security cameras. She couldn't see any, and the people milling on the street barely spared them a passing glance.

Among the grey stone buildings were smaller, rickety ones of wood. Wood had been used as a building material when Bellona was first colonised, but the process was quickly switched to stone and brick when the factories were established, where wood could be burned to produce building materials instead. That made the buildings here about one hundred and twenty years old.

The heat was becoming unbearable. Directly in the sun was hot, yes, but it was the air itself that attached to your skin like a parasite, sucking and weighing you down. She thought longingly of the way the tree in the Angel's Marbles had moved its leaves and lifted stray hairs from her face and neck.

Leo ducked into the first cafe that appeared, *Beans and Bolts*, a small, quaint place with dark brown furniture and exposed brick walls covered in newspaper clippings and memorabilia. Gerdie breathed in the coffee smell that hung richly in the air; Dad never let her have coffee often. *You're hyper enough already.*

She preferred tea, anyway.

They chose a booth in one corner, away from the handful of other customers, the table sticky and the vinyl of the seat slashed so that the foam beneath poked out. A middle-aged woman with bright lipstick and a small, electronic device in one hand approached their table.

'What can I get you, loves?'

Gerdie and Leo ordered tea, and after Fell only tilted his head in curiosity at the menu Gerdie shoved under his nose, she ordered tea for him, too. Leo reached into his pocket and pulled out some change, counting the ki as the waitress watched with a dumbfounded expression, like she'd never seen loose change before.

'Where's your Tap card?' she asked.

'Oh, um... we don't have that,' Leo said.

The woman raised an eyebrow. 'It's the latest technology, loves.'

'I've never heard of it,' Gerdie said with a worried glance at Leo.

'Are you from Goliath?' she asked.

'No,' Leo said, 'I'm from Balthasar.'

Gerdie raised her hand. 'Rendip Quarry.'

'And the banks are still operating with cash there,' Leo added.

'Huh,' the woman said, eyebrows furrowed. 'Conqueror Seki ordered this new system over six months ago, I would have thought Balthasar at least would have it, too.' She glanced around her. 'Look, I'll give you these drinks for now, because you look like you need them, but you'd best get yourselves to the bank straight after. They'll sort you out with one.'

As they waited for their drinks, Gerdie rose from the booth to circle the cafe and read what was stuck to the walls. A couple of quotes and jokes about coffee were scattered around; advertisements about the companies artificially growing coffee beans; tribute posters to the famous poet, Scott Teo, who had been born in this town in 2205. Framed newspaper clippings were dated just over one hundred years ago, when the mine first opened in 2217. There were other framed achievements, like best breakfast, a thank you certificate for donating to the local school, and finally, a clipping of the mine's closure in 2263.

When Gerdie eventually returned to the booth, their drinks had arrived, and she slid in beside Fell. Leo's eyes were downcast, watching the steam rise from his cup.

'It's strange,' he murmured.

'What is?' Gerdie asked, dunking the teabag a few times.

'That Mallincroft should operate under different currency rules. Shouldn't the whole country, the whole state at least, be the same?'

'Maybe what that nice lady said is true, though. It takes ages for anything to reach Rendip.'

Leo kept his eyes on his drink, but the set of his mouth said he wasn't convinced.

Gerdie brought her own cup to her lips when the hairs on her arms rose. There were eyes on their booth, she could feel them. When you worked with Conqueror Seki's Actions, you grew used to the feeling. She glanced over her shoulder. Four people sat a few booths down, and all had craned their heads to stare at her, Leo, and Fell.

No, not her and Fell.

Leo.

Murmuring among themselves, they glanced between each other and Leo, serious looks on their faces, seemingly oblivious of Gerdie's notice.

'Leo,' Gerdie whispered, pressing back into the booth. 'Do you know those people? They've been staring at you.'

He flicked his eyes up for a second, a flash of brown and green, before quickly lowering them again. 'I don't know them... Maybe it's because we're not from around here.'

Now it was Gerdie's turn to be unconvinced, but she didn't say anything more. She turned to Fell instead. His drink was untouched in front of him, steam still rising from its surface, and though he was looking a tiny bit better, worry still tugged at her.

There was a scraping of chairs; their audience of four had risen from the booth and started to make their way over.

'They're coming,' Gerdie whispered.

Leo sunk so low in the booth that only his forehead was visible above the table.

Two women and two men. Well, one man. The other looked barely older than Gerdie, but the rest looked to be in their twenties. One was missing an arm, the prosthetic stamped with black *T*, and Gerdie relaxed slightly. They were against Seki's reign and therefore orders, at least, and she didn't think that made them a threat. Their clothing was smudged and dull-coloured, and as they got closer, Gerdie could smell them: dust and sweat. They stopped when they reached the booth, eyes on Leo, who was still refusing to look up. It was almost as if he were deliberately hiding his face.

'Are you who we think you are?' one of the women asked. She had golden skin and a network of scars crisscrossing one arm. Her dark brown hair was cut short, she had a heart-shaped face and small plump lips. She was beautiful, and Gerdie raised a hand self-consciously to her cheek. The stupid birthmark there was so ugly. Even then, the newcomers found it in their hearts to tear themselves away from Leo to glance at her as they noticed the pink-purple stain. She lowered her hand; they were going to stare whether she tried to cover the mark or not, everyone always did when they first met her. For once, though, their gazes didn't linger for very long before they were back on Leo.

'Who do you think he is?' Gerdie asked.

The woman's hard eyes flicked to her. 'I wasn't talking to you.'

Gerdie opened her mouth to argue, but Leo chose that moment to finally raise his face, and the strangers sucked in a collective breath.

'It *is* you,' the older man breathed, sounding reverent.

'Will someone please tell me what's going on?' Gerdie demanded. 'Leo, you just said you didn't know them.'

'Your boy here,' the other woman said, eyes fixed on Leo, 'is the rightful heir to Treshane's throne.'

DO YoU thiNk you cAN rUn?
TherE Is noWheRe yoU cAn run
THis Is My domAIn
YOu canNoT surVivE heRE
CHAOS
MinE

NINE

LEO WATCHED WITH TREPIDATION AS GERDIE stared blankly at the admiring, awe-struck faces, sweat prickling at his palms. 'No, he's not. The royal family has been gone for years and years, ever since Seki overthrew them and killed them all. It's not true, is it, Leo? Tell them. Otherwise, that would make you a—a prince, right? Go on, tell them.'

Leo winced at the word *prince*. But there was no denying it now. Wearily, he said, 'Gerdie...It's true.'

Gerdie's mouth dropped. 'How is that possible? Why didn't you tell me? We've been friends for over a year, I thought I knew...' She trailed off, brow furrowing. Leo knew what she was thinking. How he'd never invited her into his house despite spending countless days with her in the orphanage. How he avoided most public places. How he always lowered his eyes and turned away when an Action was near. The realisation was clear on her face, and so was the sense of betrayal. It turned his stomach.

Leo shrugged, feeling thoroughly glum. 'If I don't talk about it, I can pretend it's not real.'

If you tell yourself something enough, eventually it becomes true.

Gerdie opened her mouth, but the woman raised a hand to stop her from speaking.

'Not here,' the woman said. 'Come with us. Come to our centre, we can talk there.'

'Your centre?' Gerdie asked.

The other woman winked at her. 'Our hideout, if you will.'

Gerdie sat up a little straighter. 'Hideout?' *Now you're talking.* Leo sank lower into his chair.

'We just want to talk,' the man said, seeing Leo's discomfort and uncertainty. 'Just hear us out.'

Gerdie was practically bouncing in her seat, staring at Leo with pleading eyes. Fell blinked serenely between them.

Finally, Leo sighed a sigh of inevitability. He could listen to whatever they had to say, it didn't mean he had to act on it. 'Okay.'

They drained the last of their drinks and followed the strangers out into the main street, then back on the tracks they'd followed earlier. He could practically feel Gerdie vibrating with excitement at the thought of going into the mine. To Leo, it felt like he was walking straight into a gaping mouth, about to be swallowed by a giant beast. The mine wasn't so horrible on the inside, though. It was pleasantly cool, the air dry and dimly lit, though not enough to prevent him from stumbling on the unevenness of the tracks. The woman with the scarred arms walked with Leo, her companions ahead, Gerdie and Fell behind, Gerdie jabbering away to Fell, who said one word in reply to her every thirty. It was only after about five minutes, when the tunnel began to gently slope downward, that the woman stuck out a hand. 'I'm Jessica,' she said. 'My dad is the leader of this group.'

Leo shook her hand. 'Leo.'

'Dad won't pressure you into doing anything you don't want to do,' Jessica said. Leo swallowed.

It was nothing like he'd expected. The cramped space opened into a large cave, the roof so high all he could see was black. They must be very deep underground. Several tunnels branched off from the cavern, some with old cart tracks, and the place smelled warm; metallic and earthy. Huge tyres from old mining trucks had been transformed into furniture, and some were painted into a variety of cartoon characters—He recognised Everly the Earthworm, a popular round-eyed pink worm who taught children about Earth.

A few other people were milling about, their clothes just as dirty. Who were these people, and why did they have a 'centre' in an old mine? Why choose to live underground in the dark and cold instead of in town?

Their curious stares, the *T* marked prosthetics on nearly every third person, and their hopeful faces was enough to answer his own question. The marks on his back throbbed.

'How are they recognising you?' Gerdie whispered. 'Why don't they think it's me? I could be an heir, too, you know.'

'Because of my eyes,' Leo whispered back. 'The green one is the mark of royalty. It runs in my family.'

Jessica led them to one side, where a large man with thick greying hair sat on an old plastic chair with three other men, surrounding a map stretched out on a box, lit by an oil lamp beside it. Leo braced himself as Jessica went to tap the largest man on the shoulder.

These were the rebels that made life complicated for Seki, who resisted his tyrannical rule, who had no idea that their acts caused Leo to be whipped as if Leo had any idea who they were.

Well, now he did.

These were the Cats.

He didn't know how to feel. Blood was rushing to his ears. His back still throbbed painfully.

Jessica conversed with the big man, who straightened, shoulders stiffening. He turned and regarded Leo, his expression softening. He came over and shook Leo's hand in a strong, callused grip, his kind blue eyes roving Leo's face.

'My dear boy,' he said in a smooth, deep voice. 'Welcome.'

Leo didn't reply. He couldn't find his voice, let alone form words. Even the man's gentle presence wasn't enough to put him at ease.

'Luca Du Bois,' the man said. 'It's a pleasure to meet you, Leo Catell. Come with me, we have a lot to talk about.'

'These two were with him, Dad,' Jessica said, waving a hand at Gerdie and Fell, hovering further back.

'They're welcome, too, of course,' Luca said. 'Any –'

The lights flickered then died. Luca gave a heavy sigh in the darkness. 'Damned generator again.'

'I can help,' chirped Gerdie.

Two torches clicked on, their beams cutting through the darkness and revealing Luca's surprised expression. 'Well, sure,' he said. 'You're welcome to take a look at it. It's just through here.'

Luca accepted a torch from one of the men and bid Gerdie follow him into a nearby alcove, Leo, Fell, and Jessica trailing behind. Metal shelves had been fixed haphazardly to the stone wall so that the alcove resembled a walk-in pantry. The shelves stocked with bottles of oil for the lamps, the smell of kerosene strong, and sitting on the floor in silence was the generator. Gerdie knelt beside it under the dirdcted torch beams, removing the metal slats from the side and fiddling with one of the wires. Leo glanced at Luca, who looked amused. Leo guessed he knew how to fix a generator but was humouring Gerdie anyway.

'It's blown a fuse,' Gerdie announced.

'We only replaced that one last week!' Jessica exclaimed.

'I've got a spare right here.' Gerdie rifled through her bag, retrieving a small transparent container. A few moments later, the generator was humming, and a cheer rose from the main cavern behind them as the lights flickered back on.

'Excellent work, little one!' Luca boomed. 'Welcome to the Cats.'

Gerdie gasped loudly at the name, then rounded on Jessica and fired questions in such rapid succession that Leo wasn't sure if she was even breathing between them.

Luca led them back out of the alcove and down one of the tunnels. They followed the old mine cart tracks around a short bend, before ducking into a smaller room cut into the rock. Maps were tacked onto the wall, some with pins stuck into them as markers, and a big round table was set up in the middle of the room. Jessica leaned against the stone archway and folded her arms while Luca dropped into one of the chairs and invited Leo, Gerdie, and Fell to do the same.

'Here's the thing, Leo,' Luca said, clasping his hands together on the smooth tabletop. 'I know what you've been through. I know what happened to your parents. The rumour was that you had died with them. Our priority is to remove Seki from the throne, not to restore the Catells, since we all thought they were gone for good. But now that we know you're alive, it's only right to give you this choice to act. But the thing is, son, it would help us a great deal if we had the sceptre. And it's only you who can find it.'

'What's the sceptre?' he heard Gerdie whisper, presumably to Fell, but she received no reply.

'And of course you know that if you find the sceptre –'

'I can't give it to anyone else,' Leo finished. 'I can't just find it and pass it on. It has to be me who puts it back on the throne and reclaims it.'

'Right,' Luca nodded. 'No pressure on you, son.'

No pressure, Leo thought bitterly to himself. *Yeah, right.*

'Can I think about it?' he asked.

'Sure,' Luca said. 'You and your friends are welcome to stay the night.'

He managed a weak smile of thanks as Gerdie clapped her hands with delight.

A buffet-style dinner was put on, and they each grabbed a bowl and spoon and joined the line. The man serving the stew was so fixated on Leo's face with an expression of awe that he missed Leo's bowl, and some of the stew dribbled onto the floor.

The mood inside the mine was one of excitement and anticipation, whispers running across the cavern like electricity through a wire. Every pair of eyes were on Leo, and even in the low illumination of the cavern, it felt like a spotlight was trained on him. He retreated into a dim corner with his bowl, hoping he could sink into the shadows. Staring glumly into his stew, pushing a piece of potato around with his battered metal spoon. Peller would have noticed his absence by now. Would he report it to Seki? Did he wonder where Leo was?

He sighed around a piece of tough beef. How could he do it? How could he become king when he was a nobody? He'd been born with a mark of royalty... so what? He couldn't even stand up without help, so how was he supposed to support an entire country?

He put his bowl down by his feet, suddenly not hungry, and rested his head in his hands, palms to his eyes.

He could easily hear Gerdie from across the cavern, her loud bubbly voice carrying through the stone.

'What is the sceptre?' she asked again.

'The sceptre, my dear girl,' Luca began, lowering his voice and adopting a lilting rhythm, making Leo think this wasn't the first time he'd told the story, 'is the symbol of Treshane's power, and when wielded by the rightful person, is capable of a many great things.'

Leo shifted his head so he could see them. She was sitting with Luca and one of the women from the cafe. They were huddled together on a rock, Gerdie on the very edge of it to hang on to Luca's every word.

'It was made shortly after people arrived on Bellona, using Melia root. There was only one of its kind on this planet. James Catell, a prince on Earth, led the mission to Bellona. He was courageous and headstrong, saw his finding of something so rare as a sign of his right to be leader of Treshane, and wanted to bind this idea with physical proof. He had plans drawn up for a beautiful sceptre, something that encompassed the planet itself.

'But when exposed to such high temperatures, the root created an explosive reaction. James didn't look away in time. His left eye was permanently damaged: blinded and leeched of its pigmentation, turning it green-grey. This didn't deter him, though; James had travelled so far and risked much, he wasn't one to give up easily. So as soon as he was healed, he returned to the Melia root – with proper protection this time, of course.'

'Of course,' Gerdie grinned.

'And so, the sceptre was made. A symbol of power passed down from parent to child, as was James' eye. While his children and their children were born with sight in both eyes, their left was always without proper colour. It became a signature of royalty here on Treshane. Marked by the sceptre, they were.'

'And what happened to it?' Gerdie said in almost a whisper, completely entranced by the story, her own bowl of stew forgotten in her lap.

'After Seki threw the coup that ended the royal Catell line,' Jessica said with a sigh, 'he hid the sceptre. We can only assume it's somewhere impossible to find. Seki wouldn't risk the rightful heir being able to find it.'

Gerdie frowned. 'Why didn't he just destroy it?'

'It can't be destroyed,' Luca said. 'Nothing is powerful enough. All Seki could do was hide it and keep a watchful eye on the Catell family members that were left.'

'You mean there's more than just Leo?' Gerdie asked eagerly. 'He still has family? Does he know? Can we find them?'

Even though Gerdie couldn't see it, Leo shook his head slowly in answer.

Jessica cleared her throat. 'No, we don't believe so. He's the last one, after his parents died. For a long time, we all thought he died with them...'

Leo tuned out the conversation, squeezing his eyes shut again. Yes, he was the only one. But he still believed he wouldn't be able to help them. Sure, he could look for the sceptre, but he'd probably die in the process, especially if Seki caught wind of what he was doing. There'd be Actions and police bots on his tail in seconds. He laughed darkly to himself. At least people would say he tried. Maybe in death he'd be more noticeable than he had been in life.

Are you giving up? You can't give up. Why would you say something like that?

Giving up was what he did best. When things got too hard, or he grew too scared, he withdrew. To do otherwise, to keep fighting, meant bringing Seki's wrath down on his head. Or his back.

Gerdie's laughter, boisterous and unashamed, cut through his thoughts. He glanced over at her again. A girl with short, curly blonde hair and a round face had joined them, and it was she making Gerdie and Luca laugh. Gerdie could make friends with anyone.

Fell was smiling, too, just a little bit touching the corners of his mouth. His eyes were on Gerdie, as if her happiness was what made him happy. As if, despite only knowing her for what Leo assumed was a few days, he was pulled into her orbit like a planet to a sun. What was it that made her so strong in the face of hardship? How did she always have a smile to share? Why couldn't he be more like that?

Leo rubbed his forehead with the heels of his palms. He wished he could be more like Gerdie. Ever since they first met, he'd wanted an attitude like she had, when he'd caught her tinkering with one of the factory's machines with only her satchel and a dream to make things better. That's why he'd wanted to help her make a difference, to be a better person. He was faced with a real chance—a chance to do more than yearn as he lay down to sleep.

He rose and walked over to the little group. Their conversation stopped as he approached, and they looked to him.

'I've reached my decision,' he declared. 'And I'll do it. I'll find the sceptre, help you weaken Conqueror Seki, and take my place as k-king.' He inwardly cursed himself at stumbling on the word.

If anyone noticed, they didn't show it. Their grimy faces broke into wide smiles of relief and hope, rising from their seats to shake his hand and pat him on the back.

Gerdie came up beside him. 'But Leo,' she said quietly. 'It could take you ages to find the sceptre, if you even find it at all. Do you have any idea where to start looking?'

'No,' he admitted. 'And I wouldn't ask you to come with me anyway. It could be dangerous. And once he realises I've left Balthasar, Seki will send people after me. He'll know what I'm doing. He's never exactly seen me as a threat, but he knows that's what I am.'

'If the comet hits before I can stop it, none of this will even matter. We can't rely on Seki to do anything about it.'

'You go on,' Leo said. 'Take Fell with you.'

'But what about you?'

Luca appeared between them, making the both of them jump. 'We wouldn't let you go on your own, son. And Hadrian has kindly offered to go with you.'

He pulled a boy into view, and Leo's pulse stopped, then raced. Hadrian had grown a few inches in the two years Leo had seen him last; he was all legs and arms and neck, pale-skinned and sandy-blond-haired. His Adam's apple was more prominent, bobbing as he swallowed.

'Hi,' he said, his voice breaking on the single word. A simple word, like they'd only seen each other last week, and not like Hadrian had disappeared two years ago without a word, leaving Leo heartbroken. It *could* have been last week, for all his emotions were betraying him. Like muscle memory, one look at Hadrian's face surged memories of late-night movie-watching, so tired that everything became funny; of stolen glances as Leo looked down from the overseer's office and Hadrian looked up from the factory floor; of eating lunch at school together, pressed side by side in the shade of a boulder behind the classrooms.

'Do you already know each other?' Luca asked, swiveling his head between them.

'A long time ago,' Leo said, coldness in his voice. 'I'm afraid I don't need anyone to come with me.'

'Sure you do,' Luca boomed, throwing an arm around Hadrian's shoulders. Hadrian's knees buckled. 'And trust me, you'll want Hadrian with you. He joined us about a year ago, he's already proved invaluable.'

Hadrian was staring at Leo, his big hazel eyes even wider, imploring for... forgiveness? Understanding?

'I've travelled,' Hadrian said, and Leo wondered if it was an explanation to Leo or proof of Luca's words. 'I know this landscape quite well.'

'You see?' Luca said, looking at Hadrian with pride.

'I...'

'Just say yes, Leo,' Gerdie said, eyes rolling behind her glasses. 'Travelling will be fun with a friend. We've travelled together and look how much fun we've had!'

Leo made a choked noise and pointedly placed a hand on his side, where it was still tender from Gerdie landing on him in the old automaton factory.

'And I'd feel much better,' she continued as if she hadn't noticed, 'knowing you were out there with someone else to watch out for you.'

'It's settled then,' Luca said, clapping Leo on the shoulder. 'I'll leave you all to get acquainted.'

In the awkward silence that followed, Leo cleared his throat and Hadrian shuffled his feet. It was only then he noticed Hadrian was wearing a faded and scuffed blue backpack.

Leo had spent two years imagining the reunion, but now that it was here, he didn't know what to say. They'd once come to the other for everything: Hadrian after a fight with his mum, Leo after a punishment from Seki. Even after his leg had to be amputated, Hadrian had been there, taking advantage of Peller's hours at Sweene & Sons to visit Leo. If anyone had been watching the house, word of Hadrian's visits either went unreported or – more likely – unnoticed, and Leo had been grateful for it. Still was. If it weren't for Hadrian's company while his leg healed, Leo would have given in to his depression. The physical pain was easily numbed by medication, and in fact it was a relief to have the leg gone instead of dealing with the constant infection and inflammation.

It was the pain inside his own head that was killing him.

But Hadrian had been with him nearly every day, letting Leo know that he wasn't alone. Even on days where they didn't talk at all, Hadrian would just sit with him, sometimes with the television playing in the background, sometimes in complete silence. Leo always knew Hadrian was there if he needed him. Did he know this Hadrian?

Gerdie broke the silence. 'You said you've travelled, Hadrian?' she asked. 'Where have you been? What was it like? Did you go with other people? Where is your family? Are they here?'

Leo almost felt sorry for him as the target of Gerdie's rapid fire, but he wanted to know the answers, too. They were supposed to have been best friends, they had known each other for nearly ten years. Hadrian had been the one to keep Leo from spiraling into darkness after his parents' deaths, when Leo thought he would be next.

'I've travelled on my own because my dad died, and my Mum might as well be for all the –'

'Your dad died?' Leo repeated faintly. It was like two punches to the heart. One for Mr. Hatch; his gentle voice and kind face. The other...

Why hadn't Hadrian told him?

Had he really chosen to run away without a word, instead of coming to Leo like he always had? When this huge, life-shattering thing happened, had Leo's friendship not mattered at all?

Hadrian's dad... dead. And Leo hadn't known. No wonder Mrs. Hatch hadn't answered the door those last few times he'd tried to check on Hadrian, eventually giving up after weeks of no word.

'Oh...,' said Gerdie. 'That's the same with me and Leo. And Fell too, I think,' she added with a questioning glance at Fell. When he only glanced down at his feet, Gerdie said, 'But we're not alone anymore.'

'Yeah,' Hadrian said. 'I guess we gotta be each other's family now, right? Anyway, to answer your other questions, I've been to most of the major cities in Treshane, like, New Londinium, Malberg, and Opler, and I even went to Goliath, once. Treshane is…' He glanced at Leo. 'Chaotic, in comparison. That's what made me join the resistance here. Under Seki's rule, the world is suffering. I wanted to help change that.'

'You *have* been busy,' Leo muttered.

Hadrian flashed him a look of irritation and Leo felt instantly guilty.

'That's very noble of you,' Gerdie said, seeming to have missed the exchange. 'I want to make changes too, you know. Rendip Quarry is a terrible and dangerous place to live, and I'm going to become a famous inventor so I can tell Seki and I can fix it. Well,' she said, looking at Leo. 'If you *do* become king, Leo, then you can make changes. You've witnessed first-hand what the factories are like. You can make it easier; *you'll* be the one making all the rules.'

'It's the same everywhere else in this country,' Hadrian added. 'Seki has a far reach.'

Leo swallowed. 'Let's not get too hasty. I'm nothing without the sceptre.'

'That's not true,' Gerdie said softly.

Leo stared at his shoes. It was true. He felt a soft squeeze of a hand against his own, but before he could pull away, Gerdie let go and rounded on Hadrian again. 'So how do you two know each other?'

Hadrian answered her but kept his eyes on Leo. 'We grew up together.'

'Oh, *wow*,' she said with glee. 'I've never had a friend for that long before. Leo and I have been friends for maybe a year, we met at the factory, you know. So, what's Goliath like?'

Leo listened in silence as Hadrian answered her questions. He was patient at first, speaking kindly as they all accepted a cup of bitter tea from Jessica, but then his replies became shorter as his irritation grew. It didn't seem to be directed at Gerdie, exactly. He started to bounce his leg, hazel eyes flicking around as if he suddenly realised he'd rather be anywhere else. It always made Leo nervous, Hadrian's short temper and how the smallest things – so small that sometimes Leo didn't even know what they were – would set him off.

Gerdie didn't know that, so Leo yawned pointedly, and the others got the hint, pushing stiffly to their feet and stretching. Fell rose gracefully, not looking the least bit tired. He was a strange one. Hadrian calmed down a bit, eager to move, and an awkward silence settled over them. Leo could almost feel those unexplained two years hovering between him and Hadrian. The silence only lasted a second, of course, before Gerdie started chatting away, but the look Hadrian gave Leo told him that he had felt it too. It said, *later*.

As the lanterns in the main cavern were dimmed, Jessica hustled them off to bed. Leo went to follow the others, but Luca stepped in front of him. 'Let's take a walk,' he said. 'I think we should chat.'

Nerves filled Leo's belly like he was being summoned by an Action to Seki's palace. Leo swallowed, then glanced at Gerdie.

She nodded encouragingly. 'Catch you later, then,' she said with a small wave before she disappeared down the corridor with Fell, Hadrian and Jessica.

Luca placed a huge warm hand on Leo's shoulder, steering him in the opposite direction. As they twisted and turned through the mine, the tunnel darkened. The Cats obviously had no use for this part of the mine, and the deeper they went, the more nervous Leo grew. The tunnel narrowed, and the lights were few and far between until eventually they disappeared altogether, leaving them in utter darkness. Where was Luca taking him? Was he going to leave Leo in the middle of the mine, in the dark and with no way out because he'd finally realised that Leo wasn't the heir they'd been searching for? All sorts of accidents could happen inside an old mine like this, and they wouldn't find Leo's body for days, maybe even weeks, Luca would know all the best places to hide a body –

Luca chuckled as if he'd heard Leo's thoughts. 'Don't worry, kid. I know this place like the back of my hand. We're nearly there. Relax.' He squeezed Leo's tense shoulder, and Leo tried not to flinch as the gesture put pressure on one of the bruises there. Despite Luca's soothing tone, Leo found it hard to relax, his breathing becoming fast and shallow as the darkness pressed in on him.

Then the soft glow of a light appeared, and Luca steered him into a small cavern that was lit by a single oil lamp. Dark metal crates were stacked to one side and dusty old mining tools on the other. Luca sat beside the oil lamp and turned up the flame, then gestured for Leo to sit beside him.

'So,' Luca began, his voice softer than Leo would have thought possible for such a large man. 'Have you been hearing it, then?'

Leo shifted on the wooden crate; eyes fixed on the floor. 'Hearing what?'

'The sceptre.'

When Leo glanced up, Luca was watching him with kind eyes. 'How did you know about that?'

Luca rested his elbows on his knees and slowly rubbed his big hands together. 'Even if I had not seen your eyes, Leo Catell, I would know who you are. You look just like your mother.'

Leo straightened. 'You knew her?'

'I did. Your dad, too. My family, like yours, goes back and a long way, and the Du Bois' have always been guards to the Catells.'

'I didn't know that,' whispered Leo. 'How come I didn't know about you?'

Even as he said it, he remembered. Murmured voices in the next room when his parents thought he was asleep. Someone returning home late at night, soft sounds of movement telling him that his parents were conversing in sign language. And a booming laugh that woke him up one night, a laugh that could only have been Luca's, now that Leo had heard it again.

Luca smiled in a way that told Leo he was remembering right. 'That tradition didn't stop just because they were over-thrown. My great-grandfather followed your grandfather into hiding after the king was killed, and it's been that way ever since. Until of course...' His mouth turned down, and he gave a mournful sigh. 'I did the next best thing I could: join the resistance and fight.'

Leo nodded, unable to speak. But Luca didn't seem to need a reply; he straightened and went on. 'You know Lane heard the sceptre, too? That's how I know. We were getting ready to set off and find it when Seki found out. I don't lead this resistance group just because I hate Conqueror Seki—although that *is* a big reason. I'm fighting for what I believe is right. Your parents were not only incredibly kind and generous people, but the true leaders of this country. Seki isn't from Treshane, maybe not even from Bellona. He's a virus, spreading quickly on this continent. Now that your parents are gone, I fight for *you*, Leo.'

'I'm nothing like them,' Leo mumbled.

'Great leaders aren't born, kid. They're made. Your dad had no idea what he was doing, either.'

Leo tried to smile his acknowledgement, but all he managed was a tiny tug at the corner of his mouth. His father had heard the sceptre too? Had he also been plagued night after night with the whispering voice?

'Now,' Luca said, pushing to his feet, 'the real reason I brought you here.' He took a few steps back to look at the crate he'd just been sitting on. Leo joined him, finally noticing the faded black logo stamped onto the metal. *For the Forest.* His stomach swooped, heart beating faster as he read the logo over and over to make sure it wasn't a mistake.

'Where did you get those?' He sounded breathless. 'I thought they'd all been destroyed.'

'Most of them have,' Luca said grimly. 'This might be all that's left. These had been passed down to your mum and dad, kept after the initial destruction after Seki took power.'

For the Forest was a conservation and sustainability company that worked to plant trees and regrow flora, to introduce nature back into a world that had tried to destroy it. Once Seki gained control of the country, he shut down *For the Forest* and ordered supplies and equipment to be eradicated. Seki hated nature, anything green and growing, something Leo never understood.

Before they died, Mother and Father showed him these very crates. Mother especially was so passionate about the program; she would sit Leo down, open the cryopreservation crate and explain with her graceful hands how they were going to use the supplies to reintroduce a wide variety of plants and trees when they overthrew Seki.

When. It had always been *when* with his mother. She had been so gentle and kind, but strong and determined, as well. If she and Father were still alive, they would have been the Catells to finally defeat Seki and regain the throne of Treshane. Instead, it was just Leo. He wished he could have taken after them.

To have these crates in front of him... The way his heart had *soared* when he recognised them. It felt, for the first time, like there was a real chance for the future.

Leo glanced up at Luca, who watched him with eager anticipation. 'Thank you,' he said quietly. 'This is...amazing.'

Luca beamed at the crates. 'It's no trouble, kid. We all share this world, so we all have a responsibility to take care of it. But best get you to bed now. You've got a long journey ahead of you, and you'll want a good night's rest.'

Back in the main cavern of the mine, Luca pointed down one of the many snaking tunnels.

'Down there, then it's just the third on the left,' he said. 'There's always someone around, so just come back to the main cavern if you need anything.'

Boys and girls had been separated, it seemed. Leo stepped into a long room lined with five small beds. Two were occupied: Fell was perched on the end of one, his silver hair glowing in the light fixed above his bed. Though Fell had saved his life, Leo felt awkward without Gerdie there between them. He found himself missing her incessant chatter already. There was another boy on the next bed, lying on his back. He lifted his head as Leo entered, then sat up.

'Oh,' he said, as Leo drew closer. 'Thought you were that other new kid.'

Leo took the bed on Fell's other side. 'You mean Hadrian?'

'Yeah,' the boy said, swinging his legs over the side of the bed. His light hair was cropped short, and freckles dotted his face and arms. 'I don't trust him. I'm Emmett, by the way. Who are you?' His look of surprise as he saw Leo's eyes meant he already knew the answer.

'I'm Leo.' He took a breath to defend Hadrian, then hesitated, surprising himself. Even after two years of hurt, with no word from Hadrian at all, he had still been quick in wanting to stand up for his friend. But were they still friends? Did Leo even know Hadrian anymore? Anything could have happened in those two years; Hadrian could be a completely different person. 'Why don't you trust Hadrian?'

'Turns up out of nowhere, he does. Claims to have all these secrets about Seki and the Actions. But how d'you reckon he knows all that? It's because he's one of them. Don't listen to anything he says.'

Hadrian entered at that moment, shrugging off his faded blue backpack. He smiled tentatively at Leo, then his face darkened when he saw Emmett. Leo couldn't help but look away, which clearly told Hadrian they had just been talking about him.

'What have you been saying, Emmett?' he growled, sitting his backpack on one of the beds.

Emmett stood. 'Only the truth. That I think you work for Seki. I saw you—'

SMACK.

Hadrian had pulled back his fist and punched Emmett in the jaw.

'Shit!' Leo sprang forward, but he didn't know if he was going to pull Hadrian back or see if Emmett, who had fallen over the side of the bed and disappeared, was all right. In the end, he grabbed Hadrian's arm. Hadrian's cheeks were a mottled red as he took a step forward. His eyes fixed on Emmett, who was using the bed to pull himself upright, blood speckling his lips.

Leo threw a desperate glance over his shoulder at Fell, to appeal to the other boy for help. Fell had risen from his bed, but just stood there watching, subtle distress on his face, a furrowed brow and strain around his eyes. Leo opened his mouth, but before he could say anything, Fell outstretched his arms. He closed his eyes. Leo swore Fell's pale skin began to glow, but that was impossible. He didn't have time to think about it further because Hadrian suddenly relaxed under Leo's fingers. The tension was leaving his body in such a rush that Leo felt the muscles deflating under his skin. Hadrian's angry expression faded, the red staining his cheeks and neck draining away.

The same effect was happening to Emmett as well. Both

boys stilled as if someone had pressed pause on a remote. Emmett's hand, raised in defence, slowly lowered, his tense expression relaxing. Seeing they weren't about to kill each other, Leo let go and hesitantly stepped back. The boys blinked, breathing slow and deep.

'No more fighting,' Fell said.

Leo's scalp prickled with unease. Hadrian's and Emmett's aggressiveness was completely gone. They looked relaxed now, if a little confused, glancing around the room as if unsure how they got there, just like the Actions at the Angel's Marbles. Gerdie had yelled at Fell to do something then, he remembered.

'How did you do that?' Leo whispered to Fell.

Fell stumbled back onto his bed, breathing heavily. A bead of sweat rolled down his temple. He glanced up at Hadrian through long pale eyelashes, a strange expression on his face, like Hadrian was a puzzle he was trying to solve.

'We should just...go to sleep,' Emmett said, his voice sounding dreamy.

'Sure,' Leo said slowly, watching Hadrian and Emmett crawl into bed. He turned to Fell, stomach knotting. Fell hadn't touched anyone, but he'd obviously done *something*. Who was this strange boy? Fell lay on top of the covers, curled into a little ball, his back to Leo.

Once Emmett and Hadrian were under the covers, Leo lowered himself onto his own bed, watching as Hadrian's bony chest slowly rose and fell with sleep, backpack under the covers with him. He'd wanted to talk to Hadrian, to settle things between them, to ask about his dad, to find out where Hadrian had been all this time, but it didn't seem like the right time. Still keeping a watchful eye on the boys, Leo slipped under the covers. Emmett tossed and turned, his breathing shallow, as if he were afraid of falling asleep with Hadrian in the room.

TEN

Gerdie woke early in the morning despite the late hour she'd finally fallen asleep. She shared a room with three other girls, Tammy, Mei, and Lori, who were fifteen, sixteen, and seventeen respectively. They were very nice and very interested in Gerdie's inventions – the other orphans often weren't. She'd stayed up introducing them to the M.O.R.T., and showing them her notebook, explaining where her ideas and plans came from. The way the girls' faces lit up when they saw the M.O.R.T., the way they cooed... it made Gerdie's heart soar. Her inventions made her interesting. Her inventions made her likeable.

Between the four of them, they covered nearly every corner of Treshane, and swapped stories about their experiences living under the conqueror's reign. Tammy was from the very north of the country, near the One Sea, where they were only allowed to have mail delivered if their house-number was odd.

Mei, who had lived to the west, said her mother worked at the palace as a chef before her fatal heart attack.

'She'd come home with her hands bandaged and bleeding,'

Mei had said. 'Seki forced them to multi-task; everything had a real sense of urgency when there didn't need to be.'

Somehow, there was satisfaction to knowing the rest of the world was as in dire need of change as Rendip; it only strengthened her determination to make a difference. In fact, she'd have loved to have joined the resistance and stay here in the old mines, but the blueprints in her bag were heavy with questions she needed answers to.

The girls slept on as Gerdie slipped out of bed and pulled on a clean white shirt with long billowy sleeves and brown pants that were a tad too big until she threaded her faded belt through. Jessica had given her the spare clothes the night before. There was plenty of pocket space in the pants, she was pleased to note, and the shirt even had a pocket at the breast, which she slipped the M.O.R.T. into. The poor thing had been in the cramped satchel and jostled around for ages.

'Best seat in the house,' she said, as the M.O.R.T. peered over the edge of the pocket with an excited whistle.

Gerdie's own overalls from yesterday were dirty and torn. She guessed rolling around a factory with an automaton and squeezing through the rocks in the Angel's Marbles and sleeping on the ground by the tree would do that to clothes. Her heart still gave a twinge when she thought of the tree, of the heat on her face as the wood was engulfed. It would be a pile of ash now. Maybe already blown away to nothing by the wind, like it was never there at all.

Slipping into her worn brown boots made her wince. Despite landing on Leo in the old factory – *everyone say 'thank you, Leo'* – the impact had still made her side tender, and the adrenaline wearing off made it that much more noticeable.

Fell was already in the large cavern when she entered, along with a handful of Cats going about their business. She wondered how early it was. It was impossible to tell, underground like this, and they weren't exactly forthcoming with clocks.

'Good morning,' she said, sitting beside him on a small round table. The spindly chair wobbled beneath her, and her heart nearly evacuated through her mouth. '*Whoop.* How are you feeling?'

Fell thought about this for a moment. A plate of margarine on toast sat untouched on a plate in front of him. Gerdie helped herself to a slice.

'Not good,' he finally admitted.

'Yeah, you don't look too well.' While he couldn't get any paler, there were circles under his eyes she hadn't noticed before, like fingers had pressed against his skin and it was yet to bounce back. 'Are you sick?'

Fell pressed his fingers to his temple. 'I don't know.'

Gerdie watched him for a moment, chewing contemplatively on the toast, but short of finding medicine for him, there wasn't much else she could do.

'Crazy about Leo, hey?' she said. The toast turned thick and sludgy in her throat. Leo... a Catell. *Royal.* It made sense now, how he'd wrapped meekness and secrecy around him like armour. But it was a pretty big piece of information about him, and he'd been Gerdie's friend for over a year. It hurt that he hadn't trusted her with it. She let out a little sigh, and despite his own weariness, Fell patted her arm.

She asked, 'So, Fell. Moment of truth. What are you going to do? Stay here with the resistance, or come with me to find Cadschel?'

'I'm coming with you,' he said. 'I can offer nothing further for the people here.'

'And you need to talk to Seki, right?' She tried to keep the obvious curiosity from her voice.

Fell furrowed his brow. 'Yes...' he said slowly. 'Seki. I need to talk to Seki.'

She pushed the plate with toast towards him. 'You might feel better if you eat. Food is like a good oil; it fixes everything.'

Fell smiled and nodded, but he didn't reach for the toast.

Over the next half hour, more people trickled in for breakfast. Once everyone had finished eating, and they'd all helped to pack up breakfast (everyone was equal, as Jessica barked), Luca called a meeting. They were a weekly habit, Gerdie was informed, where Luca updated the resistance on events that had gone wrong or right for them lately. The most recent successful operation had involved the blowing up of a liquor supplier in Lemtra, a town just outside New Londinium, that supplied the conqueror directly. Leo squirmed beside her during Luca's rundown, like he couldn't quite get comfortable. He'd also been given a change of clothes, his dirty and bloody ones replaced with a light brown shirt and wide-legged dark pants that left room for his prosthetic underneath.

Luca continued. There had recently been rations put on the nearby city of Cosy. Was there a shortage of food and supplies? No. Was there an unfair distribution of resources taking place? No. From what they could see, it had just been another confusing, irritating rule that Seki had imposed on just one city.

'So, we break into where the supplies that have been collected are now being held,' Luca said, 'and we distribute food back to the people, where it belongs. We'll be tearing down the barricades against the shops, too.'

Once the plan was put in place and a handful of members chosen for the mission, the rest of the resistance dispersed to begin the day. Gerdie stayed where she was beside Leo and Fell, watching as everyone bustled around them.

'This sounds like fun,' she said to Leo. 'Hey, when you become king, would you mind if I started up a resistance group?'

'I would, actually,' he said. 'If there's something you

shouldn't be playing with, it's dynamite. You cause enough trouble on your own.'

When they were the last remaining in the cavern, Luca approached them, appraising Gerdie and Fell with hands on his hips.

'Sure you don't want to stay?'

'I'm sure,' Gerdie said, though a little reluctantly. 'I have important things to do first.'

'Where are you headed?'

'I'm not sure, exactly,' Gerdie admitted. 'I'm looking for a blueprint company called Cadschel.'

Luca rubbed at his beard. 'Don't ring a bell. But I guess you'd try going into the city. That's where all the big companies are, working under Seki and the like. Start heading north until you read the Grimbald Highway, runs right to the capital. Or you can pick up some maps back down in Mallincroft. Back roads might be in order.'

'Thanks, Luca. For everything.'

Luca nodded and strode away, leaving her to say goodbye to Leo.

Leo shuffled, his metal leg squeaking faintly. 'Well, good luck, I guess. Try not to get into any trouble.' He held out his hand.

Gerdie glanced at the hand, then threw her arms around his neck. It felt different from their hug in Balthasar; more real, somehow. Definitive. 'I'll try. And good luck to you, Leo. I still can't believe it; you could rule over Treshane, how exciting!'

Leo's arms tentatively came up to hug her back.

'I mean it,' she whispered. 'Good luck and be careful. You might be royal and all, but more than that, Leo, you're my friend. I want to see you again when all of this is over.'

He didn't reply, but his arms tightened around her briefly. When they pulled apart, Leo turned to Fell. He stuck out his hand again, and Fell shook it. Neither looked the hugging type.

'And good luck to you,' Leo said. 'Take care of Gerdie, won't you? And *be careful*. There's still a warrant out for your arrest, remember. I don't know if news made it out of Balthasar, but I'm guessing it would have.'

Fell nodded. 'Be safe,' he said quietly.

Gerdie offered a final wave. 'See you later, comet crater!'

Leo rolled his eyes good-naturedly. 'In a while, engine dial.'

After goodbyes had been said, Gerdie and Fell left the mine and headed back into the main street of Mallincroft. She went into the visitor's centre for a map, as Luca had suggested. The visitor's centre was a small, dingy room with a bit of local art for sale on the wall—mostly the bleak landscape surrounding the town—and small plastic toys. Fell was fascinated by these, so Gerdie left him to fiddle with the toys while she went to the wall of pamphlets and maps. She found one and spread it across the small table. She frowned. Luca had said New Londinium was north, but on this map it was south. Was Luca wrong? But no, there was Mallincroft, which should have been west of Rendip Quarry, as Leo had said, but here it was more of a south-west. She shook her head and grabbed for another map of a different brand. This one was different again! Rendip was in a corner, much farther than it was in relation to other towns. Mallincroft wasn't on the map at all, and there were two towns supposedly right next to Rendip that Gerdie had never heard of and didn't even mention Balthasar.

She scanned the display of maps again. There were two more published by different companies, and she knew before she even opened them that they would tell different stories, and they did. She turned them over. All were marked with a

Conqueror Seki Approved stamp, and she felt anger boil inside her. She couldn't believe how ignorant she'd been in Rendip, where she thought dangerous factories were the only problem facing the country.

She hoped with all her heart that Leo found the sceptre, and soon. How could Seki be trusted with destroying a comet before it hit the planet? From what she'd seen and heard so far, Seki would probably relish in the destruction, the chaos.

Gerdie put down all the maps she'd gathered. They'd go north, like Luca said. She trusted him, at least.

'Come on, Fell,' she said.

He somewhat reluctantly placed down the spinning top he'd been examining and followed her out of the visitor's centre, into the hazy sunshine.

The Cats had equipped Gerdie and Fell with food supplies and water—which she pulled onto Fell's shoulders because her own satchel was heavy enough as it was—but the sight of the dry landscape stretching out before them made her feel tired. With buildings few and far between, there wasn't going to be many chances for shade and rest. It also meant there were no buses or trains. Could they hitchhike? Better not. Stranger danger and travelling with a wanted person and all that.

They kept to a dried-up river. Deep enough to stay hidden and close enough to the road that Gerdie could pop her head over the bank every now and then to check on their progress, careful to stay hidden from the cars that passed above them. They walked in companionable silence, with Gerdie occasionally mentioning something about the landscape that interested her or remembering something amusing one of the girls had said last night.

'...and then Mei said, "That's not my—" wait, what's that?' She halted as something small came scuttling toward them along the dry riverbed, the sunlight glinting off its shiny surface.

It was a little robot, only slightly larger than the M.O.R.T., and cylindrical in shape. It twitched as if to look up at them, a thick strip of black across the top looked like a blank screen.

'Oh, hey, little guy.' Gerdie squatted, holding out her hand as if for a dog to sniff.

A wide red laser light beamed from the bot's screen, running up and down Gerdie's body. She froze, unsure of what it was doing. Another red light beeped, and the bot moved on to Fell. She relaxed as the light left her body; whatever it was scanning for, she obviously didn't have it. Maybe this was this just a routine inspection? Another weird custom she wasn't familiar with out of Rendip?

The wide laser beam appeared again and scanned Fell as he watched it through squinted eyes. The screen turned bright green,faded to black, then turned an angry red. A thin silver antenna rose from the top of the robot as it began to blare like an alarm. The robot shot forward, and before Gerdie could move to stop it, Fell had handcuffs strapped across both wrists, and the antenna had sent out a shot of electricity. As soon as the electricity hit Fell, it bounced back as if it had hit a conductor instead, and zapped the bot. The bot short-circuited, its systems buzzing and sparking, body shuddering before it collapsed into a smoking heap. Silent.

Gerdie stared at the fried robot, trying to process what had just happened, when Fell groaned, snapping her back into focus. The metal cuffs were tight around Fell's thin wrists and wouldn't budge no matter how hard she tugged. She searched the robot's crumpled form, careful not to touch any metal in case it was still conducting the electricity it had absorbed but couldn't find a key or anything that would help her remove the cuffs. What she did notice was that the antenna, still sticking out from the robot and now emitting a thin plume of smoke, was a satellite. She didn't know if it had had the chance to transmit their location, but she didn't want to wait around to find out. She rifled through her bag, looking for a screwdriver that would fit the cuffs. *A #1 should do*, and she pulled it out, brushing off the few safety pins that had attached themselves to its magnetic surface. Slotting it into the screw between the cuffs' hinges, she fiddled as she tried to get a good grip, glancing up at Fell's face as she did so; it was pinched, and he watched her progress intently. A bead of sweat rolled down her temple, but the hinges refused to budge. She met his gaze with a helpless expression of her own.

Gerdie poked her head over the edge of the riverbed, scanning their surroundings. A large road sign a little way ahead declared that the city of Lanirose was only a kilometre and a half away. Surely Lanirose would have a locksmith, or someone who could help. *Surely.*

She rubbed Fell's wrists as best she could with the coconut oil she had on hand—her own skin dried easily under all the soap she used to get the machine grease off her hands. It wasn't enough to slip his hands through the cuffs, but she hoped it would be enough to ease his skin, which was quickly reddening beneath the metal. Angels, an allergic reaction was all they needed right now.

'How did you do that?' she asked.

'Do what?' The words came out strained and distracted, like being able to resist an electric shock was not nearly as big a deal as wearing handcuffs.

'The bot *zapped* you,' she pressed. 'And you zapped it right back.'

'Oh.' Fell shifted agitatedly from foot to foot. 'I'm not sure.'

The *whoosh whoosh whoosh* of traffic above them as they

walked had ceased to just the occasional *whoosh*; Gerdie guessed the morning rush to work over, so she helped Fell climb out of the river to walk along the top, where they could reach Lanirose easily. Continuing in the riverbed would have taken them in the opposite direction. The city began as attached brick houses and slowly grew to wide structures, and literally *grew*; the buildings reaching a dozen stories high. There wasn't a soul in sight, but Lanirose's residents were probably at work, Gerdie told herself. Every...single one of them. She glanced around with apprehension. Like a ghost town. Hm.

After about five minutes, she and Fell reached a crossroads, shops and cafes spread out before them. The street was deathly quiet despite the cars parked along the sides of the streets. When Gerdie looked closer, she saw shop signs flipped to *open*, and figures moving behind the windows. She relaxed slightly. Not a ghost town, though the street still had a haunted feeling.

Gerdie chose a direction at random to head in. 'Why do you think it's so quiet here?' she whispered. 'Coincidence? Sunlight allergy? Is it going to rain, maybe?' She glanced up. There *were* clouds gathering overhead, providing a temporary relief from the sun. As she lowered her gaze again, she caught a hanging sign overhead: *The Lanirose Locksmith Company.* She clapped her hands together and dragged Fell inside.

The shop was empty, though a faint drilling sound came from out of the back. A small gold bell was perched on the front counter with a note inviting customers to ding for assistance, so Gerdie slammed her hand down. The drilling stopped.

A middle-aged man with a balding head and a fat round nose appeared from the back room.

'Sorry 'bout that,' he said, coming around the side of the

counter. 'I wasn't really expecting anyone to come in today. How can I help you kids?'

Fell lifted his imprisoned hands and Gerdie gestured to them.

'Ah, had a run in with one of them police bots, did you?' The man started to rifle through a clear plastic container of small keys. 'Those things can be faulty sometimes, shootin' out cuffs left, right and centre. Yes, here it is.' He pulled a small silver key from the pile.

'Yeeees,' Gerdie said, bouncing on the balls of her feet. 'This one was definitely faulty. We were just out for a walk, minding our own business. You know. It approached us for no reason. We're not important or wanted or anything...' She trailed off as both the locksmith and Fell stared at her with bemused expressions. Gerdie cleared her throat. 'Why is this city so quiet, anyway? Where is everyone?'

The locksmith grunted, turning his attention back to Fell's handcuffs. 'Bunch of Actions arrived yesterday. They got some sort of machine in tow that they're testing. They generally use Lanirose for stuff like that 'cause we're so isolated from other towns.'

With a small *click*, the handcuffs loosened, and Fell's thin wrists slipped out.

'Thank you,' he said, rubbing the reddened skin. Even as Gerdie watched, his skin faded into the almost translucent white once more. Luckily, the locksmith was too busy picking the cuffs up from the floor to notice.

'Yes, thank you,' she said hurriedly. 'What do we owe you?'

The locksmith waved a hand. 'Don't worry about it.'

Good thing, because she didn't have any money, anyway.

'But be careful out there, all right?' the locksmith added. 'They've asked that everyone stay indoors in case something goes wrong.'

'Will do!' she said, rushing to the door. 'And thanks again!'

As soon as they stepped outside, Gerdie's arm was roughly seized, and she shrieked in surprise. An Action appeared out of nowhere, and now had both she and Fell in his grasp, his metal mask dull silver with a smoke stain on one side. Gerdie lost her stomach somewhere around her feet. They'd been caught, they'd been recognised, this was all her fault, how could she have been so stupid—

'What are you two doing out? Your instructions were clear: stay inside until further notice.'

The Action didn't wait for her reply, even if she had one. The Action hauled her and Fell across the road and towards a grand building opposite – tall and made of sandstone, columns lining the entrance at the top of a flight of stairs. She could hardly believe it—they hadn't been recognised.

When they were under the pillared overhang, the Action let them go. Gerdie stumbled at his roughness, but Fell regained his composure with grace.

'Get in there,' the Action growled. 'And don't come out until you're told.'

Gerdie didn't need telling twice. She dashed through the revolving glass door and into the...

It was a museum.

The entrance room was huge, with an arched roof and columns on either side. A massive stone staircase at the far end led to a second story that was framed by an elaborate banister. It smelled of varnish and old things, and full of people milling about—she and Fell probably weren't the only ones to have been shoved in here—and their murmuring voices and soft footsteps bounced around the giant room. Suspended by wires above them was a flock of stuffed birds, poised as if in flight. There were about ten different species she could see, all so small and beautiful. She'd never seen a bird fly in real life, only in movies and documentaries about Earth, and the diagrams in her school textbooks. Treshane used to have birds that could fly, when there were still trees for them to live in, but now it only had big, flightless birds like the tarawer ostrich, farmed for its meat and eggs. And a butt-load of flying insects, of course.

Gerdie lowered her gaze. In the middle of the room was a giant statue of Seki, made from tonnes of gold she was sure, and so tall she had to crane her neck to see his fat head. She poked her tongue at it. How did they even get it into the building?

She tore her eyes from the statue with some effort—you know when something is so ugly you just can't stop staring? —and turned around to peer outside the wide, thick-glass window; the Action was standing by the door, another posted a little farther down the road. She filled her cheeks with air then let it out noisily. Clearly, they weren't going anywhere anytime soon. She cast her gaze around the entrance hall again, her eyes falling on a sign by the reception desk: *Free admission, open daily from 9:00—17:00.*

Well, they might as well. She couldn't deny that she had always wanted to go to a museum, and this one seemed as good as any. She elbowed Fell, who was also staring at the glinting statue of Seki.

'I wouldn't stare too long,' she said. 'Might make you ill.'

'Who is it?' he asked, eyes still glued on Seki's golden face.

'That's Seki,' Gerdie said in disbelief. The statue might have been too tall to see the details of his face, but *everyone* in Treshane knew what the conqueror looked like. His portrait hung wherever a wall existed.

'That's Seki?'

'Seriously?'

Fell finally looked at her, brows pulled together.

'How can you not know what Seki looks like? And don't you need to talk with him or something?'

Fell winced, raising a hand to his head, like a sudden

thought pained him. The action tugged at her chest. She couldn't imagine forgetting her purpose or not knowing what her next move was.

Gerdie placed a sympathetic hand on his shoulder. 'Let's kill some time before we're allowed out again.'

Fell gave her a small nod. They made for the stairs into the exhibitions when a voice barked, 'Hey, you two. Where are your tickets?'

A museum guard eyed them suspiciously, the keys on his belt jangling as he walked over.

'Oh, we didn't get any,' Gerdie said.

'No ticket, no entry.'

'Okay, may we have a ticket then, please?'

The man crossed his arms over his chest. 'Tickets are five ki. Each.'

Gerdie's jaw dropped in indignation. She waved her hand toward the sign above the reception desk. 'But it says free admission!'

The guard didn't look back. 'Well, it's wrong.'

'But that's not fair!'

He took a step closer. 'Do I need to call the Actions?'

Gerdie swallowed. 'No,' she mumbled. 'We'll go.' She took hold of Fell's arm and marched him to a stone bench along the opposite wall, beneath a white sculpted bust of Martin Petrov, the Angel who first discovered Bellona. She dropped down onto the seat and Fell lowered himself beside her. The Seki statue loomed over them, and it still seemed as if, even though he faced the other direction, he was watching her out of the corner of his eye. She glanced past the statue to where the guard was speaking to the receptionist, both glancing back at her and Fell.

'Any ideas, Fell?' she asked. 'I don't want to be stuck here with that statue for Angels knows how long.'

Fell reached for her satchel, pulling it from her shoulder

and onto his lap. His small white hand rummaged around for a little while before re-emerging empty. He looked at Gerdie, pale eyes narrowed, then pointed to her shirt pocket. 'Ah. There.'

Gerdie glanced down to where the M.O.R.T. peeked over the edge of the pocket. When she looked up again, Fell wore a mischievous smile, making him look the most human she had ever seen him. She loved it.

'Distraction,' he said.

Gerdie felt her face split into an answering grin. 'Why, Fell,' she said. 'I do believe I'm rubbing off on you.'

ELEVEN

Drip, drip, drip.

The dream felt alive, something lurking in the darkness with him. Watching, waiting. Leo walked through the black tunnel, gaining momentum as the dripping grew louder. Was he finally getting close to voice's owner?

'*It is time. It is time.*'

Water dripped somewhere nearby. A tap? Was this tunnel near a lake? Was it...?

Leo came to, the dream pierced by artificial light overhead through cracked eyelids. The cot creaked as he shifted, scanning the room; he was alone. He rolled over, and his stomach swooped as the day before trickled back into his consciousness. Gerdie, leaving yesterday with Fell. The boy seemed nice enough, just so quiet and secretive. Who knew what Seki wanted him for? Maybe the conqueror's reasons were uncharacteristically justified, and Leo had let Gerdie go off with a murderer or something. No; Fell had healed Leo's leg after the automaton. But even if Fell was innocent of whatever Seki thought he'd done, there would still be Actions out looking for him, and who knew what they'd do to Gerdie if they found her with him. He was sure Fell had done something to calm Emmett and Hadrian down last night, he just wasn't sure what. Something wasn't... normal. Nothing Leo could do about it, anyway. Once Gerdie and Fell left, Leo, Hadrian and Luca spent the rest of the afternoon in one of the mine's many alcoves, with a cup of burnt coffee, going over ideas of where the sceptre might be.

Hadrian had said, 'Seki might have hidden it in a place he knows well.'

'You mean like the palace?' asked Leo.

'No, nothing as obvious as that.'

'Where, then?'

Hadrian's eyes, big and round, met his. 'Trumble.'

'But there's nothing left of Trumble,' Luca said. 'It's a wasteland since the last comet hit.'

'Exactly. And no one ever set up a cleaning operation; they just left it, like a shrine or something. Can you imagine how impossible it would be to find anything there?'

'I am filled with confidence,' Leo said flatly.

But neither Leo nor Luca had had any better ideas, and while they brainstormed into the evening about the sceptre's location, with horrifying ideas like the bottom of the One Sea or somewhere in the Core, nothing sat quite as well like Trumble did. It meant something to Seki, and that had to count for something.

Leo pushed the scratchy blanket back and reached for his prosthetic. Absentmindedly, he smoothed down his hair and made his way to the main cavern, following the hum of conversation. As he entered, every eye swiveled in his direction, which immediately made him want to turn around and flee for the safety of the bed. But his stomach rumbled, so he swallowed his embarrassment and made for the food, keeping his head low.

He took his plate of toast and dry biscuits into a corner of the main cavern, chewing slowly as he watched the morning bustle of the Cats. Thankfully, their attention had quickly shifted.

'Mind if I join you?'

Hadrian didn't give him a chance to answer before dropping down in the seat beside him, plate in hand, backpack on. Leo watched him out of the corner of his eye, his breakfast turning lumpy in his throat. This was the first time they'd been alone since reuniting.

'So,' Hadrian began. 'I thought we'd start –'

'Why didn't you say goodbye?' asked Leo quietly.

Hadrian lowered his plate. Swallowed. 'I regret that. You deserved better. I got into a fight with my mum that night... before I left. A really bad one.'

Leo believed him; Hadrian had always been getting into fights with the other boys at school with his *attack first, ask questions never* attitude.

Hadrian scraped his knife absentmindedly across the plate. The sound grated Leo's ears. 'I just wanted to escape for the night.'

'You could have come to mine,' said Leo, even though it wasn't entirely true. He'd never been allowed visitors after Peller took him in, and the times when Hadrian snuck in were carefully calculated and never without risk. In those early years, Seki was under the impression that Leo was capable of conspiring against him, and it was Peller's responsibility to keep Leo isolated. It was only in the last two years or so that Seki relaxed his monitoring, correctly realising that Leo wasn't brave enough to make a stand. But by then, Hadrian was already gone.

'No, I couldn't have. Eventually I ran too far to ever come back. Speaking of secrets...' he said with a glance that was playful at first but quickly turned serious. 'Why are you here? What made you finally change your mind?'

Instead of pointing out the hypocrisy of keeping secrets, Leo dropped his gaze to the unfinished meal on his plate. 'Accident,' he answered truthfully. 'And still, I... I don't know. Let's just see if we can find the sceptre first. I can't think beyond that right now.'

They cleaned their breakfast dishes and returned to their room, equipped with food and water for their journey. Emmett had thrown a dirty look at Hadrian as he passed him in the cavern earlier, but he'd disappeared shortly after, which put Leo a little more at ease.

'It won't be impossible,' Hadrian said as he threw the last of his things into his bag. 'The sceptre *wants* to be found by you, don't you see?'

Leo gave a little shrug. 'Well, I have no better idea.'

Hadrian grinned. 'That's the spirit.'

Shouts came from the main cavern, and Leo shot to his feet in alarm, his prosthetic squeaking in protest over the sudden movement.

'What's going on?' he said.

'No idea!' Hadrian said.

Leo ran into the tunnel, ignoring Hadrian's hasty whisper of, 'Wait!'

The main cavern was filled with people running around. It was like watching a disturbed ant nest.

'How did they find us?' someone yelled.

Leo grabbed Luca as he ran past. 'What's happened?'

'Actions,' Luca wheezed. 'Run, Leo! We'll hold them off for as long as we can, but you can't let them get to you! There's another exit—through there!' Luca pushed him hard, and Leo stumbled toward the tunnel as dozens of uniformed Actions flooded the cavern, tasers drawn. He watched in horror as they quickly had several resistance members on their knees and had bots clamping their hands behind their backs.

Hadrian had too tight a grip on Leo's arm. He might have been skinny, but he was strong. When had that happened?

'Don't worry about it!' he hissed. 'You're too important. Without the sceptre, their efforts will have been for nothing!'

Leo let Hadrian drag him away, but he was unable to help throwing glances of despair over his shoulder at the scene. Hadrian led the way through the tunnels, stumbling often on the uneven ground. They burst out of the mine and into daylight. The sudden brightness made pain flare behind his eyes.

No Actions remained outside; all had gone in, a full attack. Leo and Hadrian dashed around the other side of the mound that marked the mine, away from Mallincroft's centre. They didn't stop running until they were in a rocky area, where they could hide behind boulders. Hadrian fell against one, panting and holding his side. Leo was out of breath as well, but he didn't feel tired. He felt angry.

'This is what I'm talking about!' he yelled, scrubbing a hand through his hair. He walked in circles, unable to keep still even though his legs burned from the run.

'This is my fault. They watch me, I led them here. What's the point of looking for the sceptre? I can't do anything!'

'This wasn't your fault, Leo.'

Leo whirled to face him. Hadrian's pale ears were now pink, made even more noticeable by the way they stuck out from his head.

'Yes, it was.'

Hadrian's expression softened. 'The best way to help the Cats now is to find the sceptre.'

What made him feel worse was that, with the Cats gone, the responsibility was on him, and him alone. Yes, the sceptre would weaken Seki, but Leo had been relying on the resistance to take the lead on bringing Seki down. It was a selfish thought, but what was he going to do now? He couldn't take

Seki on. Seki was too large, too strong, too powerful, and Leo was...

Scared. Weak. Small.

Leo put his hands behind his head, trying to calm his breathing. Exhaled long and slow. 'You know the way to Trumble, then?' He sounded resigned, even to his own ears.

'Yeah. It's not far from here.' Hadrian pushed himself to his feet. He pulled a device – not quite a phone, but Leo couldn't keep up with the changing models – out and tapped it a few times. 'It's toward Mount Sydney.' He placed a hand on Leo's shoulder as he passed, and the gesture suddenly made Hadrian feel more real, like he'd been a ghost for the past day. 'They'll be okay. I haven't known them for very long, but I've seen that they're good people, prepared for anything. They would have known something like this was going to happen one day.'

It didn't make Leo feel better.

'I've got an idea,' Hadrian said.

They'd been walking for about half an hour, following a quiet train track as it cut through the rocky landscape. A highway ran parallel in the distance, cars rolling along it like marbles. Hadrian stared at his phone, following their progress on a directory app. He'd made small talk with Leo as they walked, friendly and casual, like the missing years between them meant nothing. When Leo had pictured time alone to finally talk, he thought it would be secrets revealed, and truths uncovered. Everything was just like it used to be, just like those two years apart never existed, and Leo started to wonder if their reunion was not so big a deal as he had thought. Did people do this to each other all the time? Had Hadrian not missed him at all? Had he not spent night after night crying himself to sleep with loneliness?

Hadrian ducked behind a large rock beside the curving train tracks, easing himself against it to get comfortable. Leo peered around one side, but he saw nothing that might constitute to any idea behind this but a nap on the hard ground.

'What are we doing?' Leo said.

'Wait for it,' Hadrian said, closing his eyes. 'Should be just a few minutes.'

Leo lowered himself onto the ground and leaned back against the rock. It was only just wide enough to cover the both of them. As if it was trying to be helpful, Leo's brain suddenly remembered that Hadrian's *I've got an idea*-s usually carried a sinister undertone. Once, he switched the non-fiction and fiction sections in the school library when they were ten. When they were nine, Leo had to stop him from handing a bottle of fuel (which was a story in itself) to their teacher to douse the fire that started in the lab.

He was pulled from his nervous thoughts by a faint rhythmic chugging, steadily growing louder and louder. Leo turned to Hadrian in silent question, and Hadrian grinned wide enough to show his dimple. 'That's our ride.'

Leo went to rise, but Hadrian grabbed his arm and yanked him back down. 'Not yet. Don't want the driver seeing us.'

Leo glanced around the side of the rock. A black steam train was puffing along the tracks toward them, white smoke escaping from its chimney.

'But there's no station,' Leo hissed.

Hadrian gave him an exasperated look. 'We can hardly buy a ticket at a station, there'll be Actions out looking for you by now.'

Leo didn't need to be told this, but he still couldn't believe the alternative Hadrian was suggesting. 'You mean we're about to board a *moving train?*'

Hadrian waggled his eyebrows, filling Leo with dread. Not everyone found the idea of death exciting. While he remembered Hadrian's scary pranks and bad attitude, he also remembered the way Hadrian made him laugh, made him feel alive. So, when Hadrian pushed to his feet, body tensed like he was ready to run, Leo found himself doing the same, though his heart clenched painfully in his chest.

The train slowed as it approached the bend near their hiding place—must have been the reason Hadrian chose it in the first place. As it passed, Leo saw the number on the front: 394. Trains with only three numbers instead of five meant they carried cargo, not passengers. This, at least, was something Leo was okay with. Shipping crates rolled past, covered in graffiti. Hadrian waited until about six carriages passed before he cried, 'Go!' and he took off.

Hadrian was a fast runner, much faster than Leo. He was on the train in a single leap, forcing his way into a container, leaving Leo sprinting desperately behind. Hadrian leaned out of the container and held out his hand. Leo reached for it, but the train was coming out of the bend and was speeding up again. His legs were burning, and even though Gerdie had made his prosthetic more comfortable, it had never been built for heavy running. The train was moving too fast, Hadrian was slipping away, he wasn't going to make it—

He finally grasped Hadrian's hand, and Hadrian hauled him into the container. Pulling Leo's weight made Hadrian lose his balance, and they both fell back, crashing to the hard and dusty ground. The train vibrated beneath Leo's back as he fought to catch his breath, the smell of metal filling his nostrils.

'Whoo!' Hadrian said. 'That was exciting.'

'Speak for yourself,' Leo panted, but he was smiling. He had done it. They were on the train.

The container they'd landed in carried wooden crates of various sizes. Leo dragged himself toward the back of the container and leaned against one of them, trying to catch his breath. Hadrian was also breathing hard, but his brown eyes were bright with excitement at their success as he took in their surroundings. 'What do you suppose is in all of these, then?'

Each crate was stamped with *FOR INCINERATION* in big black letters. Whatever was inside was being sent to burn.

'No...idea...' Leo said between breaths. He rubbed the skin surrounding his prosthetic, trying to relieve the ache from running. But since Gerdie tweaked the prosthetic, the usual redness had subsided; it was like the leather of the socket had been molded to his own skin. He felt silly for letting himself be in pain for so long. As he examined the prosthetic, he heard the creaking of wood and the sounds of Hadrian shifting through the contents inside the crates.

Silence. When he looked up, Hadrian was staring into a box, a pensive expression on his face.

'What is it?' Leo asked.

Hadrian quickly replaced the lid. 'It's nothing.'

Clearly it wasn't nothing. Leo pushed to his feet, stumbling a bit at the train's rocking. He braced himself with a hand against the side, the metal rough against his fingers. Hadrian made no move to stop him as he approached the crate, but he didn't meet Leo's eyes, already busying himself with the next crate.

Leo steeled himself before peering inside, expecting something gruesome. At first, the crate appeared empty, filled only with darkness. As he searched the gloom of the crate, he realised he was looking at the tops of stacked gilded frames. He lifted one and rested it on the top of the crate, his stomach dropping as he recognised it.

It was a painting.

The girl in the frame stared back at him with soft eyes, one brown and one green. Her dark skin smooth with brush strokes. An official portrait of a royal family member – she was glittering, even through the painting, with jewels and a tiara. A

Catell, his ancestor, though he didn't know who she was for sure. Why was it being sent to be destroyed?

Leo tore the lid off the next crate, wobbling as the train shook beneath him. More paintings were stacked inside. He pulled out *Girl with a Pearl Earring*, her thoughtful face staring back at him. He was numb; these were some of Earth's greatest treasures, brought to Bellona before the comet hit Earth, being sent to the fire.

'They must be from the National Museum in New Londinium,' Hadrian said grimly. Leo hadn't even noticed him come up behind him. 'There's busts and jewelry and all sorts in the rest of the crates.'

Leo swallowed the lump in his throat. 'I –'

The train slammed on its brakes. He and Hadrian flew toward the front of the container, crashing into the wall, Leo's vision flashing white for a second as he banged his head before falling to the dusty floor. The train gave a final shudder and came to a complete stop, sending them stumbling back.

Someone was shouting.

Leo pushed himself to his feet, wincing as his back throbbed anew, and peered through a gap in the door. Since they were toward the back of the train, he couldn't see much. The tracks were curving right, cutting through the dry, rocky landscape. Leo's stomach dropped as he saw it: the tracks ended suddenly just ahead of them. If the driver hadn't stopped when they did, the train would have derailed. Work vans with flashing orange lights were parked beside it.

A few men stepped into view toward the front of the train. One of them – Leo assumed was the train driver – was waving his arms furiously.

' – idiots! What the hell are you doing?' His voice was just audible from this distance and beneath the hissing of the train.

Hadrian joined Leo at the door and used his height to peer through the gap above Leo's head.

'What the hell are *you* doing?' one of the workers shouted back. 'This line is no longer in use; Conqueror Seki has ordered the track to be pulled up and used to build the Lemtra line.'

'Bloody useless!' the driver said. 'I've been told no such thing, and I'm carrying a service under the conqueror's orders.'

The worker glanced down the length of the train, and Leo pulled back, though it would have been impossible for them to be seen from that distance.

'Time to go,' he whispered. 'End of the line, anyway.'

'But where are we?'

Hadrian crossed the container and peered through a gap in the other side.

'That looks like Mount Sydney,' he said, and Leo had to squint through the haze to see the raised shape in the distance. 'We've passed the state border. I reckon we run for it. Be out of sight before anyone notices. It'll take them ages to sort this mess out.' He slid the door open.

'But what about...' Leo glanced helplessly back at the crates that held some of Earth's and Bellona's culture.

'I'm sorry, Leo. But we can't take it with us.'

He knew that, but his heart ached as he tore himself away from the crates carrying such precious artifacts and joined Hadrian at the door. He hoped they would be saved from their fates by the track disruption, even if it was just for a few days more.

The whole world seemed to stretch before him. Flat, brown, and hazy, then the dark hump towards the horizon that was Mount Sydney. Small dark spots covered the landscape like scars: tree stumps, or the hollows where stumps had been pulled. A darker line to their left: a scar left behind by a river, now dried up because of a rising climate.

After living within the closeness of the factories and smoke of Balthasar, he felt too small, the world too big, like he might become lost in it, never to be found again. The heat was relentless; it felt like a heavy layer of clothing, one he couldn't shed.

They dug into their packs as they walked. The Cats supplied them with dried meat, hard biscuits and water, but not a lot. Not that Leo could hold that against them, of course, when they had so many mouths to feed, but it meant that they would have to be careful.

'Wish we'd jumped onto a train carrying food,' Hadrian grumbled.

Leo was inclined to agree. His mouth was dry, and the heat only made him dry up even faster.

'You know,' Hadrian panted, 'you can buy these mini-water filters that let you drink clean water from anywhere. Saved my life after I left home. Not that there's any water around here,' he added. 'But still.'

'Why did you need one of those?' Leo asked tentatively, afraid pushing too far about the last two years would make Hadrian run away again.

Hadrian was quiet for a moment, as if choosing his words carefully. Their footsteps crunched in unison.

'I didn't take anything with me when I left. Just the clothes on my back and the couple of ki in my pocket. I stole a lot.' There was no apology in his voice. 'I got caught a few times, had to keep off the streets. Survived on water from the rivers that service the factories.' He shuddered. 'Even filtered, it's disgusting.'

'But where did you go? What was your plan?' *Why didn't you tell me?*

'I walked to New Londinium. Found Luca there. Joined the Cats and been with them ever since.'

Making a difference. Fighting back against Seki. And what had Leo done in those two years? Nothing changed for him. He'd continued his miserable existence while others fought his battles.

After an hour or so of walking, a long hill rose into view. At first Leo thought it was another quarry, but it was too still, too silent, the sides too high and steep. This was a crater. This was Trumble.

Or what was left of it.

'There's barely anything around,' Leo remarked. No other towns or cities, only one major road. Just the ghost of the forest. 'And as the place *For the Forest* operated from, it's almost as if the comet were aiming for it.'

'Some say it was,' Hadrian said as he picked his way over the rocks and started to ascend the side of the crater. 'You know what comet it was, don't you?'

'The Death Comet.' Everyone knew that. It was taught in school, but even those who hadn't received an education knew because of the annual Trumble Day celebrations. Trumble and Seki were Treshane lore.

'Yeah,' Hadrian said. 'And the Death Comet is attracted to harmonious and beautiful things, because it wants to destroy them. Trumble was one of the last spots of nature left. The people there took all manner of pains to protect it; they were against the deforestations and building of quarries and factories. This had been beautiful and green once.'

Leo looked around again at the bleak landscape, at the tree stumps surrounding them. He tried to grow them in his mind, picturing them tall and strong and sprouting branches and leaves. 'It's hard to imagine.'

'I know. I can hardly picture it myself, but my mum had paintings of all kinds of plant species on the walls at home. She

and my dad had a project going on to bring back the plants…
before he died.' Pain made his voice hitch.

'What happened?' Leo asked quietly. 'To your-?'

'I don't want to talk about it,' Hadrian snapped. His
hands made angry fists at his side, red creeping up his neck.
Leo was rarely the target of Hadrian's anger, but he had been
witness to it enough, had seen others wither beneath it, that he
quickly clamped his mouth shut.

As the crater loomed above them, Leo's apprehension
grew.

'What will we see in there?' He couldn't keep the fear and
uncertainty from his voice.

Hadrian didn't answer for a little while, and when Leo
looked over, he caught Hadrian's throat bobbing as he swallowed. 'I don't know,' he said, 'but it won't be good.'

And it wasn't.

Once they'd climbed to the top – the going slow as Leo
struggled on loose rocks and the steep side – and surveyed
what stretched before them, all he saw was devastation.
Mounds of blackened rubble, shells of entire buildings
stretched horizontally, the ground thick with ash. Apart from
their heavy breathing from the climb, there was silence. Not
even the hum of an insect. The presence of death settled on his
skin like a heavy blanket.

Leo went to speak but his voice was dry. He swallowed and
tried again. 'Why did no one recover anything?'

'Seki's orders,' Hadrian said. 'I guess maybe he didn't want
to disturb the dead, or the whole process was too painful…I
dunno. Scavengers have been here, though.' He pointed, and
Leo noticed the footprints pressed into the blackened ground.
The thought of people trying to make a profit off such a
tragedy made him sick.

'Can you feel anything?' Hadrian asked quietly.

'I'm feeling a lot of things,' Leo said, gazing out over the destruction, voice hoarse.

'I mean the sceptre. Can you feel if it's here?'

'Oh. Um...' Leo continued gazing out over the crater. 'I don't think so. But I don't know what I'm meant to be feeling for.'

'We should get closer.' Hadrian began to pick his way down the sides of the crater.

Uneasy, Leo followed. The steep descent required careful maneuvering that his prosthetic made stiff and difficult. By the time he finally reached the bottom, where the other end of the crater was just a line on the horizon, Hadrian was already gingerly walking through the rubble, eyes trained to the ground.

Leo joined him, but he knew this wasn't right, and not just because they were disturbing a site that shouldn't be disturbed. In his dreams, he was in a cave. Well, he'd been in a dark cold place. Could that have been the ash remains of Trumble? The more he thought about it, the more he wasn't sure. And though he didn't know what it meant or who the voice even belonged to, he knew it was sceptre-related. Luca had cemented the thought.

After several minutes in which he found a mangled metal structure that might have once been a bus stop, several crushed cars, and a tiny pair of shoes, Leo straightened, about to tell Hadrian they should move on, when movement out of the corner of his eye caught his attention.

There was someone else in the crater with them. A stout man, his head cocked to one side as he regarded Leo and Hadrian. Then he started walking towards them. Leo tensed – did he work for Seki? Had they been followed?

'Hadrian,' he whispered.

Hadrian glanced up from where he was bent over a pile of

charred bricks. When he saw the man, he straightened and stormed over. 'What do you want?' he snapped.

The man had no weapons that Leo could see and was looking at them only with curiosity. He didn't think Hadrian's aggression was justified, but the man was still a stranger. Unease made the hairs on the back of Leo's neck stand up.

The man was close enough now for Leo to see his grey hair and whiskers. He stopped a few metres away and gesticulated gracefully with his hands. *Who are you?*

Leo signed back. *We mean no harm. We are looking for something.*

Nothing to be found here but death, the man signed.

Hadrian looked nonplussed. 'How do you—' His eyebrows lifted as he remembered. 'Your mother, of course. I remember you telling me she was deaf. What's he saying?'

'He's wondering what we're doing here.'

'You didn't tell him, did you?'

'You don't think he could help?'

'This is too important,' Hadrian said.

Leo turned back to the man. *Do you know of any caves close by here?*

The Quinn Ranges are fifteen kilometres from here. He pointed west. *Mount Sydney. Maybe there.*

Thank you. Leo reached into his pack and pulled out what was left of the dried meat.

The man's weathered face lit up as he accepted the package, free hand a blur against his mouth as he signed, *Thank you, thank you, thank you.*

'I know where we have to go,' he told Hadrian once the man had wandered off. 'The mountain range.'

'Mount Sydney? Why?'

'I think I've been dreaming about the sceptre,' he said. 'It's in someplace dark. A cave, I'm pretty sure. It's in something old and big.'

Hadrian cast a final glance over Trumble, then nodded. 'All right, I trust you know best.'

Leaving the devastated remains behind, they scrambled back out of the crater. Hadrian helped Leo up some of the steeper parts where his prosthetic wouldn't cooperate.

When they reached the top, they both took a moment to catch their breath. Leo braced his hands on his knees, and as his breath steadied, he heard a faint, whirring sound. He peered ahead, through the rippling heat, at a small metallic thing rolling toward them. He glanced at Hadrian, but he was staring back down at Trumble, hands braced on his hips. As the little robot drew closer, Leo noticed it was made of the same dark patterned metal of the Action masks, and cylindrical in shape. It stopped by his feet, an antenna rising from its top.

'Um...' Leo rarely left Balthasar and had only ever travelled to the capital by air. Were the bots common on the ground? Or, and the thought hit him like cold water, had it been sent by Actions?

A little red light appeared on its antennae and Hadrian cried, 'Look out!' He pushed Leo out of the way as a blast of light shot from the robot.

Leo lost his balance and hit the ground, rolling halfway down the crater away from Trumble. He watched as Hadrian kicked out at the robot, barely dodging another shot, then whipped his hand to one side, jabbing at a spot behind the robot and making it fall still.

Leo got shakily to his feet. 'What was that?'

'Police bot. They'll stun you and send out coordinates. Some have handcuffs. Either way, you'll be helpless when an Action arrives, which they will. We're being tracked.'

'How did you know how to turn it off?'

Hadrian kicked the bot; it rolled down the crater's side

towards Trumble and out of sight. 'I have experience with these little bastards. The conqueror uses them quite a lot.'

Hadrian joined him and they descended the rest of the way, those two years stretched out between them again. 'Did you... get in trouble with him? Is that why you stayed away for so long?'

A muscle in Hadrian's jaw twitched. 'Something like that.'

He went to turn away, but there was something in his expression that said there was more to it, something that made Leo ask, 'Why are you really here?'

Hadrian was quiet for a moment, as if trying out his words before he spoke them. 'Let's just say... that you aren't the only one looking for something.'

Leo waited, but Hadrian didn't look as though he was going to say any more about it, so Leo let it drop as well. Conversing with Hadrian felt like fixing a faulty machine, one that could blow up at any minute, and he didn't want to ruin things. Not when he finally got his friend back and he'd been willing to come with Leo on his mission. But for the first time, it occurred to him that maybe Hadrian's disappearance and subsequent absence hadn't just been a result of his anger issues, his inability to stay still. That maybe there had been a very good reason.

The secrets between them burned a hole in his chest.

An old road weaved beneath them as they walked through the afternoon, torn up during the shock wave after the Death Comet hit. Jagged lines cracked the gravel, but the road provided the quickest, safest route. Their boots crunched on the rocky ground in unison, and the noise was calming, grounding, which was why Leo noticed when it suddenly went down to one pair. Hadrian had stopped, and as Leo glanced over his shoulder to see what the hold-up was, Hadrian had gone very pale.

'Are you okay?'

Hadrian closed his eyes, throat bobbing as he swallowed.

'Yeah, I—' He was breathing heavily, sweat beading on his forehead. 'I just need a moment. I'm sorry...' He lowered himself to the ground, stretching his long body out on the road, head against the gravel.

Leo dropped down beside him, quietly grateful for the rest. Hadrian's eyes were closed, and his body began to stiffen. His chest arced upwards, the tendons in his neck straining. Leo went cold all over. Was Hadrian having a fit? What should he do? He'd never seen something like this before. Hadrian kicked, his skin turning red. Oh, Angels, he was going to die right there, and Leo could do nothing—

'Hey, it's okay,' Leo said, voice calm and strong, though it wavered slightly. He didn't even know if Hadrian could hear him. He pulled Hadrian's head onto his lap so that it was off the hot hard ground. He was stiff and unresponsive under Leo's hands, but his mouth was clear, free from vomit and saliva, and though his breathing was hard and fast, he *was* breathing. Then he was moaning, hands clawing at his chest like he was trying to stop something from getting out – or help it stay in. He was scrabbling so hard that he ripped one of the buttons from his shirt. Through the gap in the fabric this created, Leo saw pink lines, long and thick, across Hadrian's pale chest: old fingernail scratches.

Leo gripped Hadrian's hands to prevent him from inflicting anymore damage on himself. 'It's okay,' he kept murmuring. 'I've got you.'

After a few seconds, Hadrian calmed. Legs stilled. His body slackened and his breathing remained laboured, but he opened his eyes. Sweat beaded on his forehead.

He stared past Leo's head, seemed to be waiting for something, then glanced down at his chest, eyebrows rising in surprise. His hands were still clasped in Leo's, but Leo loosened his grip.

'You were trying to scratch yourself,' he said. 'I stopped you.'

'Thanks,' Hadrian panted. 'No one's ever...That is, I've...'

'It's okay.'

'No,' Hadrian said, struggling to sit up. Leo pushed him gently upright, staying close in case Hadrian fell ill again. 'Really. That was the fastest I've ever come out of it, and there's usually a lot more blood.'

'How often does that happen?' Leo asked. 'Did you get those in Balthasar?' If Hadrian had gone through this in the years they knew each other, it didn't happen in Leo's presence.

'It—' He cut himself off. The astonishment and vulnerability that had been on his face when he thanked Leo was gone in an instant, and Leo didn't realise how much the glimpse at the Hadrian he used to know had lightened his heart until it was gone. Hadrian had begun to feel like home again. But his expression hardened, and he shifted away until their arms were no longer touching. He cleared his throat and pushed to his feet, swaying as he did so. 'We're wasting time,' he said curtly. 'We have to keep moving.'

hOw DO yoU liKe MY plANeT?
caN YOu SMelL thE chAoS?
I KNow You havE FounD hIM
buT it mAKEs
No
difFerENCe
I aM a cRUShEr oF WoRLds
WaTCH Me deStroY

Twelve

Gerdie peered around the columns that flanked the interior entrance to the museum. The guard was chatting to the receptionist. They were absorbed in their conversation, but not absorbed enough that Gerdie and Fell could sneak past without notice. The plan was a-go.

She glanced down at the M.O.R.T. in her hands. 'Ready?' she whispered.

The M.O.R.T. let out a quiet, wheezing whistle that sounded suspiciously to Gerdie like it was saying, *If I have to be.*

She pulled out her screwdriver and made final adjustments to the little bot's latest feature.

'Okay, M.O.R.T.,' she said, placing it down onto the marble floor. 'Remember, you want to go that way,' she pointed to the archway to the left, 'so that we can go that way.' She pointed in the opposite direction.

The M.O.R.T. stood on his stumpy legs, took a few wobbly steps, then was off in the direction Gerdie indicated.

She watched with bated breath as the little robot *tick-tick-tick*ed across the floor and disappeared into the next room. A few seconds passed in which Gerdie nearly chewed off all her fingernails, then there was a small, muffled explosion. Thick smoke poured from the archway as an alarm blared, and people screamed and ran from the room. The two guards on duty ran into the room amid panicked shouts, hands to their security belts. Fell made to go, but Gerdie held him back.

'The receptionist!' she hissed.

The receptionist had risen from her desk and was looking on in alarm at the scene in front of her. Distracted though she was, she would still be suspicious at the two people decidedly not panicking. But she was taking small, cautious steps forward, as if unsure what to do.

'Come on,' Gerdie murmured under her breath.

Among the screaming visitors running for the door, a woman fell over, and finally the receptionist sprang into action to help the woman up.

'Let's go!' Gerdie said, and she and Fell weaved through the wave of the crowd, past the receptionist's desk, and into the next room. She hoped the M.O.R.T. would be okay, and at least if any authorities came, they were on the *other* side of the museum to the bot. She and Fell passed the history exhibition, and the few visitors still in the wing were leaving through the archway they had just come through, motivated by the alarms. Gerdie wanted to stop and read through the exhibition – Treshane was colonised nearly one hundred and fifty years ago! – but they were too exposed in this area. She glanced to either side as they passed quickly through the exhibits. Old tools, parts of old spaceships, pottery, models and sculptures of green plants like the ones in Ada's house. The museum was a tribute to Earth, as nearly everything in Treshane was, maybe even in all of Bellona. Gerdie loved it, Earth had been so fascinating, but large stone words carved above the next door caught her eye: *SPACE ROOM*. The room beyond was dark.

Fell was by the plant models, his skin taking on that ethe-real glow again as he stared at the plastic leaves

'I'll be in here,' she told him.

The space room was dark, but the walls were lit with little lights to look like stars, and constellations had been drawn in white lines around them. She recognised the Cat's Tail, Emily's Arrow, and the Cloaked Lady. It felt like being in space itself.

Large glass display cabinets were lined up in the middle of the room, holding instruments and mineral and rock samples. A giant telescope was set up inside rope barriers.

'Wow.' Gerdie tilted her head back, trying to take it all in as she wandered further inside. This room was the most beau-tiful thing she'd ever seen.

She passed the information and displays on the moons Maylow and Oriana, and stopped at the information on Goodhue, Digetoria, and Albina – the other three inhabited planets in the Hector-Nero system. Digetoria was the smallest and strikingly blue because it was ninety percent water, she read, and had only one tiny continent with a population of around one million people on that small patch of land. Dige-toria was also vibrant green, and jealousy spiked in her chest. She wished she could travel there, breathe clean, unpolluted air, feel grass against her fingertips Maybe one day she would. Maybe they would commission her to invent something once she was famous.

Albina was the biggest planet of the three, but she'd heard it was the least populated because of bad air conditions – less to do with polluted air and more to do with high levels of carbon dioxide. As she stood in front of the 3D model of Albina, an orange and white orb, she read on the information card that the people there lived in little oxygen-supplied pods, and that if they went outside they had to wear protective helmets and suits The planet was mostly used for research. No one lived there for long periods of time.

Something tugged at her pant leg, and she looked down. The M.O.R.T. was at her feet; she scooped him up and placed him back in her shirt pocket with a 'Good work, little guy,' before she continued around the room.

Next was the section on Earth.

The old planet of Earth was given a place of honour in the middle of the room, slightly raised on a platform. Naturally. A huge orb of the planet, lit from inside, was suspended in the air. Gerdie never tired of hearing about it. The beautiful green and blue of it looked so alive and refreshing, nothing like Bellona's hard, dry surface that seemed to be the same colour no matter where you were.

She stood on a large white dot and triggered the display. The Earth exhibit began to slowly spin, and a cool computerised voice began reciting facts about the now-extinct planet. She'd heard most of it before: how the people had treated Earth badly for years – first accidentally, then without care – until the planet's health reached a point of no return; rubbish-filled oceans and chemicals in everything. The younger generations managed to bring it back and sustain it... until the Death Comet hit. The Angels of Bellona could have taken a page out of that instruction manual instead of making the same mistakes as the people on Earth. There was nothing else on the information cards she didn't already know, so she made her own way slowly around the platform.

As if sensing its presence, her eyes landed on the Death Comet. It had an entire stretch of wall ahead dedicated to it.

The Death Comet came around every few hundred years, destroying planets completely. Bellona had been incredibly lucky when the Death Comet hit, as it only destroyed one town. It was sad, of course, but it had the power to obliterate the entire planet. There were many arguments circulating that it hadn't been the Death Comet, since all of Bellona would have been destroyed if it was. The DC wasn't one for failure. Maybe it was finally wearing itself down, losing steam, as it were.

The back of the display was an illustration of the Death Comet. It was an angry being, Gerdie could feel that even through the artist's interpretation. With the rippling red and orange energy surrounding it, it almost looked as if it had horns. And even though it was hard to tell in the drawing, she knew it was huge, enough to destroy a whole planet with a single collision. It sent a shiver down her spine, but she didn't get that feeling when she looked at the current comet streaking toward them. Her brain told her the one in the sky was a threat, but her heart didn't entirely believe that. She didn't feel anything malicious from it, nothing like the feeling she got just by looking at a mere painting of the Death Comet.

The Death Comet had blown up at least ten planets across a thousand years, perhaps even longer than what the astronomists could track. Why was it so angry, why was it so intent on destruction?

A tall painted display beside it read *Chain of Destruction* and had details on the planets the Comet destroyed in the past. Neptune, Cicero, Hortensia...until finally, those that had been habituated by people: Gaius, Mars, and Earth.

Fell appeared so quietly beside her as she read that she nearly jumped out of her skin. He didn't even seem to notice: he was looking over the display on the Death Comet, a slight furrow between his brows.

'Do you think that's the Death Comet up there?' she asked him. 'Coming back to destroy what it didn't last time?'

'No,' Fell said. 'The Death Comet is already here.'

'You're right. In poor Trumble,' Gerdie sighed. 'I hope it doesn't come back, though.'

'No,' Fell said again. 'In Seki.'

It took a moment for Gerdie to process what he might mean. She turned to him. There was something in his expression that made her blood turn cold. Some grim determination that was so different from his usual soft expression. He looked more aware than she'd ever seen. 'What do you mean? Are you remembering?'

Fell nodded. 'Being here... seeing all of this...' He gestured to the Death Comet exhibit. 'I remember now. This is Seki.'

'Seki is a...comet?'

'The comet up there,' he said, raising his blue eyes as if he could see through the Space Room's dark, star-speckled ceiling to the comet in the sky, 'is here to stop it.'

'How is it going to do that?' she whispered.

Fell rubbed a finger under his nose. 'I don't know yet.'

As he walked away, the artificial stars seemed to glow brighter, and his skin shimmered in their light.

It hit her all at once.

'It's you, isn't it? You're the comet.' There was something so ridiculous and impossible about it, but she suddenly knew it as well as the birthmark on her face, as something that had always been there, she just hadn't had the words for it.

He nodded. 'Yes.'

'So when you said you were from the Hector-Nero System... You meant literally.'

'Yes.'

'You're a comet.' Just checking once more.

'Yes.' Fell looked a bit concerned now, coming back to stand beside her.

She leaned against the wall, blocking the tiny lights of the Emily's Arrow constellation. Her heart beat faster, and she braced her hands on her thighs.

'How come you didn't make a crater?' She thought of the Fell-shaped hollow in Odds and Ends. 'The Death Comet left a big one.'

'It's about intention,' he said slowly, as if figuring out how to explain it. 'Seki, and others, seek to destroy, to cause chaos or harm. Most of us, though, seek peace or exploration, or to simply be—orbiting suns.'

Gerdie suddenly pictured several comets conversing in the sky as they took a stroll around the sun. 'And how come there's still a comet in the sky if you're here on Bellona?'

Fell raised his eyes, only to be met with the black 'I draw power from it. I have not been to many planets and was unsure of my ability to return to comet form. I've chosen to separate myself to come down here, but not all comets do.'

'So why *are* you here?'

'The Great Comets sent me –'

Gerdie held up a hand. 'The Great Comets?'

'Comets are under the supervision of three Great Comets, the first to be born of the Merten Cloud.'

The conversing comets in her head grew long beards and wore glasses. She shook the thought away.

Fell swiveled his head left and pointed. 'There. See?'

She followed his finger. Further down the room was a display of the Hector-Nero System. An illustration of the particle-filled cloud that encircled the solar system, with facts too far away for Gerdie to read.

'You were born there?'

'Yes. When I had completed three orbits, the Great Comets sent me,' Fell continued, 'to stop Seki from destroying this planet. He cannot continue his reign of destruction.'

'So you remember now?'

'Yes. Being in this place, seeing the statue.' Fell rubbed his fingers against his forehead. 'But this planet... Seki has ruled for too long, he has influenced it too greatly. It has made me... ill.'

'I feel that,' Gerdie murmured.

'It is Seki's only purpose to destroy,' Fell said. 'He

succeeded, but one city is not enough for him; he is looking to the rest of the planet. Only, he is weakened, and he won't be able to take comet form anytime soon, at least not enough to cause an impact. He will want to use other means.'

'The automaton,' she whispered in horror. 'It's a weapon, but only a prototype. What if he's building more? What if he's planning a whole army?'

What if Dad helped him?

Tears pricked her eyes. It didn't make sense. She pushed off from the wall and wiped her eyes. 'Well if you're here to stop Seki, I want to help.'

'It will be dangerous,' Fell said.

'Life is already dangerous,' she replied. 'Especially under Seki's reign. I want to help.'

Fell smiled. It crinkled his eyes, made him look human, and not at all like—beneath his skin—he was part of the universe itself.

'How old are you?' she blurted.

Fell looked taken aback by the question, then his brow furrowed slightly. 'Time passes differently up there, but on this planet... a few hundred years, maybe?'

Gerdie blinked slowly at him for a few seconds. He didn't look older than fourteen... how could he have been around for so long?

'What's your real name?'

Fell paused, thinking about this, too. 'I do not have one,' he eventually said. 'Not in the sense that you mean. When we are in comet form –' his words slowed, as if he were searching deeply for each one – 'we sense each other's energy and are able to communicate directly. There is no need for names until we take human form.' Fell smiled, like this conversation was completely normal, and turned away to continue scanning the exhibition. Gerdie stared after him, mouth hanging open. The miracles Gerdie had witnessed had been miracles of technology – impressive, yes, but things that could be taken apart and studied. Things that could be explained and shared as equations and diagrams. But the boy in front of her... he was a miracle that couldn't be resolved with a pencil in a notebook.

Eventually she glanced at her watch; about an hour and a half had passed since the M.O.R.T. cleared the building.

When they came out into the entrance hall, the street was full of cars and people again. Whatever had been keeping them all inside was evidently over, like someone had pressed play on the remote of life.

Gerdie sidled over to the receptionist, who had returned to her desk and was clicking away at a computer. 'What's been going on? Why did we have to stay inside?'

Without looking away from the screen, the receptionist replied, 'Actions arrived to test something yesterday up on Stockton Hill.'

'Test what?'

The woman shrugged. 'Some weapon. Think they're trying to shoot the comet off course or destroy it all together.'

Gerdie looked at Fell in alarm. His own eyes were wide.

'But they can't!' Gerdie cried.

The receptionist finally glanced at them and raised an eyebrow. 'Better than the alternative, isn't it?'

Stomach turning, Gerdie left the museum with Fell.

'What will happen to you if they shoot it?' she asked quietly as they descended the stone steps.

'I will be destroyed,' Fell replied, sounding oddly calm. 'I will become a million pieces of rock and ice, floating in space forever. Perhaps parts of me will join other floating matter eventually –'

'That's all very poetic, Fell, but we can't let that happen.'

'Seki knows I am here,' he said. 'He will do everything in his power to see me gone, either in this form or the sky-bound one.'

'Not if we stop him first.' Down the left end of the newly bustling street rose a pallid hill. Two round structures were on top but were too far away for her to make out what they were. It must be Stockton Hill.

'Come on,' she said, setting off down the street. 'It's a nice day for sabotage.'

Stockton Hill was just outside of the city. Gerdie left Fell at the bottom and began the climb. The going was steep, her lungs burning, but she didn't dare slow. She passed a graveyard, covered in bright, glittering flowers made of thick glass. She climbed the rest of the hill on her hands and knees, small sharp rocks pricking her skin, trying to avoid detection while she peeked over the top. Luckily, she'd happened to climb a side with a gazebo and used its short walls to hide behind. If she didn't move, the Actions wouldn't see her; their attention fixed on the machine they surrounded. Three Actions all together, and behind them was a large iron machine that resembled a cannon, except for a small computer screen installed on top beside a satellite. The craftsmanship on it was amazing, and the way the barrel –

No, she chastised herself. *This machine was created for something horrible.* She shouldn't admire such a creation.

Even so, something about the weapon looked familiar, and Gerdie scanned every detail, trying to figure out where she might have seen something like it before. Then, when one Action pulled off a cover, revealing a thin cylindrical gun, she knew. She'd seen it on the blueprints in the old automaton factory.

One Action mentioned an early dinner and the others agreed. Two of them threw a black tarpaulin over the weapon, securing the ends down with rope, while the other packed the equipment that was scattered around the site into a large bag.

As soon as they'd disappeared behind the other side of the hill, Gerdie sprang into action.

As she crept around the machine, she collected a handful of rocks and lifted the tarpaulin to drop them through the air vents along the side. *That should make the blades jam and possibly snap when the machine is switched on.* She poured water from her bottle down the barrel to dampen the gun powder, and slashed at the little wheels beneath it with her pocketknife. She stepped back to admire her handiwork and noticed a dark figure climbing the other side of the hill; an Action had returned. With no time to replace the tarp, Gerdie crouched and made her way quickly and quietly back down the other side, grinning to herself as the Action reached the machine and gave a cry of, 'What the hell?!'

It wasn't a good idea for them to stay in Lanirose overnight, not with the Actions milling around, and not when they might be hunting for whoever sabotaged their weapon. She knew the Actions were planning to stay, too – she'd found two bedrolls close by the machine. They could still stay, if they didn't mind sleeping on the rocky ground of Stockton Hill while Gerdie and Fell enjoyed their bedding.

About an hour's walk outside of Lanirose, she'd chosen their bedroom for the night beside a covered performance stage in a park. The grass lay around the concrete paths was artificial, of course, and very soft. She wondered if real grass had felt like this. They lay down on their backs, Gerdie's stomach rumbling wildly with hunger, but there was nothing she could do about it for the moment.

Shiny plastic trees were few and far between, so they had an uninterrupted view of the night. The comet was domi-nating the sky, tail streaking behind it. It was impossibly bright, now, and tinged with green; larger than any star she'd ever seen.

'What's it like up there?'

'It's endless,' Fell replied softly. 'Peaceful. And beautiful.'

She tried to imagine floating in that vast black space and found she couldn't, not without feeling overwhelmed, like the way she'd felt after Mum left, and when Dad died. So, her thoughts quickly shifted back to the present. Since she'd stopped moving and let her body—and mind—relax to rethink everything that had happened, she realised with a lurch that she was without a purpose, back to the beginning of trying to make her life mean something.

No need to invent something to stop the comet and gain Conqueror Seki's attention when he was to blame for most of Treshane's problems anyway.

'What do I do now?' she asked the night. 'Building a machine to stop the comet was my best chance of becoming something, it would have been so epic, and now that's impossible.'

'Are you angry at me?'

Gerdie closed her eyes. 'Of course not, Fell. It's not your fault. And I don't want to see you leave, or destroyed or anything. I only wanted the comet gone because I thought it was going to hit us. But I know that's not the case now, and I won't let anything happen to it – to you.'

A beat of silence. 'Why did you have to build this machine to become something?'

Gerdie turned her head, but Fell was still gazing up at the sky, eyes moving slightly as if he were reading the stars. Two little white moths were resting on his stomach, and her mood lightened, just slightly. *Fell the Moth Magnet.*

'No one will ever notice me or what I can do if things stay the same. This world is so big – I even thought that when all I knew was the bottom of Rendip Quarry, and now that I'm *here*, well...' She gestured aimlessly, then let her hands fall by her sides. 'I feel very, very small. And I want to be worth something, to make people's lives easier with new inventions, like Mr. Tulk or Mr. Jameson or...' She swallowed. 'Or my dad. If I could get someone to notice me, then *I'll* be someone. I'll be important.'

When Fell didn't reply, Gerdie's thoughts inexplicably drifted to her mum, and she hated when that happened, but once the thoughts started trickling in, they broke her mental barrier like an overheated machine, exploding into a torrent of parts. Did Mum know Dad died? Did she care? Maybe she did and was just too busy digging her minerals to come back for Gerdie.

Fell remained quiet, and she thought he might have fallen asleep. But as she glanced at him, he had his hands up near his chest and was twirling them together. Over and over, his hands performed a complex dance that was beautiful to watch. Light appeared between his hands and the movements slowed. The white light left his palms and became small balls that drifted around them, some in clusters, some travelled way beyond their feet, some with rings and the rocky texture of other planets, until they surrounded her like they had in the museum, only this was so much better.

A galaxy, right before her eyes.

A small sound of wonder escaped her. 'How did you do that? They look like tiny stars.'

'They are,' said Fell.

The real stars in the sky beyond faded into the inky black, dimmed by comparison; all she knew was this tiny constellation and the strange, magical boy beside her.

Fell lifted a finger toward one of the smaller stars, hovering by their noses. It lit the planes of his face as he brought it down on the tip of his finger to hover above their faces, shining red, yellow, blue, green, twinkling like a precious diamond. The more she stared at the tiny bright orb, the more she saw swirling in its depths, threads and whisps, like an entire world was contained within it.

'This star has received no recognition,' Fell said. 'It lives its life, shining brightly like it has always done since the day it was born. It has no name, but look at how beautiful it is, how bright it makes your sky.'

'Beautiful,' she repeated glumly. The stars might be beautiful, but she was not. Not with her ugly purple-pink stain, her fingers darkened by grease, her frizzy red hair. The last thing Mum said to her before she left was, *You are so beautiful, my girl, and I love you.* If Gerdie really was beautiful, wouldn't Mum have chosen her over work?

'Beautiful.' Fell was looking at her now, and she gave him a small smile of thanks. She reached out a finger to gently prod one of the stars, and it felt cold, bouncing lightly away at her touch.

'You were wrong, Fell,' she whispered. 'When you said you weren't magic.'

Softly, Fell said, 'We are all magic. The elements in your body originated in stars. As a star cycles through its life, it produces the components that make up the universe and everything in it.' He reached his hand toward where hers was still bouncing the little lights, and gently ran a soft, cold finger across her knuckles. 'There is stardust under your skin.'

She wished she could believe him.

They left the swags in the park in the morning, too bulky and heavy to take with them. A shame, because they had actually been comfortable and warm, even if they did smell a bit like aftershave.

Gerdie pictured a map of Treshane in her mind, trying to calculate how far Lanirose was from New Londinium. The only problem was she didn't know where Lanirose was on a map. She knew Rendip Quarry, of course, and Balthasar. She knew Trumble was near Mount Sydney and the Quinn Ranges, but that was about it, except for the fact that the capital city was a long way from Rendip. She supposed they were going to have to ask someone and avoid the Actions at the same time.

'Right, well,' said Gerdie with her hands on her hips. 'I guess we got a lot of walking to do.'

'Or we could fly,' Fell said.

Gerdie pursed her lips in thought, then shook her head. 'We couldn't. Quad-wings are expensive, and I think you have to book in advance, and I don't even know where the nearest port is, and there's *no way* we could hire one and drive it ourselves, but one day I'd like to –'

'I can fly us there.'

He held his hand out to her and, confused, she took it, his skin cold and smooth against her palm. He closed his eyes, and a breeze picked up, ruffling through her hair, and then they were flying, or what felt like flying. The world flashing past in a dizzying blur of colour and light. She was weightless, the ground gone from beneath her feet, stomach completely left behind. She opened her mouth to scream –

Then it all stopped. The sudden feeling of her feet hitting solid ground again made her stumble, letting go of Fell's hand. Everything kept spinning, spinning, spinning and she squeezed her eyes shut. *That's enough comet magic for today, thanks.*

When her head cleared, she cracked an eyelid open. She opened the other and blinked them both in surprise.

'Is this it?' she asked.

She expected Treshane's capital city to be full of ginormous buildings bursting with the latest technology, the streets filled with flash cars and the monorail track she'd seen pictures of running high above their heads, the train itself zooming past, hanging low from the track like a fat snake. *This* city was white and sterile, rows of uniform office buildings, standing straight and tall. And above them, even taller, were trees, their trunks a textured brown and their three branches –

The realisation hit her in a rush of disappointment. Not trees: oxygen turbines, the ones designed to resemble trees. The air felt cool and light, helped by the turbines, and there was a huge amount of them around this place like giant sentinels, blades revolving slowly. She breathed in. It smelled like mint. No smoke, no thick, heavy air.

She looked to Fell. His skin had a touch of yellow around the edges and had lost its ethereal glow. His forehead, beneath his pale hair, was shiny with sweat—the first real bodily function she'd seen from him.

Tentatively, she touched his shoulder. 'Fell?'

He shook his head. 'This is as close as I can reach. Seki… His power is like a barrier. He knows I'm close.'

'Is that how you knew where to go? You can sense each other?'

He nodded.

'Huh, weird. But handy. So, where are we, then?'

She spotted a notice board nearby and scanned it: Some poor person had lost their cat, Juliet; a recent graduate was offering tutoring; and finally – *Join Malberg's first cricket team!*

'Malberg,' she read aloud. She remembered seeing the name on one of Seki's pamphlets. It was one of the newer districts being developed around New Londinium. New buildings and houses meant a fresh demand for building supplies and resources, and the reason why the quotas for the already overworked factories had been raised. Something gleamed out of the corner of her eye, and she glanced over. Nearby was a large white table with a long list of carved names, and Gerdie only had to catch the words 'bos virus' to realise what it was: a memorial to the thousands of people who had lost their lives to a pandemic shortly after arriving on Bellona when it was first colonised, the virus infecting the cows brought from Earth that then transmitted to humans. And beside the memorial, a street map displayed the area, pointing out points of interest, train stations, and information on the development program.

'New Londinium is here,' she said, pointing. 'It's not far at all.'

As they moved through Malberg, passing rows of new houses, the air began to smell like cinnamon. And then lavender, and then orange. Soon they were all blending together and becoming unpleasant, strong enough to bring on a headache.

'Where are all those smells coming from?' she asked, wrinkling her nose.

A woman emerged from a house nearby with a bin bag and exclaimed to a man washing his car in the driveway, 'Oh, the smell!' she said. 'I do wish the conqueror would choose just one smell to infuse in the oxygen turbines.'

'I heard he couldn't make his mind up,' grunted the man. 'That's why we have all of them.'

Gerdie wondered what it was like inside Seki's mind, what it was to be so indecisive and hateful and unfeeling all the time. She turned to Fell to mention this and was alarmed to find he wasn't by her side. She whirled around, panic rising – the city was so big, she'd never find him, they had no way of contacting each other, what if he'd been spotted and arrested – but he was lingering back behind her, sagging against number twenty's mailbox with his eyes closed.

'Fell...' she asked tentatively, taking soft steps toward him. 'Are you okay?'

His forehead was still damp, and he was breathing heavily,

and when he opened his eyes to meet hers, the blue was dull and filled with pain.

'Just a little further, okay? The business district is right there, see? Just there. It says business district. We're so close, Fell, then you can rest.'

Fell nodded wearily, pushed off from the mailbox, and followed her down the street.

Ha.

HA.

ha.

hA.

HA.

Ha.

ha.

Thirteen

With Hadrian's insistence that he was fine, they carried on with their plan to walk on until nightfall. But when evening revealed an illuminated town in the distance, they both agreed to keep going until they reached it. A bed and hot food sounded much more appealing than the hard ground. Hadrian pulled a torch from his pack, and they picked their way around rocky hills until they found the main road, then passed a large blue sign that informed them they were entering the town of Courtoff.

Faint music grew louder and louder as they passed houses towards the larger buildings of the town. A band playing, maybe. Or an out-of-control house party.

A firework went up into the sky with such a *bang* it made Leo jump. Hadrian placed a steadying hand on his shoulder. 'Must be a street party of some kind,' he said.

Leo craned his neck. A gap in the buildings was packed with people, laughing and cheering. Flags and the colourful tops of market stalls between them.

'I wonder what they're celebrating.' He stopped as a thought occurred to him. 'What date is it today?'

Hadrian's brow furrowed. 'The nineteenth. I think.'

'It's Trumble Day.' Every town and city on Treshane would be celebrating tonight.

Hadrian gazed into the town, his face lit red, orange, blue as more fireworks exploded in the sky. When he turned to Leo, a wicked smile played on his lips. 'I think we can afford to relax. We made good progress today.'

Leo cast a glance at the crowd. They were a roiling blur from here, but there were a lot of people. 'I don't know...'

'Oh, come on. When was the last time you had fun?' Hadrian grabbed his hand and pulled him toward the music.

The street was a crowd of bodies and thumping music, smells of roasting meat and candied nuts. Balthasar celebrated with a concert from the local schools, and market stalls. He supposed every town celebrated differently. He couldn't help but think of how Gerdie would love this; the noise, the food, the energy. He could imagine her fingers tapping against one another like they always did when she was excited or taken by a new idea.

Colourful flags hung between buildings, and the music thumped through his feet and into his chest like a second heartbeat. As one song ended and another began instantly, he recognised the catchy tune as an old Earthen one by a girl called Taylor...something. He couldn't quite remember.

As he took in the overwhelming number of people in the street, Leo was confident he and Hadrian wouldn't be recognised, if word had even spread this far yet. The people of Courtoff were laughing, dancing, and drinking. No one would be worrying about looking for two wanted boys.

This celebration wasn't about Seki, it was about the dead, and, more importantly, about the living.

Hadrian disappeared into the crowd but was back a few seconds later with two plastic cups, handing one to Leo. Leo raised the cup to his mouth, bubbles fizzing lightly on his nose, and took a sip. The liquid was strong, like fumes filling his mouth, but with a sweet lemony aftertaste.

'What is this?' he choked out.

Hadrian grinned. 'I have no idea. But I like it.' He downed his drink in one, and Leo did the same, spluttering only slightly as the liquid burned his throat. But as it settled in his stomach, it warmed him like a small fire, and he let Hadrian pull him into the thick of the crowd. Everyone jostled together as they jumped and danced to the music. At first, Leo hated the proximity, so much sweaty skin pressed close to his, people breathing hard and shouting. But the bass thudded its way into his chest, and he felt nothing else. Hadrian jumped around maniacally, and Leo was *laughing*, laughing so much that his cheeks hurt, like the muscles were resisting the movement.

A man in a cap accidentally bumped into Hadrian, and the transformation on Hadrian's face was instant: features darkened, animosity narrowing his eyes. Leo saw the way his hand bunched into a fist and caught it in his own before Hadrian could raise it.

'Let's move,' Leo shouted, though he could barely hear himself over the music. Hadrian relented under Leo's tugging, and as they pushed towards the outskirts of the crowd, Leo was struck by a memory. A throng of bodies like this, music blaring through tinny speakers: the school dance, when he was twelve. Leo had been permitted to go – though with strict curfew and Peller in attendance the whole time. He had still managed to enjoy the evening... until Bryan Musgrave appeared. Leo couldn't even remember what he said now, but it would have been the same old taunts. Hadrian had grabbed Leo's hand and pulled him outside (though they could still be seen by Peller through the windows) where the fresh air and muted music quietened his mind. He remembered thinking, as long as Hadrian was beside him, everything would be okay.

They stopped beside a table, abandoned drinks and plastic plates littering its surface.

'Okay?' Leo asked.

'Yeah. Fine.' Hadrian's tone was snappy. 'I want to go back in, I like this song.'

'Are you sure that's a good idea?'

Hadrian grabbed one of the half-finished drinks from the table and brought it to his lips.

'You don't even know what's –' Leo started, exasperated, but Hadrian had already downed the contents.

'Woo!' Hadrian shook his head. 'Come on, let's go.'

He dragged Leo back into the crowd before Leo could protest, and started the stupid dancing that had made Leo laugh, and it worked again. Hadrian's laugh was infectious, drawing Leo in until he jumped around beside Hadrian. It was chaos, yes, but it had already crawled into his veins and set his blood on fire. If this was how Seki felt, Leo was beginning to see the appeal. He forgot about his prosthetic, he forgot his real name, he forgot Seki. The night carried him away the way he had dreamed of doing for years.

'You are nearly here.'

Leo snapped his eyes open, nerves prickling his stomach at being woken by a strange voice. Only, there wasn't anyone close by, and he realised the voice didn't belong to a stranger. Not completely, anyway.

The voice from his dreams was louder than he'd ever heard before. He was close.

He closed his eyes, waiting for them to accommodate to the bright morning sunrise. When he could open them again, though with some difficulty, he took stock of his surroundings. He and Hadrian were on the sandy bank of a river beneath a stone bridge. He wrinkled his nose as the smell of the water hit him: sulfur. There must be a factory upstream somewhere, leaking its chemicals into the water.

His head was pounding. Hadrian still slept beside him, sprawled out over the sand, one arm clutching his backpack to his chest, mouth open.

Leo tipped his head back and tried to relax his shoulders so that his tension didn't wake Hadrian. How had they ended up under the bridge? Hazy images from last night gained slow clarity in his mind. He remembered downing drink after drink with Hadrian. That explained the headache, then. And he had been dancing—well, he wasn't much of dancer; his mother had loved it, he remembered, and would often scoop him onto her feet so that he could move as she did, and when she died, he never danced again. But last night, he had moved to the beat, had completely forgotten himself.

As he gazed up at the rose-gold sky behind the underside of the bridge, a dark shape in his periphery made him turn his head.

A mountain.

It must be Mount Sydney, appearing on the horizon as they'd walked in the evening, too dark to see it, then. The comet was flying just above it, a streak at the tip of the mountain. When he finally tore his gaze from the mountain, Hadrian's big hazel eyes were blinking awake.

'Hey,' he said, voice husky from sleep.

Leo replied, 'I found the mountain.'

A scream made them both bolt upright.

Leo winced as pain lanced through his head at the sudden movement. As they scrambled to their feet, an explosion shook the ground, almost making Leo fall back down. Panic spiked in his chest as he cast his gaze wildly over the bridge above them, to where a thick plume of smoke billowed from the town.

An automaton marched into view.

Distantly humanoid in shape. Taller than the one that had attacked him, Gerdie, and Fell outside of Rendip Quarry. Coppery-gold shell gleaming. Leo's stomach vanished completely. Had the key been found already? Was Gerdie too late?

But no - as the automaton stomped past the small buildings of Courtoff, its movements were slow and sluggish like it was running out of battery. An old model or a prototype, perhaps, but that didn't make it any less dangerous: its arms swung, destroying the tops of buildings with one swoop, and flames shot from its hands to finish off the rest. People spilled out into the street, screaming as they ran.

'Oh, Angels…' Hadrian said under his breath.

Leo stood, completely transfixed with horror, even as his every nerve screamed at him to move. The automaton swiveled and Leo saw a blinking red light on the top of its head. It was searching for something, and he was pretty sure he knew what —or who.

He made to run across the bridge when Hadrian grabbed his hand and yanked him back. 'Are you crazy?'

'We have to help them! It's my fault it's here!'

'Yeah, Leo, it's looking for you and you want to run right over there and let it crush you?'

'But…' he said weakly, as another building crumpled, and more people screamed. Some had started running for the other side of town, where sirens sounded. But Leo doubted any fire or police department would be equipped enough to take down something that Seki had built.

'The quicker you find the sceptre,' Hadrian said, his grip tightening on Leo's arm, 'the quicker all of this will be over. *Seki* will be over.'

Leo's whole body tensed. He couldn't just *leave*. It was like being at the Cats headquarters all over again. Being the reason for destruction without staying behind to help clean the mess.

'There's nothing you can do, Leo.' Hadrian shoved his bag into his arms. 'What, you're going to stop it with your bare hands? We have to go. Now.'

Casting a last helpless glance over the town before following Hadrian away from the town at a jog.

'Once it realises you're not there,' Hadrian said, breathing quickly, 'it will keep looking. And its legs are a lot longer than ours.'

Leo's own legs felt stiff as he forced them to move, like something in his body was resisting. *That's right, run away. Run away like you always do.*

But Hadrian was right, wasn't he? The automaton would be fitted with the latest technology and would find him in an instant if he ran out right under its nose—it had already tracked them this far. If it didn't kill him on the spot, then it would take him to Seki, who probably *would* kill him on the spot.

The terrain between Courtoff and Mount Sydney was relatively flat, sporadically dotted with boulders and stones, but that didn't mean the going was smooth. The uneven ground tripped both of them up more than once.

Leo glanced behind him so often that he pulled a muscle in his shoulder, but the view behind them remained the same: a thick column of smoke. His palms were slick with sweat no matter how often he wiped them on his pants. Eventually the smoking town disappeared from the horizon, but Leo felt the worse for it. When he finally swiveled his head forward, neck aching and Hadrian a few steps ahead, his senses tightened. His mind jumped around, imagining something following them, and again he was turning around every so often, expecting to see the automaton gaining on them.

Electricity towers loomed overhead, power lines buzzing. The comet burned above the mountain like a beacon. As the ground became rockier, and the gentle upward curve of the mountain base turned sharp, Leo's stomach began to turn. Not with nerves, he realised, as his nausea moved around like a compass needle, but with purpose. He might have had to leave Courtoff behind, but here was his chance to make it right. To make everything right.

It wasn't just a sense in his dreams now—it was a tangible, physical pull.

The feeling pulsed so strong it was making him nauseous. He couldn't see the cave entrance or any sort of gap in the rocky mountainside that surrounded him that matched what he'd seen in the dreams.

His heart sank. What had he been expecting? A neon sign pointing to the entrance, flashing the words *"HERE IT IS"*?

Desperation had him continuing to frantically scan the jagged mountain wall. He was vaguely aware of Hadrian speaking, probably suggesting they keep climbing, but Leo ignored him. It *had* to be around here, if the feeling in his stomach was anything to go by.

Then... there!

The entrance was so small, so well concealed, that the fact he had found it made his heart feel full...like he really was meant to be there, that he was wanted there.

'It's here,' he whispered, and Hadrian was at his side in an instant.

He grimaced at the tiny dark opening. 'There? Are you sure? Wait, can you sense the sceptre?'

'I don't know,' Leo said. 'I just have this feeling. I think I've seen that cave before. In my...dreams.' He glanced at Hadrian, afraid the other boy would think he was crazy.

Hadrian only nodded, seeming to accept his explanation. He watched Leo expectantly.

Leo gave the comet a final glance before letting the darkness swallow him.

His footsteps echoed as he stepped tentatively inside, totally unsure about what was waiting for them. Water dripped from somewhere nearby.

Hadrian flicked his torch into life, pointing the yellow beam into the shadows. There was nothing particularly special about the cave, nothing to suggest it housed the answer to Treshane's troubles, but the feeling in Leo was growing stronger. He had a sense that he was meant to be here, that this place had been waiting for him.

'This is it,' he whispered, and even then, his voice sounded too loud in the darkness.

'Excellent,' Hadrian breathed.

The blackness of the cave seemed to swallow the torch beam, so they walked close together to follow the narrow light breaking through the darkness. They walked for a long time, seeing nothing but damp rock walls and the occasional spider. With every minute that went past, the deeper they descended, the more nervous Leo felt. He wiped his palms on his shirt, sweaty despite the chill of the cave. It felt like anything could be lurking in the darkness, and while he had never felt threatened by the voice in his dreams, it didn't mean it wasn't threatening in real life. He had never, after all, understood where the voice came from.

'*You are here.*'

Leo jumped out of his skin as the voice sliced through the quiet. Hadrian yelped, and when he asked what the matter was, Leo realised he hadn't heard it.

'I heard something,' he said, voice shaking slightly as his fear subsided. 'I think we're close.'

After just another minute of walking, the cave tunnel

opened into a large space with a high ceiling, and a heavy presence pressed in on Leo so suddenly that his stomach swooped like he had missed a step. They weren't alone. Stalagmites jutted up from the floor, and the air felt damp. And most remarkable of all was the single beam of sunlight that shot from the roof – surely they were too deep for light to reach them like this – and lit a lush mass of green.

Leo felt his jaw drop, and heard Hadrian gasp as he saw it, too. He thought the tree in the middle of the Angel's Marbles had been spectacular, but this... Big and sprawling, and so commanding in its presence—Leo felt it in his chest like it had its own gravitational pull. Wide green leaves and thin twisting branches spread across the cave wall as if to claim it for their own.

'I've...never...' Hadrian began.

Leo was speechless too. He recognised the leaves on the plant as those on a Lona; wide and faintly heart shaped, with white veins reaching out from the midrib down the middle. Memories of his mother flooded him, of her graceful hands as she showed him pictures of different plant species. Preparing him, as every surviving Catell had prepared after Seki's coup, for a future where nature was returned from the chaos that had conquered it. The Lona hadn't grown on Earth; it was unique to Bellona, but Leo never thought he would ever see one.

The branches on the Lona were thick and could probably stretch throughout the cave for Angels knew how long. The sceptre, if it really was here, would probably be hidden in the very depths of the green mass.

Hadrian reached into his satchel and pulled out a knife. Leo's blood turned cold – had he been carrying that the whole time? Hadrian advanced on the mass of green.

Leo grabbed his hand. 'What are you doing?'

Hadrian yanked his arm away. 'The sceptre's in there, isn't it?'

Leo glanced back at the Lona. His blood was pulsing in his ears, and he was sure he could hear a similar beat pulsing from the plant. 'I – I don't know. But you can't destroy it. It's too rare, and –' *Powerful*, he wanted to say, but he didn't know if Hadrian would understand. 'You just can't,' he said again.

'How are you going to get it, then?'

Leo took a few tentative steps toward the mass of green. As soon as he was an arm's length away, the Lona shivered, leaves rustling with a loud *shh*. A leafless branch whipped out and struck Leo's hand, sending him stumbling back. His prosthetic caught on a loose rock, and he fell hard, clutching his now-bleeding hand to his chest.

Hadrian sat behind him and held the knife, handle-first, toward him. Leo ignored it. The branch slunk back into the rest of the Lona and was still once more.

Seeing Leo wasn't going to take the knife, Hadrian sighed and said, 'I'm going to start a fire.'

'So how do you know Gerdie?' Hadrian asked.

Leo tore his gaze from the fire. They'd had their meager dinner of whatever rations they had, but his stomach still felt empty.

'She works at Sweene & Sons,' he replied. 'A year younger than us. We met because she was always tinkering with the machines, trying to make the factories better.'

Hadrian made a noise in the back of his throat, almost like a laugh. 'Good old Balthasar.'

'Did you go back?' Leo asked. 'While you were with the Cats?' It had struck him how close Hadrian had been.

Hadrian's expression darkened. 'No. I didn't go and see Mum, if that's what you're asking.'

'I wasn't –'

'We should go to sleep,' Hadrian said shortly. He rolled over without another word, clutching his backpack close to his chest.

Something woke Leo in the night. He lay, frozen now that the fire was out, straining his ears to listen, but all he could hear was Hadrian's breathing and his own heartbeat in his ears. When he couldn't discern anything like immediate danger, he rolled over. Hadrian was on his back, one hand resting on his stomach, head cushioned by his jacket.

Then he heard it: a whisper. He sat up, careful not to wake Hadrian. The whisper was speaking only to him. Where was it coming from?

He pushed himself quietly to his feet, careful not to wake Hadrian, and careful to take his torch.

Goosebumps rippled across his skin at the cold. He pointed the torch, the uneven natural stone casting weird shadows across the walls, until the Lona appeared in the yellow beam. Slowly, quietly, he approached, stopping when the leaves stirred. Mother had always explained that nature was a living thing, but he had never really understood it until now. It was always hard to imagine something you saw in a photo as once being alive. He lowered himself onto the cold damp ground and crossed his legs like he was about to begin a casual conversation with the Lona.

He let the torchlight roam gently over the plant, over its thick leaves and the brown branches beneath them and inhaled deeply. He couldn't determine exactly what the Lona smelled like—the freshness of mint, the lightness of orange, the strangeness of chlorine—but he recognised what it made him feel. It smelled like Father's strong arms play-tackling Leo to the ground for a football, and like Mother kissing him goodnight.

It felt right in a world full of wrongs.

The light passed over the centre of the Lona, and wrapped in the folds of the leaves, hugged protectively by thick and twisted branches, something glinted gold.

'Oh...' he breathed. He rose shakily to his feet.

Clutched in the arms of the plant was the sceptre; a wand of gold about the length of his arm. He could just make out the rounded tip, surrounding a blue-green gem. He reached a hand toward it, but the plants quivered, snatching it back, out of his reach.

'*Ours...*' something whispered. The voice was a harsh, raspy whisper, and it left no doubt that this was what had filled his dreams for years.

Not the sceptre, but the Lona.

He replied quietly, 'My name is Leo Catell. I've heard you in my dreams. You have it. The sceptre.'

'*We found it. It was thrown away, no longer wanted, but it called to us. We claimed it.*'

'I understand,' Leo said. 'You're right to say it is yours. It belongs to Treshane. But I am the rightful heir to the throne, and it calls to me, too. I am one of you. With the sceptre returned to its rightful place, Seki will lose his power. I'll make this country a better place to live. A safer one for you. Please.'

The Lona made a harsh sound that could only be a laugh.

'*Prove it.*'

'What?'

'*Prove that you are worthy of this sceptre. We don't believe you. See here...*' One of the branches snaked forward to hover its leaves around his prosthetic. '*You are metal. You are one of them. You are not one of us.*'

His heart gave a painful squeeze, and he momentarily lost his breath. 'I didn't choose this,' he whispered.

Prove himself worthy? The thing he was most afraid of. He realised how much he'd been counting on this moment—when he finally found the sceptre—to make everything better, and he felt his heart crack under the realisation that even the sceptre didn't think he was worthy. He didn't know what to do.

'How can I prove it?' he asked.

The Lona whispered indistinctly, its voice fading away as leaves thickened around the sceptre. The glint of gold disappeared from view.

'Wait—' Leo said, but the Lona fell silent. He wasn't aware of Hadrian beside him until he felt the warm, bony hand on his shoulder.

'Are you okay? I thought I heard voices.'

Leo stared at where the sceptre had disappeared. It was right there; he was so close. All he had to do was prove himself worthy of earning such a valuable part of Treshane. He had to be strong, complete the impossible, convince the Lona that having a metal prosthetic meant nothing. He glanced up at the ceiling as if he could see through the rock.

'I have to climb this mountain.'

Fourteen

Gerdie and Fell avoided Malberg's central district and walked around its outskirts, through the area that was being demolished to accommodate the new development. They picked their way through sandy areas and concrete foundations and portable toilets. There were no workers tending to the machinery despite it being midmorning, the sun already burning the back of her neck. *It must be the weekend* – she'd completely lost track of the days.

Then they were in a derelict area, where old buildings still stood... but only just. Cranes and heavy vehicles waited nearby with malice. Whether this was old Malberg or just an unlucky area subject to the conqueror's wishes Gerdie couldn't say, but it was a deserted street—the surrounding buildings had their doors and windows boarded over with dull metal planks, and rubbish drifted feebly down the gutters like tumbleweed.

A tiny grunt made her tear her eyes away from the eerie scene before them, to where Fell was hunched over again, face white and scrunched up in pain. She rushed to his side, throwing an arm around his limp shoulders.

'Talk to me, Fell. Please tell me what's wrong.'

'I...' Fell closed his eyes. 'I underestimated him. His power has weakened, that is why Treshane was not destroyed when he landed, that is why he stayed. But it has not weakened enough.'

Gerdie's stomach flipped. She'd watched him grow weaker but had been powerless to stop it. She couldn't help but think of her dad then, as she took in Fell's sweating brow and pinched mouth, and how if Dad was sick then he should have looked like this and then she would have known, but she hadn't known.

'What can we do? How can I help you?'

He swayed a little on his feet, and Gerdie took hold of his arm. 'Fell? Can you take power from your comet? *Please.*'

He took a shaky step forward. 'I –'

And then he collapsed.

I aM ALMosT gLad yoU aRE hEre
liTTLe One
THat IS wHat You arE
LItTle. heLpLESs
i ReLIsh iN GEtTing To wAtCh yOu WitHeR aND die
THIs IS mY planEt NOw
wAtCH as I DEStroy It
If You LAst tHat LoNG

i am not so little as you may think
a drop of water is little, but drop after drop
makes an ocean
snowflake after snowflake makes an avalanche
i am not so little
and i will last long enough to see you fall
only you shall be destroyed
this... i... promise

FIFTEEN

'I don't understand, Leo,' Hadrian panted behind him. 'Did you see something last night? What exactly is your plan here?'

Leo continued to march through the cave, ignoring his questions until Hadrian's hand fell tightly on his shoulder.

'I'm not worthy of the sceptre.'

'Leo, you –'

Leo stepped out from under his hand. 'I'm not looking for a confidence boost or praise or anything. I'm just stating a fact here. I've done nothing to prove that I'm worthy to be crowned a – a *king*. To govern over an entire country. The sceptre won't let me just pick it up and take it back to the throne.'

'We haven't even found it yet,' Hadrian said. 'You don't know that.'

Leo turned to face him. 'I do know it. And I want to prove that I am worthy, even though I don't feel like it. I want to do it now.'

Hadrian scrubbed a hand through his light hair, making it

stick up in all directions. 'Okay, well...Why would climbing the mountain prove that?'

Leo's heart swelled in gratitude for his understanding. 'I don't know, exactly,' he admitted. 'It's something that requires strength, I guess. Proves I'm strong enough to support this country.' But he didn't feel strong, and he felt stupid for saying these things out loud.

Hadrian nodded, but his pale eyebrows were drawn together.

This would be what proved his strength... if he had it. He had come this far, and he would not return empty-handed.

Daylight glowed ahead and Leo stepped outside into the warmth of the early morning. He picked a random direction and started walking around the mountain, stumbling every now and then as loose rocks tripped him up. After a few minutes, he found an area made of jutting ledges and boulders. He wedged his left foot between a gap and hoisted his other leg up, resting his prosthetic on a flat rock. The thin metal design of the foot had no grip, and he felt himself falter like the loose rocks beneath him for just a moment. It was just enough for those familiar thoughts to creep in and wrap themselves around his resolve. He pushed them away and continued to make his slow way up the mountain, Hadrian climbing behind him.

At what he guessed was about a third of the way up, the going evened slightly, and he stopped to catch his breath and take in his surroundings. He had a clear view of the land around the mountain: storm clouds gathered on the horizon, but he didn't know how to tell which direction they were heading. Just beyond was the devastation of Trumble; below him was Courtoff, thin plumes of smoke still rising from the town. Something in the distance moved toward them, easy to spot amongst an otherwise still landscape. Leo shielded his eyes to make it out; it wasn't moving as a vehicle would.

Marching like a toy soldier was the automaton, maybe a few hours away. Leo clenched his jaw, turned and scanned the rocky mountain face. He didn't know what he was looking for, exactly. He was just hoping *something* would present itself, a magic answer. He heard Hadrian before he saw him; the other boy was panting hard as he pulled himself onto the ledge.

'Leo...' he said, his blonde hair matted to his forehead with sweat. 'This is...ridiculous...'

There's nothing here, he realised, and of course there wasn't. He wasn't at the summit yet. The Lona wouldn't consider him worthy if he only made it partly to the top of the mountain. No, he had to go all the way up and make it back down again.

He gripped the next ledge, feeling around for a brace for his feet.

'*Leo,*' Hadrian said behind him, but Leo ignored him. He had to reach the top of the mountain. It was the only way.

His next reach was too hasty: the rock crumbled under his hand, and he was falling. He landed hard just a second later, sharp rocks stabbing into his back and the still-healing whip marks there. He let out a cry, rolling onto his side to ease the pain, and then he fell again in a flash of blue sky and orange rock.

Something grabbed his wrist, yanking his arm from his shoulder but keeping him from falling to the very bottom. When Leo opened his eyes, Hadrian was there, straining to hold Leo's weight without going over the ledge himself. Where their hands met was slick with sweat, and Leo could feel his grip quickly sliding from Hadrian's. He scrambled for the ledge, filling his fingernails with dirt and small stones. His left leg found purchase, and with Hadrian's help he pulled himself onto the ledge and collapsed on the solid ground. Hadrian dropped to his knees beside him.

Leo's heart was beating wildly, like it had only just realised how fast it had come to serious injury or even death, and the after-effects of adrenaline were weighing his limbs down and making them shake. His right arm throbbed with pain, overwhelming everything else. Wincing, he pulled himself into a sitting position, glancing down at his arm. A wide red gash ran from nearly shoulder to elbow, blood dripping freely.

'Shit,' he muttered, biting on his bottom lip. The intense sting of it made his head spin, he breathed sharply through clenched teeth.

Hadrian raised his head, then sat up when he saw the blood running down Leo's arm. He pulled his satchel onto his lap – he had carried it up the mountain, unable to let it out of his sight even for this – and pulled out a small vial of Bolander's Solution. He shifted closer, and Leo proffered his arm. As soon as a few drops of the yellow-brown liquid hit the wound, his skin began to knit together, and the pain subsided until only a jagged red line remained, surrounded by blood that was already drying.

They both watched his arm for a few moments longer, though Leo didn't think either of them were really seeing it. What a disaster all of this was. To come so far but still feel no closer. To already be bleeding before he'd even attempted the steepest part of the mountain. He didn't know why he should feel so surprised that he failed. It was inevitable, really.

Weak. Useless. Failure.

'Come on, Leo,' Hadrian said quietly. 'This is too dangerous. Let's go back.'

Leo didn't realise he was crying until a tear rolled down his cheek.

They were quiet on the way down. The dark clouds Leo spotted earlier rolled over to them after all, to mirror his mood, and just as they reached the cave, a clap of thunder was the only warning before a torrent of rain fell. Leo hurried inside, shivering at the coolness of the cave.

Once they were back in the cavern with the Lona, Hadrian started a fire with a kerosene fire-starter block he procured from his backpack, and they shared the last of the food. The rain was thundering outside, pouring in through the hole in the roof and soaking the Lona, drops bouncing off the leaves and pooling in shallow dips in the rock.

'We could just cut through it, you know. I'm sure it would grow back.'

Leo tore his eyes away from the newly formed mini water-fall to where Hadrian was staring at the plant, his legs drawn up to his chest.

'We can't do that,' he said quietly.

Hadrian scoffed and fed another fire-starter to the flames. As the fire flared, the light caught the sceptre within the Lona, glinting at them from between the leaves.

'Leo, the sceptre! It's there! I see it!'

He leapt to his feet and rushed forward as if to grab it, but a thin branch lashed out like a whip, cutting into Hadrian's arm. He howled and fell back. 'Grab it, Leo, now!'

Leo watched the scene, dumbstruck. Blood trickled down Hadrian's arm, but he didn't seem to notice. Blood filled his face, too, his expression feverish and desperate. This sudden mood had come on so fast that Leo couldn't help but stare. He'd seen Hadrian angry, but nothing like this. An uneasy feeling started in his gut.

Leo peered between the leaves, to where the sceptre was lodged between the branches. But instead of feeling excite-ment, he only felt deflated. It might be here, but what difference did it make if the plant would never let him have it?

'It won't give it to me,' Leo said. 'I'm not worthy enough,

I told you. I thought reaching the summit would be enough, but I guess I'm not even capable of that.'

'This is useless,' Hadrian snarled. 'The stupid plants are right. You aren't worthy of anything.' He reached into his satchel and pulled out what was inside for Leo to finally see.

Shackle bots.

Hadrian flung them too fast for Leo to even react, and then they were shackled around his wrists, binding his hands together. They whirred and chittered as they tightened.

'What the...?'

Leo was so stunned he didn't even make a move as Hadrian marched over. All he could manage was to search Hadrian's eyes, looking for some hint that this betrayal had been there all along.

'Why?'

Something flickered in Hadrian's eyes at Leo's simple question, but they soon hardened again.

'I'm sorry, Leo.' And there was something in his voice that was almost believable. 'I need that sceptre. It's nothing... personal. Seki, he...he's given me a lot. I have to do this for him. He has all the power. Not you.'

Anger stirred inside Leo. 'Because he took it from me. From my family.'

Hadrian turned away, pulling his phone from his pocket, a portable charger dangling from it. He keyed in a few buttons, held it to his ear. 'Captain Walton,' he said. 'I've got him. And the sceptre.'

It only took twenty minutes for the quad-wing to arrive. Hadrian dragged Leo, still bound, back to the cave entrance to wait, not trusting him alone with sceptre even though it wouldn't have mattered. Even without his hands in shackle bots. They didn't speak, though Leo had a thousand questions. As the quad-wing arrived, a whirlwind of water sprayed in the cave, soaking Leo's clothes. Once the large quad-wing landed and the blades slowed, Leo tried to keep his head up as he eyed the cave entrance with defiance, ready for whoever was about to step through. But when Captain Adam Walton stepped out of the quad-wing, his knees shook slightly despite himself.

Captain Walton kept his eyes fixed firmly on Leo while three other Actions filed out of the quad-wing. Their thick black cloaks reached their booted ankles, shiny gold buttons and clasps adorning their chests.

'We know your game, boy,' he growled. 'You stay quiet and meek for years, let Conqueror Seki think he can trust you, all the while planning to betray him.'

Leo hung his head. There was no point in arguing. There was no point in saying anything. It would only be twisted and used against him later anyway. He'd been on this road too many times before.

Leo was restrained to a stalagmite as a couple of Actions surrounded the Lona. Hadrian spoke in hushed tones with Walton to one side. Only one Action flanked him, and she remained relaxed, metal mask hanging limply from her fingers as she watched the progress of the others. She knew Leo from the palace; they all thought he was weak, and they were right, even with Walton's false idea that this had been Leo's plan all along.

A sudden shout made him flinch. The Lona lashed out its branches, whip-like, and the Actions were forced to quickly step away. Leo's heart rose, just a tiny bit, that maybe it wasn't as hopeless as he thought. The Lona would fight back in a way that he couldn't. But there were more Actions than the branches could keep up with, and the Actions were armed with more than bark and leaves. Metal slid on metal as the Actions unsheathed their guns and knives. Leo turned his head, looking away and swallowing against the tightness in his throat. *Oh, Angels.* They were going to kill the Lona, destroy this last remaining hidden patch of nature, and it was all his fault. They would burn it and retrieve the sceptre, and he would have failed like he knew he would all along. He couldn't protect anything or anyone and here was the proof. Anything he encountered was going to end up punished, he would never have made a good king, and all of this was for nothing –

He let out a choked breath. When he looked up again, no attack was working on the Lona. Bullets bounced off the leaves, and even fire didn't have an effect, the flames licking at the leaves like they were made of cement. A tiny weight eased from his chest. While the Actions conversed in low voices about how they were going to get through the Lona, Leo leaned his head against the coolness of the stalagmite and closed his eyes.

What had his father told him about the sceptre? Not enough. Was it because Leo was too young at the time? He'd been ten when his parents were killed, maybe his father thought he'd been too young. Or, most likely, Father had simply assumed that he would be around long enough to find the sceptre himself, like Luca said he'd been planning. Death was so hard to imagine when you were alive.

Father only ever told him the history of the sceptre, of their family.

'*This is our destiny, Leo,*' he'd said once. '*It's up to the Catells to restore harmony to this country. The sceptre is the one thing Seki fears.*'

'*And you're going to find it?*' Leo had asked with little interest. He'd been eight at the time, his favourite cartoon playing in the background.

'*I'm certainly going to look.*' Father had run a hand over Leo's hair, glancing fondly at the television. '*What's Chicken-wick up to today?*'

If Leo had shown more interest, would he know how to get the Lona to grant him the sceptre?

When it became clear they weren't going to get it released anytime soon, the Actions set up camp for the night, telling themselves if they hadn't got the sceptre by morning they would leave; take Leo to the palace and let the conqueror decide what to do next. Leo wouldn't be getting his hands on it – clearly no one was – and that was what mattered most.

The shackle bots around Leo's wrists were replaced with cuffs the Actions had brought with them: if he moved even just a few meters away the cuffs would sound, the Actions alerted to his movement. At least it meant he wasn't chained to the stalagmite anymore.

As Walton joined the fire, coming back from circling around the Lona one last time as it hissed and rustled under his gaze, he said, 'If we can't get it, Catell here can't either. But just for good measure...' He lifted his foot and brought it back down hard onto Leo's prosthetic.

Leo couldn't stop the cry that left his mouth. The beautiful contraption that Gerdie had fixed for him cracked under Walton's boot like an eggshell, and pinched the skin below his knee, exposing the jagged scars there as it came away. Walton turned away without a backwards glance. Through blurring vision, he noticed Hadrian biting down on his bottom lip, throat bobbing as he swallowed. Did he regret calling Walton? Feel guilty over betraying Leo?

Leo dragged himself further away from the fire, curling up against the cavern wall.

He heard a shuffling, and glanced up to see Hadrian coming toward him, crouching at his side. He peeled away the broken prosthetic since Leo could not.

He didn't meet Leo's eyes, but he whispered, 'I... I'm...'

'It's okay,' Leo said hollowly. Was it? Was he just too tired to really care whether Hadrian was sorry or not? Or did he just want some silence?

'I really am sorry,' Hadrian said, placing the prosthetic to one side. He blew out a breath. 'It's complicated.'

It was a weak excuse, but Leo believed him. He knew something was going on with Hadrian beneath the surface – his worsened temper, his illness, two years away without word – and who was Leo to judge someone for keeping secrets?

'I forgive you,' he said, then turned his head, tucking it into his shoulder. Hopefully it had been all Hadrian needed to hear, and he would leave. Leo realised with a small jolt that he meant the words. Hadrian hovered for a few seconds, but got the hint and rose to his feet. It wasn't until his footsteps had faded as he rejoined the Actions by the fire that Leo raised his head again, watching in his peripheral vision as they set up swags and shared food amongst them. Leo didn't receive any, and his stomach grumbled.

The fire died down, conversations quietened, and Leo's mind wandered. Even if he could move, could escape, where would he go? The Cats had been rounded up, Peller would report him straight away if he returned to Balthasar, and who knew where in the world Gerdie was. Hope left him like air from a balloon.

When he glanced over at the camp again, Hadrian had set himself apart from the group, not engaging in their conversation, only shortly answering the questions he was asked about the Cats and the journey from Mallincroft.

Leo lay down, cushioning his head on his arms as best he could, his back to the Actions and their camp. Leo grew stiffer and colder against the hard, damp ground of the cave floor, but he didn't move.

He must have slept, because the next thing he knew, he was awake in darkness. The Actions were snoring, their camp-fire dead, and at first, he thought it was the cold and the noise that had woken him, but, no, someone was whispering, two Actions talking to one another, so Leo closed his eyes to try to go back to sleep. The whispering sounded familiar, and his body seemed to remember it before his brain did. His skin tingled, and he knew without turning to look that it was the Lona.

He blinked a couple of times, hardly believing what was in front of him. In the pitch blackness of the cave, he felt rather than saw the plant in front of him. It had stretched itself across the floor, past Hadrian and the Actions; he could hear its bulk shifting restlessly behind him.

'*You forgave the boy,*' they whispered.

'Hadrian?' Leo breathed in surprise. 'Yeah, I...' Why *had* he forgiven Hadrian? Was it because of their friendship? Because it was further proof of how weak he was, and why stop at all his other failures?

'I still believe he's a good person, I guess. And what would be the point of holding on to that hate and anger, anyway? I'd rather let those feelings go, see if he and I could work things out one day, instead of carrying them around for the rest of my life.'

That was... true. The words surprised him, even though he had spoken them.

'*That is a king's answer,*' the Lona replied. '*With this forgiveness, you have proven yourself to be worthy of the sceptre and the throne of Treshane.*'

Leo fought hard to keep his voice down. 'You couldn't have told me that *before* I climbed the mountain?'

'*A man's worth is not in his physical strength. It is in his actions towards others.*'

One of the Actions shifted in his sleep, and Leo held his breath. The snoring resumed; he relaxed. 'I guess,' he whispered.

'*This belongs to you.*'

He heard the plant shift closer, pressing something cool and solid against his chest. Hardly daring to believe it, Leo raised his bound hands to hold the sceptre to him, the metal warm and smooth. His heart beat hard against the sceptre as if it was trying to reach out and grab it for itself.

'Thank you,' he said, 'but what can I do? I'm in handcuffs, my leg is gone.'

There was a soft *click*, and his handcuffs loosened. He blinked in surprise, then slid them gently off his wrists before they fell to the ground and made noise.

'Wait,' he whispered, but the plant was already sliding away, disappearing back into the cave wall.

'*It is time, it is time...*'

He adjusted his grip on the sceptre so that it was firmly in his hands. He slid his fingers along its smooth edge, marveling at the warmth of it, like it was alive. It was gleaming faintly like light was trapped inside. Its circular top was made up of five bands that joined at a point, where two small balls balanced on top to represent Maylow and Oriana, and just below the hilt before the shaft began were two horizontal points, like on the hilt of a sword. He could hear his father's voice, his teachings, as he gazed at the sceptre.

The hope swelling in his chest disappeared like a popped balloon. Without his leg, it was still no use. He was still trapped.

Maybe the Lona didn't know what he needed the prosthetic for, or maybe it just didn't care. The Lona might not like the prosthetic, and neither did he, but he needed it; it was a necessity now, and nothing he or anyone else did would change that.

As soon as he thought it, the tension evaporated from his shoulders. He hadn't realised just how heavy the idea of his prosthetic had been, how his thoughts on it were like a steel trap in his chest. It had always been the worst thing in the world to him, but it was better than no leg at all. Hating the prosthetic wasn't going to bring his leg back.

If you tell yourself something enough, eventually it becomes true.

Besides, there were bigger things to worry about.

Sleep was impossible. He clutched the sceptre to him as he lay on his side, away from the Actions, like it was the teddy bear he'd cuddled in bed as a child. His mind whirred all night as it formulated plan after plan for how he was going to escape without the Actions knowing. But each plan ended in failure, his imagination in overdrive and conjuring gruesome ends. His broken prosthetic still lay where Hadrian had put it, but it was in no state to support his weight.

Eventually, he tucked the sceptre under his shirt, against his stomach, and secured it in the waistband of his pants, praying that sheer luck meant the Actions wouldn't notice, or bother to check for it.

He replaced the handcuffs, clicking them shut just when the Actions stirred early, as Walton's phone began to buzz. *It speaks to the state of Treshane,* Leo thought, *That we can find reception in the middle of a mountain, yet no nature or wildlife.* He watched as the Actions shared a small breakfast and packed up their hasty camp, and it was only when they started walking back through the cave that Walton gestured for Hadrian to get Leo. Leo let Hadrian help him to stand, careful to keep his side angled toward Hadrian to hide the sceptre. With a few clicks, Hadrian separated the cuffs so that Leo could throw an arm around his shoulders. Hadrian supported him by the waist where there was no risk of him feeling the sceptre pressed against Leo's stomach.

They didn't speak during their slow way out of the cave. Leo's heart beat faster with every uneven step. *Was he going to do this? Could this really work?* They were nearly at the quad-wing. He was never this lucky, something was going to go wrong...

The blades of the quad-wing were already spinning as they approached, and Hadrian loaded him unceremoniously into the quad-wing, seating him at the very back. The automaton that had followed them from Courtoff was stationed at the base. As Hadrian buckled his seatbelt for him, Leo began to let himself formulate a plan.

It was an hour-long trip in the quad-wing to New Londinium. Leo watched as Mount Sydney grew smaller and smaller, Trumble like a bruise on Treshane's surface, and Courtoff a speck beside it.

As they approached New Londinium, something was different about the aerial view of the city. With a jolt of horror, he realised what it was. At least a dozen of the giant automatons had been placed in uneven intervals along the inside of the city walls. With one blow of their mighty fists, they could break the city walls in half, and Angels knew what else. Were they switched on? Had Seki found what he was looking for? Time was running out, and Leo leaned forward in his seat as much as the seatbelt would allow, to feel the sceptre press against his chest, a reminder that it wasn't too late just yet.

As they landed, Leo never thought he'd be wishing for a jail cell, but this had been a week of discovering things about himself he hadn't known before. In a cell, at least, he could be alone to figure out his next move, or even hide the sceptre more securely until he figured out what to do with it.

But some things never change, and when he realised they were headed for the throne room, Leo's mouth went dry. Despite Hadrian supporting him as he hopped, he stumbled, and Hadrian's hand shot to Leo's front to steady him, right on his stomach. Leo's heart sunk as the hand froze. Slowly, Hadrian's fingers closed around the sceptre through Leo's shirt, and he loosed a breath in a loud exhale.

'Leo...' was all he said. His hand snaked under Leo's shirt to grab the sceptre. Leo brought his elbows down, but it did nothing.

No no no no no –

Hadrian pulled the sceptre free and released his hold on Leo. The sudden loss of support made Leo lose his balance, and he fell to the ground. His heart felt like it had been placed on an anvil and the hammer was coming down.

'Captain Walton,' Hadrian said without taking his awe-filled eyes from the sceptre.

Walton glanced over his shoulder at them, freezing up.

'He had it all along,' Walton growled as he marched over. 'Bastard.' He raised his gun, hit the butt of it over Leo's head, and Leo knew no more.

Sixteen

She'd pulled Fell out of the open and into the concrete walls of either a half-built or half-demolished building. The concrete was hot on the back of her legs, but the longer she held Fell, the colder she felt. She cradled his head on her lap, tapping the side of his face, lightly at first, then harder when she received no response.

'Please, Fell. The comet is *right there*, just draw power from it!'

She shook him, but nothing worked; his eyes remained closed, his body limp. She could barely feel a heartbeat in his chest, but *did comets even have heartbeats? Had she felt his before? Did his body work the same way as hers?* She didn't know, she didn't know. He was so cold, and Gerdie felt herself begin to panic because she just didn't know what *normal* for him was. Didn't know how to help him, didn't know what to do. She rummaged one-handed through her bag, searching desperately for something that would help, but her hand came back empty.

Frustrated tears pricked at her eyes, and she let them fall, let a sob escape. It echoed through the building, reminding her how alone she was. The building was missing a roof and the blue sky felt too close, the concrete felt too hard, and she felt like the loneliest person in the universe, like her sound of despair would float here in space forever, never heard and never received. Three grey moths landed on Fell, their fluffy bodies crawling across his arms. Gerdie waved them away angrily.

'Shoo!'

They fluttered away but were soon back.

'Who's there?'

Gerdie sucked in a breath as footsteps tapped softly somewhere outside her periphery. She sniffed and clutched Fell tighter, blinking to clear her tear-filled vision. Tears fell hot and fast down her cheeks, finally clearing to reveal a small woman hovering behind a nearby wall.

'Gertrude?'

Gerdie squinted, shock drying the rest of her tears. 'Ada?'

Ada's shoes *click-clack*ed on the concrete, interspersed with the crunch of sand, as she hurried over to kneel on the ground beside them.

'What are you doing here? What's happened?'

'My friend,' Gerdie sobbed. 'I don't know how to help him, he just *fell*. I don't know if he fainted or – or –'

Ada pressed her thin hand to Fell's cheek. 'Let's get him inside.'

Together, they carried Fell through the maze of dilapidated buildings. He was much lighter than Gerdie expected, but that wasn't a good thing. It made him seem...empty. Like there was nothing left inside. Like he was already gone. Ada stopped them in front of a crumbled concrete house that looked much the same as the others in this seemingly forgotten area, with hastily nailed sheets of metal boarded up one side—oh, and at least it had a roof. With some careful maneuvering so that she didn't drop Fell, Ada removed a few of the metal sheets – which weren't nailed down at all, just propped up to look like they were – and revealed a dark opening. She secured her grip on Fell once more and led the way down a narrow flight of stairs into a pitch-black space.

'Here,' Ada said, as Gerdie followed her blindly into the room. 'Up, up, up.'

Gerdie followed her lead, lifting Fell a little higher as she shuffled forward, then lowering him again onto what she assumed was a table. With her hands free, Ada flicked a switch, and the room lit up. Gerdie's jaw dropped.

Every inch of the four concrete walls was covered in maps, blueprints, drawings and photographs. The blueprints for the automatons, scribbled over, the design more recent than the ones in Gerdie's bag. A photo of a young couple smiled down at her; the man's eyes a mismatched brown and grey-green, just like Leo's. There was a photo of Gerdie at eight, head bent in concentration as she worked on the bot in front of her, unaware that her photo was being taken. She remembered how she'd heard the click of the phone camera, had good-naturedly scolded Dad as he'd laughed.

She tore her eyes away to look at Ada, who was bustling around the room, opening drawers and cupboards. She ran a small white towel under a tap in the corner, set onto a grimy bench that held a coffee machine and biscuit barrel.

Ada noticed her staring. 'Help yourself.'

With a quick glance at Fell, Gerdie darted to the barrel and shoved her hand inside, emerging with a couple of Monte Carlos. She ate two in quick succession, then grabbed a few more before joining Ada at Fell's side. She'd placed the damp towel on Fell's forehead and was running her hands up and down one of his limp arms as if to warm him. Gerdie caught the rise and fall of Fell's chest, and all the tension left her body in a rush. He was alive.

'Is there anything I can do?'

Ada didn't reply, but she mumbled to herself as she returned to the cupboards, then back to Fell. Gerdie took a step back. Ada knew what she was doing. Hopefully.

A small archway in one corner opened to another darkened room. Gerdie went to it, pulling a lighter from her satchel and flicking the tiny flame into life. She had borrowed it from Mr. Groz, who had used it to light his pipe in the evenings, to light a Bunsen burner a few years ago. She'd forgotten to give it back. The little light didn't show much of the room, but stacked just inside the archway were a few dented metal crates, opened and empty, stamped with faded words: *For the Forest.*

'What is this place?' she asked.

Ada tore her eyes from Fell to stare wistfully at the far wall, at the drawings and photos there, as if she was seeing the room for the first time in a long time. 'This is where Stefan, Lexell, and I used to discuss our ideas.'

Gerdie's heart swooped at the mention of her dad, 'Your ideas? Like new inventions? Was your partner an inventor, too, then?'

'Not quite,' Ada replied. 'But he was just as passionate as Stefan and me in slowing, if not stopping, Seki's industrial regime, and saving the little nature we have left.'

Gerdie thought of the dozens of green paintings in Ada's house and saw Ada a little clearer. She wasn't mad. She was determined.

'How were you going to do that?'

'We had plans of developing an area especially for the healthy growth of flora.'

'Like the greenhouses?' She'd never seen one, but she knew they existed, of course. Like factories, but with glass and warmth instead of metal and smoke, and growing fruits and vegetables instead of metal sheets and electronic devices.

'Not quite, love,' said Ada gently. 'Plants don't belong in greenhouses as much as animals don't belong in cages. They need sunlight, fresh air, an open sky. Somewhere that benefits other plants and animals.'

Gerdie rather thought she felt the same, now that she had experienced life outside the quarry.

'No,' Ada continued. 'We would dedicate a space and make it fertile. We just weren't sure where. Nearly sixty percent of Treshane is uninhabited but none of it is near the amount of water we would need. And the water must be free from the waste of factories, so that it's healthy for the plants.'

Gerdie nodded enthusiastically. 'So, what happened?'

Ada's expression turned sad. 'We needed a lot of money. A project like that requires a multitude of finances as well as people to support it, and it had to be kept secret from the conqueror. It was around these early days of planning when your father was commissioned by Seki. Stefan hated Seki, but he was a father first, an inventor second, so when he was approached to design the automatons for Seki, he couldn't refuse the money. Not just for our project, but for you also, Gertrude.'

Gerdie swallowed. She hadn't known the things Dad had secretly done for her, all to improve their lives, and she wished she could have told him that she hadn't needed any more than what she already had. That as long as they had each other, that had always been enough.

'I found blueprints in an old factory,' she whispered. 'They had Dad's name on them.'

Ada went on, 'Of course, as soon as he realised what he was designing, what the automatons were for, he refused to work any further.'

Gerdie's eyes burned, throat thickening, as her mind finished the story before Ada could. No one refused the conqueror without being labelled a traitor, and her father hadn't been tortured like the others, and she'd been told he died of consumption, but she never even knew he was sick, and it had all been so sudden –

'I am sorry, Gertrude,' Ada said, watching as the thoughts and realisations flickered across Gerdie's face.

Dad hadn't died.

He'd been murdered.

She went to take a steadying breath, but a sob came out instead, and once that started, she couldn't stop. She cried so hard she thought she might break, and still her tears would spill from her body like an engine leaking oil. Ada gathered her into her arms and let Gerdie sob into her chest, until she was consumed by Ada's herby, musty-clothes smell, and her own grief.

When her breaths eventually reduced to hiccoughs, she pulled away from Ada, wiping her eyes with her hands. Ada cupped her face, using her thumbs to dry the rest of her tears. Gerdie gave a final loud sniff and shoved another Monte Carlo into her mouth to discourage further crying.

Fell stirred beside them, moaning softly, and Gerdie turned to glance at him hopefully through puffy eyes. To her disdain, his own eyes remained closed, and he stilled once again. Gerdie turned over the cloth on his forehead so that the cooler side was on his skin, and let her fingers linger on his temple after she brushed off the biscuit crumbs she'd accidentally dropped on him. She watched his face intently, as if the force of her gaze alone would be enough to wake him up.

'His name is Fell,' she whispered, realising she hadn't told Ada this. 'He's...' She paused, unable to find the words to explain.

'I know what he is,' Ada said.

Gerdie froze mid-chew. Around her bite of Monte Carlo she said, 'You do?'

Ada sighed, laying Fell's arms across his stomach. She

pulled out a chair from under the table. 'Sit down, Gertrude, my love.'

Gerdie did as she was told, lowering herself into a chair by Fell's head. She placed the last of the biscuits on the table, and Ada grabbed one. She chewed slowly, and Gerdie bounced her leg, fidgeted her fingers in her lap, wanting to see if Ada really did know the truth.

Finally, Ada swallowed and said, 'I know this boy is the comet in our sky.'

It was the truth, as Ada had promised, but it still made Gerdie's heart skip a beat to hear it spoken out loud.

'How?'

'He is not the first comet to take a human form on Treshane.'

Gerdie nodded. 'Seki. Fell said—'

'Yes, Seki,' Ada said. 'But there was another, fifteen years ago. Lexell.'

Gerdie's jaw dropped. She drew on her limited memories of Lexell; his kind green eyes, the way he moved so gracefully, a sense of calm whenever he was around. Fell was just like him. Why hadn't she seen that earlier? Exactly how many comets-turned-human were walking around Treshane?

'I met him at an inventors' conference,' Ada said, 'where we were both hoping to hear of more sustainable ideas. We fell in love.' The corner of her mouth lifted in a faraway smile that was so young and girlish Gerdie couldn't help but smile as well.

The smile fell from Gerdie's face as she asked the inevitable. 'What happened to him?' All Dad had said, when he'd sat her down two years ago, was that he was gone.

Ada's gaze dropped to her lined hands. 'Seki found out, of course. The comets have a way of sensing one another when on the same planet, and Seki has seen all who arrived after him as a threat. Which they were, of course – he is the reason they landed here. No one wants Seki to continue his path of destruction, and the Great Comets have been forced to step in. But he is weak now. He's taken on too much. This is the time for us to strike.'

Gerdie pulled a face. 'He is?' If this was Seki at his weakest, she'd hate to see him at his full strength.

Ada smiled grimly. 'Why do you think he has built such an army? Why the automatons are so full of weaponry? He has been respawning as the Death Comet too quickly; it has only been eighty-four years since he destroyed Mars—a short time for an immortal being. Seki was not able to destroy this planet when he landed, he only devastated Trumble, but that does not mean he won't try again in whatever way he can.'

Gerdie's stomach turned. The whole planet flattened and burned and bombed by those terrifying robots. No one would be left alive. They would be just like Earth.

'How do we stop him?' she whispered.

'We ensure the automatons are never powered up. But first,' she said with a glance at Fell. 'We need to wake him.'

iMAGIne iF YOu jOInEd Me
If WE cOmBIned OUR poweR
inTO one UnSToPpabLe FOrce
i Can sAVE YoU
If You'Ll lET mE

no

Night was falling as they carried Fell outside, Ada at his feet, and Gerdie at his head. Her hands hooked under his armpits, and she couldn't tear her eyes away from his unresponsive face. Ada led them further down the street and around the back of a tall building—windows all gaping holes, missing their glass panes— to where an old cage elevator sagged. They placed him gently down inside, Ada shut the door with a lot of effort and creaking – mostly from the door - and with some muttering under her breath she got the elevator moving, up, up, up. Gerdie watched as the ground fell away, past broken windows and shattered bricks of the building they were scaling, until the elevator shuddered to a halt at the building's flat, concrete roof. Only a few inches high wall separated the roof from a fall into the abandoned street below. The old steam vents were cold and still, rust and sulphur invading the back of her nose. On one side, the lights of the city of Malberg gleamed like a spotlight, and on the other, the new development was enveloped in darkness.

They lay Fell down in the middle of the roof, and Gerdie tilted her head back, keeping her hands on Fell's cold shoulders. The sky was wide open above them, the beautiful purple-pink and blue of dusk, stars winking into existence, and the moons rising high, one following the other as if they were playing a game. The comet's glow looked faded somehow, like a smear of paint on the sky and not the glowing ball of energy it should be.

'Will he, like, recharge or something?'

'I really don't know, my love,' Ada said quietly. 'I guess we can only hope.'

Gerdie squeezed Fell's shoulders. She bent to whisper in his ear, letting her frizzy hair fall and form a curtain around them. 'You have to wake up now, Fell. You must go back to the comet. You have to get better. Leave this place, it's making you sick. Seki is making you sick. Don't worry about us down here. You just get better, okay?'

He didn't respond. He was so utterly still. Gerdie sniffed. The M.O.R.T. rolled out of her pocket and landed by Fell's head. It let out a sad whistle.

Ada began to sing.

Gerdie raised her head in astonishment. Ada had never sung in front of Gerdie before, but her voice was the most beautiful thing she had ever heard. The sound wrapped around her like a blanket, it made her sad and happy all at once.

'*The things I could have shown her,*
But she was gone too soon…' the song went.

Under her hands, Fell began to stir. Gerdie gasped, turning back to him. Ada kept singing.

'*While I lived on Bellona,*
She lived on the moon.'

Gerdie squeezed his shoulders again. 'Fell? Can you hear me?'

His long eyelashes fluttered, and then his eyes opened. The ice blue irises appeared washed out in the dim evening light.

'Gerdie,' he said softly, and she realised it was the first time he'd ever used her name. She wished she could have heard it more.

She gave him a watery smile. 'I'm here.' A furrow appeared between his brows, and she smoothed it away with her thumb.

Ada kept singing, even stronger now. Gerdie wanted to hold the tune in her heart forever.

'Do you know what you have to do?' Gerdie whispered to him. 'Your home is just up there, waiting. You tried your best down here, but now it's time to go.'

Fell's gaze drifted past her to the comet.

'Please, Fell,' Gerdie said. 'You have to go. You'll die down here if you don't.'

His eyes widened, comprehension and consciousness flooding his face. Gerdie's heart lightened to see this sign of the old Fell. Then he started to vibrate, his whole body gently shaking, but growing in intensity until she could hear it through the table and feel it through the concrete at her feet.

Fell glowed, his skin lighting from the inside until Gerdie was forced to blink against the brightness. Small orbs of white light floated out from his body, slowly at first, then faster and faster, more and more, taking Fell with them. He was leaving her, his body disappearing beneath her hands. Gerdie leaned forward until her head was right by his.

So faintly she almost didn't catch it, Fell said, 'See you later, comet crater.'

Gerdie let out a laugh that sounded a bit like a sob. 'In a while, engine dial. Say hi to the Angels for me,' she whispered.

He was gone.

Gerdie and Ada stayed on the roof after Fell left, watching the flickering lights of Malberg. Gerdie could just make out an electronic banner above a highway, flashing from a mint advertisement to a poster of an upcoming movie about some superhero or other.

'Ada?'

'Yes, darling?'

'How did you know to sing?'

Ada continued staring up at the darkening sky, her face lit by Oriana's glow, while Maylow was a semi-circle of yellow. Finally, she said, 'You know I have a child.'

Gerdie nodded. Of course she remembered the closed door of Ada's son's room, kept undisturbed years after he ran away, locked to everyone but the boy who had never come back.

'He was Lexell's child,' Ada said quietly.

'Oh. So then...' Gerdie began slowly, trying to do the math in her head but failing because there simply wasn't any room in there among the information she'd gathered in the past few hours. Days, even. 'Doesn't that make him... half a comet?'

When Ada finally lowered her head, there were tears gathering in her eyes. Guilt stabbed at Gerdie for bringing up such a sensitive topic, and she reached for Ada's hands, squeezing.

'My son did have comet in him, and it was too much,' said Ada. 'He was angry, all the time, even though Lexell's spirit radiated nothing but harmony. When he was a baby, I would sing to him, and it would soothe him, appease the temperament within him. Things only got worse as he grew, and when he learnt the truth, his pain overtook him. I... I shouldn't have kept the truth from him for so long. I only told him who – *what* – he truly is after Lexell passed. We thought it would be safer that way, but my son hated me for keeping it all a secret, believed I could have done more to protect Lexell, and that's when he left me.' Quietly, she added, 'It's what I deserved.'

'Don't say that,' Gerdie whispered.

Ada dropped her gaze. 'I fear Seki has taken everyone I've ever loved.'

Gerdie opened her mouth to say something she hoped would be supportive, but when she realised that what Ada said was true for Gerdie as well, she closed it again. Seki had taken her dad, her world. Now he had taken Fell. She sniffed, wiping her nose with the back of her hand. 'What do we do now?'

Ada sighed. 'We pray to the Angels that Seki never finds the key.' And then she made her way back into the elevator, muttering something about 'more eyes than the Angels,' and Gerdie slowly followed, unable to bear looking up at the sky, not daring to see if the comet was going to zoom straight past Bellona and never come back.

Once back in the basement of the derelict building, the coffee machine buzzed loudly as Ada clattered through the cupboards for a couple of mugs. Gerdie drifted to the side to continue scanning the paraphernalia tacked up on the wall, desperate for more of her father, even if it was just a signature. Ada joined her, handing her a cup of coffee. She was glad for something warm to hold, and breathed in the rich, slightly burnt scent. As she took a sip, a small sketch caught her eye. Drawn in lead pencil in such detail it could have been a photograph and left no doubt that it was the same disc in her pocket.

She said, 'Hey, that's my coin, see?' and pulled it out to show Ada.

SMASH.

Gerdie jumped to avoid Ada's mug as it shattered on the concrete floor. Hot coffee spilled over the mug in her own hand. Wincing, she placed her cup down and sucked on her burnt fingers.

'Gertrude,' Ada said in barely more than the whisper and without taking her eyes from Gerdie's coin. 'Where did you get that?'

'Dad gave it to me before he died,' she replied, confused by Ada's reaction. 'He used to tell me all kinds of stories about it, but I never knew which one was the true one.'

Ada held out a trembling hand, and Gerdie dropped the coin into it. Ada sank into a chair, sending up a small puff of dust.

'This is the key to the automatons...The key Seki has been looking for all year.'

'What?' Gerdie dropped into the chair beside her, her skin tingling. The missing piece from the blueprints... She'd had it all along.

'It's made from Graphensilk,' Ada continued. 'A very powerful substance.'

Gerdie had heard of it, of course. A material found only on Bellona, with glowing red veins. It was rare – miners could mine for years and never find a trace of it in their lifetime. It was powerful, too. She'd heard that just one small piece had been enough to power Goliath's first city for months until they built electricity towers. She should have known, should have recognised it, it seemed so obvious. It had always looked like goldish copper to her.

Ada held the coin up, it glinted gold and red as it caught the light. 'This one piece is enough to power fifty of Seki's automatons.'

Gerdie stared at it as though seeing it for the first time. 'The other inventors wanted it, too.'

'Oh, yes,' Ada replied. 'They could power a great many new inventions with this before they inevitably handed it over to Seki.'

'But where did Dad get it from?'

'Your mother.'

'Oh. Yes. Right.' She should have guessed that; Mum had been a geologist. Maybe she still was. With a tightening in her chest, Gerdie recalled the last of Dad's stories, just over a year ago. The one, she realised now, that had finally been the truth.

'Your mum gave this to me,' said Dad as he sat on the edge of her bed, pushing aside the homework she had doodled over.

Gerdie sat up, flatly remarking, 'Oh.' She already knew she wasn't going to like this story.

'We met during our first year of university,' he said as if Gerdie had asked. 'Though she studied geology, and I was studying engineering, we both shared the Introduction to Mathematics class. It was love at first sight. For me, anyway. Took a long time before she finally said yes to a date, she always put her work first.'

Nice to know some things never changed.

Dad held up the coin. 'This was once just a lump of rock. Part of a bigger piece that Mum found within a week of her job out of university. Propelled her entire career.'

Gerdie muttered, 'Good for her.'

'Mm. She saved this little piece for me as a gift on our second wedding anniversary. I think she wanted me to use it to power something awesome.'

'Why, what can it do?'

'You know, I'm not sure. What do you think it can do?'

Gerdie sat up, sliding the rest of her homework onto the carpeted floor. 'Hm. Maybe it's currency for another planet. Ooh, no! Is it a really strong battery?

Dad chuckled. 'Maybe. At any rate, I want you to have it.'

'Really? But why?'

'I think I've gotten all I can out of it.' He held it up between thumb and index finger, pulling an exaggerated thinking face that made Gerdie smile despite her mood. He placed it in her palm and closed her fingers around it. 'Use it for something great, my girl. And keep it safe, just in case.'

Ada said, 'Stefan had this piece moulded into a form that would not arouse suspicion. But Gertrude... This is all Seki is waiting for.'

The solution came to her swiftly, and though it hurt to even think about, she forced herself to say the words out loud. 'We must make sure Seki never finds it. We have to hide it or – or destroy it. Not let anyone get hurt by it.'

Now that would be something great.

'Only extreme heat can destroy Graphensilk,' Ada said.

'A fire?' Gerdie suggested.

Ada shook her head. 'The Core.'

SEVENTEEN

ADA REPLACED THE METAL SLATS TO HIDE THE entrance to the old house before darting down the street, Gerdie on her heels.

As they left the derelict area and neared the lights and shininess of the city, Ada murmured, 'The Action on guard usually takes half an hour to reach this area from the west of the city, but if Seki has felt Fell's presence, he might have increased patrols.'

The road smoothed, buildings glowed with light, an assortment of smells from indecisive turbines assaulted the nostrils, and quad-wings whirred overhead. Gerdie stuck close to Ada's side, feeling too out in the open, like all eyes were on them, even though the people they started passing had their eyes glued to their phones.

They hurried through the spaces between bins and parked cars, ready to duck out of sight, but the town remained free from Actions. Passing menu stands, bus and quad-wing stops, and under streetlights that glowed mostly white; occasionally one was green or blue or red, which were hard to see by. Gerdie had experienced enough by then to think that was probably the point. Seki wanted the whole universe in chaos. After about twenty minutes of walking, Gerdie's heart beating fast in anticipation the whole time, a huge white wall loomed ahead of them, wrapping around what must be New Londinium, and glistening in Oriana's full white light. Just beyond the wall, she could make out towers topped with grand domed roofs she guessed belonged to the palace.

'Whoa,' Gerdie said. 'Why is there a wall around the city? What's in there that they're trying to keep in?'

'I think the point is to keep things out.'

'What kinds of things?'

Ada pursed her lips, then she nodded. 'This wall is a good sign. It means Seki feels weak and vulnerable. Were he at his full power, he would not need a wall to dispel his enemies. Nor a metal army, for that matter.'

'And the Core's in there? You're sure?' She'd always thought the Core would be in a desolate place, not here in the middle of the New Londinium. The centrality of it all made it seem so much worse.

'Yes, I'm sure.'

A squealing of breaks and a tremendous *bang* made Gerdie gasp and whirl around. Two cars had collided in the street. Both drivers had already gotten out, seemingly unharmed, but Gerdie made to go to them anyway. Ada stopped her with a bony but firm hand on her shoulder.

'Shouldn't we help them?' Gerdie asked.

'They'll be fine,' Ada said. 'These prangs happen all the time. Seki keeps having the road signs changed.'

Gerdie glanced back, and the drivers did look fine. They were conversing, waving their arms at the small street signs on thin metal poles as one car's bonnet steamed above a broken headlight. Her heart continued to thud after its fright, but she turned back to the palace wall.

Graffiti covered parts of it, turning the white into a rainbow. She could just make out the nearest piece: cramped thick letters that she assumed had read *Free Treshane*, but someone had started to clean it from the wall, so now it just read *Free Tresh*.

As they approached the gate, Ada grabbed Gerdie's hand and quickly pulled her behind a large statue of a wide square head with no distinguishable features. A quick glance at the plaque said it came from Earth. Gerdie opened her mouth, but Ada pressed a finger to her lips without looking away from the gate. She had impeccable aim, Gerdie had to admit. She ducked away from Ada's finger and peered around the side of the statue.

A single Action stood guard at the entrance into the city's heart, their features indistinguishable behind their patterned metal mask. Security cameras flanked either side of the gate, black gazes fixed on the entryway. Ada watched carefully, like she was waiting for something.

About one hundred metres down the wall, another Action monitored another entrance. She glanced in the other direction: same story.

Gerdie scanned the top of the wall again and something caught her eye. The massive, looming shape of an automaton. Gerdie tugged on Ada's sleeve, unable to tear her gaze away from the hulking silhouette.

'Yes, I know,' Ada said grimly.

Had it always been there? Unpowered, but still threatening, a warning? Or had Seki found a way past needing the Graphensilk to start them, and was getting them into position?

She tore her eyes from the automaton, wondering what Ada was waiting for when a car pulled up at the gate. The Action held out a gloved hand, and the driver slid a piece of paper into it through the window. It was only after carefully scanning the paper, getting the driver to step out of the car to ask what Gerdie imagined was a barrage of questions, checking the back seats and boot of the car, and scanning the driver's body with a metal detector did the Action finally let them pass, pressing a button to open the gate.

Somehow, Gerdie didn't think 'We'd like to enter the conqueror's favourite place in the palace to destroy the one thing he desperately wants' was going to be getting them through.

'This way,' Ada whispered, already crossing the street, moving quickly. 'Sometimes the Action on duty is tiring and easy to fool, but I don't think that one is. We can't risk it.'

'I could cause a distraction?' Gerdie said, thinking of M.O.R.T. in the museum.

Ada shook her head. 'There are still cameras.'

Gerdie rifled through her bag anyway, finding some cement tack. It was a hard material until it was warmed, turning soft and malleable. It could then be used for a minute or two before it hardened again. 'Not for long,' she said.

Ada's eyes widened when she saw it. 'That might just work, my girl. How's your throwing arm?'

'Not good,' Gerdie said, searching around in her bag again, 'but I have this.' And she pulled out an old starter gun. She had found it at Odds and Ends and was planning to dismantle it to use the springs for M.O.R.T.'s limbs.

Ada's eyes flicked towards the cameras. Gerdie broke off a small piece of tack and rolled it between her palms until it was soft like clay, then she shoved it into the short barrel of the starter gun.

Gerdie took aim; she'd only need to smash the screen, or maybe the connection between camera and wall. Or...

She curled her finger around the trigger and fired.

The tack hit the guard right between the eyes, through one of the holes in the mask. They didn't have time to react before they fell to the ground.

Ada gasped. 'I thought you would hit the cameras.'

'I thought about it,' Gerdie said, slipping the gun back into her satchel. 'I didn't kill them, did I?'

Keeping close to the wall to avoid the cameras' field of vision, Gerdie and Ada huddled by the gate. The cameras were pointed outwards, focused more on the space just before the gate entrance rather than the gate itself. Ada leaned in to inspect the Action.

'He's still breathing,' she said. 'Just unconscious.'

Gerdie let out a sigh of relief and pressed the button to open the gate. 'Alley-oop.'

They were in New Londinium. Enclosed by the wall meant it was not unlike being in Rendip Quarry, but in Rendip, evenings were quiet; workers returning home from the factory bone-tired, too exhausted to even hold conversations with one another, and the machines powered down for the night, their roaring reduced to a gentle, slumbering hum.

Here, within the capital walls, automobiles *whoosh*ed past, feet tapped, carrying jovial, casual voices with them, and music jingled from nearby restaurants along with warm savory smells. The heart of New Londinium was awake, alive; a twisting maze of brightly lit criss-crossing streets. Ada walked with purpose through it all, leaving Gerdie to hurry to match her pace. She was glad to be with Ada, though. Glad to be doing this with a familiar presence. Ada made her feel safe, even if she had always been a little eccentric.

'How do you know the way?' Gerdie whispered.

'Your dad, of course. He took the opportunity to explore areas of interest to the conqueror during his initial visits. But once we're inside, if we find the visitor's entrance to the Core, there will be signs to follow.'

Gerdie's heart beat wildly with every step that took her closer to the palace. Her hand kept ducking into her pocket to feel for the coin, as if she were expecting it to suddenly jump from her borrowed pants and make its escape.

She and Ada were anonymous among the streets of New Londinium, where no one spared them a second glance, but under the glare of the streetlights Gerdie still felt exposed, like they were right under the metal noses of Actions, right under the very nose of Conqueror Seki. Security cameras were set into each streetlight, and Gerdie swallowed as she quickly averted her eyes. Maybe if they moved fast enough, kept their heads down, they could be in and out of the Core before Seki could say 'chaos.' Even among the tallest buildings, the palace was visible from every street within the walls. Gerdie could just make out Treshane's flag flying from the highest points of the palace: two white circles on an orange background to represent Bellona's two moons. Ada had been right about the signs; directions around the palace and to the Core were printed in bold white letters on black iron posts but hanging from each was a *closed to visitors* sign.

Gerdie stayed hot on Ada's heels as they turned down the road that led to the palace. Absent of shops and restaurants, the area was much quieter. *The inside must be crawling with Actions, alarms, security cameras...* and there they were, trying to break in without being caught.

This is bad, this is bad, this is bad.

Between the two of them, was there time to invent a small bot to carry the coin to the Core for them? No, that was impossible. She knew she had next to nothing inside her satchel for what they needed, like remote controls, a GPS, or a camera, and though Ada's dress was thick, it wasn't thick enough to hide inventing materials, so she didn't have anything either. Gerdie continued to follow Ada as the buildings thinned, and the palace grounds came into view. They crossed the empty car park into a wide-open area latticed by stone paths. It must have once been a garden, but now there was only scratchy brown scrub and loose rocks.

Staff parking was allocated on this side, and wide bins slumped in a line against the palace walls. The gross, sweet smell of rotted fruits and vegetables drifted from their open tops, and, unfortunately, it was to here that Ada strode. Gerdie held her sleeve to her nose. Even if there were enough fresh food to go around, so many people in the quarry couldn't afford it, and here was Seki just throwing it out. It made her blood boil.

She followed Ada's gaze and just made out a darkened part of the brick above the bins: an opening into the palace.

'Did Dad tell you about this, too?' whispered Gerdie.

'He did. It should lead to a kitchen cellar.'

And it did.

After a few minutes of crawling through the cramped rubbish chute, slipping, gagging, and trying not to wonder *what was that?!*, Ada lifted the small square roof at the end of the tunnel, letting in a rush of warmth and the smell of baked bread and roasting meat. Despite the welcome, Ada hesitated before climbing through.

'What is it?' Gerdie whispered. 'Is someone there?'

'Just the opposite,' replied Ada, and Gerdie could hear the puzzled frown in her voice.

'Isn't that a good thing?' Gerdie squeezed beside Ada so that she could see into the kitchen herself. All she could make out were table legs and large plastic barrels – no feet, as Ada had said.

Ada made a *hm* noise in the back of her throat but began to climb out of the chute. Gerdie was glad to stretch out again, and to feel the warmth of the kitchen. The high ceiling pierced her with harsh artificial light, and the silver countertops gleamed, their edges sharp. The tiles and walls of one half were a slightly brighter colour, less smoke-stained, as if the kitchen had been recently extended. Gerdie wouldn't be surprised; the conqueror was a big greedy man, after all. Conquering a country and planning to destroy its inhabitants must make you hungry.

Pooh-pooh, she thought bitterly.

The kitchen tiles turned to carpet as they left it, lush but peeling back at the walls, and uneven in places so that Gerdie kept stumbling, and she hadn't been the first; the carpet was riddled with stains, where she guessed servants carrying trays of food and drink had fallen into the trap. The stretch of wall was dotted with lighter squares as if paintings had once hung there. Did Leo know what the paintings had been? Did he know of the family who used to live here?

The palace was quiet, but instead of feeling grateful, it only made Gerdie nervous. They should have met someone by now. It *was* getting late, though, and maybe the staff had gone home after serving dinner. Yes, that made sense. The car park was empty, there was no event on tonight. It made perfect sense for the palace to be quiet. Still, her insides fizzed fast like a shaken can of soda. She reached inside her pocket for the M.O.R.T., wondering if it would come in handy for anything, and realised with a sickening lurch that it wasn't there. Had it rolled out of her pocket? Her heart broke at its loss, but there wasn't anything she could do about it now.

They reached the area that was open to the public, and gleaming gold signs had indeed been fixed to the wall, showing the way like gilded beacons.

Turn right.

We're nearly there.

Down the passageway. She pulled the coin from her pocket as if to save time once they got to the Core.

Could it really be this easy?

Turn left.

In and out, destroy the coin, Seki's army gone forever.

Gerdie was beginning to overtake Ada, practically running as her pulse beat wildly, driving her on as she passed a ticket office and a line of queue barriers –

She rounded a corner and bumped into something cold and solid that made her stumble backward, tripping over Ada, who was right behind her, and sent her sprawling to the floor. The coin rolled from her hand and disappeared under the thick black boot of the Action Gerdie had collided with. His metal mask was pushed back to the top of his head, and a gun was on his belt. Gerdie watched in horror as he lifted his boot and saw what was beneath it. He leaned to pick it up and his nose ran with snot, dripping to the floor, but he didn't seem to notice as he scooped the coin up in his thick fingers. His mouth dropped open in surprise before it curled up in a wicked smile.

The Action, sniffing in vain against his running nose, only had one pair of shackle bots on him, and he used them on Gerdie, believing Ada to be too weak to fight back. He was right, Gerdie realised sadly; the older woman's thin frame was trembling under Sniff's tight grip on her upper arm. She longed to reach out and take Ada's hand in hers, to tell her it was going to be okay, but she couldn't do that with her hands shackled and with Sniff's other hand clamped tightly on her arm, or when she didn't believe the sentiment herself.

Sniff dragged them into a small dim room off one of the corridors, Gerdie's satchel slung around his shoulder. A gruesome display of metal masks lined the back wall, their empty eyes staring at nothing. A bald, middle-aged Action with glasses that did nothing to hide the dark bags under his eyes was seated in front of a dozen tiny televisions. They flashed with static but showed images from various rooms in the palace and grounds; Gerdie recognised the kitchens. The Action had a newspaper opened on the desk; the footage ignored. She had really been *that* close.

He barely looked up as they entered, and sighed, 'What is it, Taskey?'

'Found these two creeping around near the Core. Reckon the conqueror will want to know.'

The Action saluted at Seki's name, eyes still on his newspaper. 'The conqueror is a busy man.'

'Tell him he'll want to hear about this one.'

The Action looked up, raising an eyebrow, and Sniffy leaned close to murmur about the coin, twirling it in his fingers like he was about to perform a trick with it.

Gerdie kept her chin up, staring defiantly between the Actions, hoping they wouldn't notice the way her hands trembled in the cuffs... Was this what had happened to her father? Was she following in his footsteps, in cuffs and facing Actions, off to answer to the conqueror? They had shared so much together when he was alive, so why not this as well?

She remembered the M.O.R.T. had disappeared at some point, and it made her feel deserted. At least something would remain of her after she was gone.

'And her?' Baldy asked with a nod at Ada.

'I recognise her,' Sniffy said. 'She was with that...well.' He glanced at Gerdie out of the corner of his eye, then leaned in to whisper to the bald Action. It was more of a stage-whisper, so Gerdie heard it. 'With Lexell.'

Ada gave a jolt of surprise.

'Huh. Leave her here, then, and I'll take her to the office for questioning. Take the girl to the conqueror.'

'Yes, sir.'

Sniffy hummed a jaunty tune as he dragged Gerdie out of the security room. She cast a last helpless glance at Ada, and she found Ada didn't look frightened anymore, like the mention of Lexell had filled her with conviction. She nodded once, determinedly, and Gerdie returned it, though a little less sure. Sniffy continued to hum his song, extremely pleased with himself.

She didn't need a gilded sign to know that this was the conqueror's own area of residence within the palace. It was chaos, a mess: paintings hung askew on the walls, a table had seven lamps on it as if someone couldn't make up their mind on which one to have and so had gone for all of them. There were multiple rugs on the floor, some half rolled, others over-lapping. As she took a breath, she could pick out cinnamon, lemon, vanilla, and copper, all at once. She wrinkled her nose and proceeded to breathe through her mouth. Cupboards were open, their contents spilling out onto the floor. Gerdie didn't consider herself a neat person, but even this made her anxious for a vacuum cleaner.

Laughter and music drifted from other rooms, but it wasn't music Gerdie recognised. She wasn't sure if it could be classed as music at all. It sounded scratchy and out of tune, rather like when she tried Ada's violin for a week, as if the instruments were being played by an amateur who didn't know how to care for them. It sounded metallic somehow, too. Not like the beautiful wooden violin Ada had. Then, Gerdie supposed sadly, there were no trees anymore to make such instruments. Only metals.

An Action flanked an ornate door, his metal mask patterned with twisting raised lines. Sniffy explained the situation to him, and Gerdie saw the eyes behind the mask widen.

'Wait here.'

The masked Action disappeared inside with a swish of his

long black coat, returning a minute later with a nod of confirmation.

Seki was waiting for them in the throne room, sprawled on his throne. His presence so strong that it drew her gaze even when she tried to take in her surroundings, a planet caught in orbit. He was a big man; not fat, exactly, just built bigger than a human, sized up.

Because he's not human, she reminded herself.

She'd wanted to be so brave when confronting him, like she knew her father would have been, but her knees were shaking. She thought they might give way and send her sprawling to the floor if the Action didn't have such a tight grip on her arm. Her breathing quickened; she could feel herself panicking. She couldn't give up. She couldn't let Seki win.

But without Fell, or Ada, or even Leo for that matter, she felt even more alone than she had when her father died.

Sniffy shoved her forward, and she stumbled but managed to keep herself upright. She was before the throne, under Seki's sharp gaze, so close she could smell him. So close that he would only need to reach out and wrap his huge hands around her neck. Her fingers fidgeted in the cuffs as if searching for the coin. She felt so tiny in the gigantic space before this gigantic man. No painting had ever captured his suffocating presence.

'So, you are Stefan Sailor's daughter,' Seki said. His voice was gravelly like when something caught in working gears.

Gerdie couldn't decipher his tone of voice. Was he amused? Angry? Unimpressed? It was hard to tell. It sounded like all three, but at the same time like he was empty of any emotion.

Seki leaned forward. He was blinking hard and rapidly, and his hands were never still, just like hers, except her hands always had a focus, something productive to occupy them. The conqueror's had no such focus, just twirling and flicking as if he were trying to make something from the empty air. His expression was clear of emotion. His constant movements and blinking were disconcerting, and he made sudden movements that made her flinch.

'Your father abandoned his duties, his promises. Abandoned *me*.' Seki lifted a hand to his chest at the affront, then his fingers were back to dancing in the air. 'All I want,' he continued, 'is to protect this planet...'

That's not true, that's not true.

'Your father thought something quite different of me. But now I have what I need.' He held out his hand to Sniffy, who saluted and came forward to deposit the coin into Seki's hand. Gerdie's stomach roiled to see it in Seki's possession.

'It is made of the most precious of materials,' Seki said, gazing at the coin in wonder. 'Graphensilk. Yes. Such force; it is life-giving. With this, it will power my automatons to be the strongest the universe has ever seen.'

I'm so sorry, Dad.

Seki stared at her with such intensity she had to look away, even though she really didn't want to, didn't want to seem like she was giving in to him—she feared she would catch on fire otherwise, like an ant under a magnifying glass on a sunny day.

He reached out a hand as if to touch her birthmark, when Sniffy chimed in with, 'She meant to destroy it, Your Highness. On her way to the Core, she was.'

Seki sat back again, blinking hard at her. 'Well. If she wants to see the Core so badly...'

Gerdie's throat turned dry. *Anything but that.*

'Which part, Your Majesty?' the Action grunted.

Her heart threatened to burst out of her chest. What did he mean by what part?

Seki sat back and then leaned forward again. He blinked hard, utter delight dancing in his eyes as his fingers danced in the air—an emotion she understood but liked the least. 'Just throw her in.'

There was a definite spring in Sniffy's step as he dragged her from the throne room, like he was a dog, and his master had called him a Good Boy. Gerdie rolled her eyes in disgust. He dragged her through a passageway and down a cold flight of steps, steps that seemed to go on and on and on. It was such a contrast to the plush and marked entrance she'd glimpsed before she was caught – something didn't feel right.

'Wait,' Gerdie said, her nerves unable to take the confusion. 'I thought we were going to the Core.'

Sniffy barked a laugh. 'Eager, aren't you? Don't worry, you'll get your chance. Only Captain Walton can do that, and he's not here right now.'

'Oh, lucky me, yes, the Angels are really looking out for me today.'

'He should only be an hour or two,' Sniffy grunted. 'Think you can wait that long?'

'I'll try my best.'

There was movement inside some of the other cells, but the Action unlocked the first cell and shoved her inside before she could get a good look at the rest of the prison –that's what this was. He locked the door, and left, still chuckling at her presumed eagerness. She sank to the cold floor as silence descended once again. She sniffed, hoping Ada was okay, and prayed to the Angels that Leo would find the sceptre. He was their only chance now.

The planet was about to be destroyed, and she'd helped make it happen. Her father had tried everything in his power to stop it, and Gerdie had ruined that, like she ruined everything else. She had failed, Fell had failed, and now Seki was going to win. She let her head fall onto her knees.

Fell.

Was he okay? Had he made it back to his comet form, back to the Merten Cloud? Anger flared in her, hot and fast and irrational. He was supposed to take down Seki, that had been his mission. Fell was the one with magical powers, the one most equipped to destroy a cosmic form like Seki, but that hope was gone too.

And now she was going to die.

EIGHTEEN

When Leo blinked his eyes open, he caught a two second view of plush grey carpet before the back of his head throbbed violently and he was forced to squeeze them shut again.

'Sleep well?'

Seki's voice.

Leo shot upright, wincing as pain lanced through his skull before horror dulled everything else.

He was in one of the palace's many chambers, this one crammed with furniture bought for the palace that Seki later changed his mind about. The delicately plastered ceiling was spotted with mould, a corner darkened with damp.

Seki crouched beside him, and Captain Walton was just behind, watching with his arms crossed, flanked by three other Actions with their masks pushed back to the tops of their heads.

Leo shifted, taking stock of his body. Hands were in cuffs again, secured behind his back. He forced himself to raise his face. Tried to conjure every word that Luca had said, every kind word that had come from Gerdie's mouth. The Lona's final words. All that he learnt of himself in the past few days, even if his stomach rolled with fear.

He was the heir. He was a Catell.

This was *his* kingdom.

And Seki had stolen it.

Leo glared at the conqueror, but Seki didn't look as angry as he had expected. He looked curious at Leo's appearance. Amused, even.

'Ah, Leo,' Seki sighed, as if Leo were a naughty child who had eaten the last biscuit in the barrel without permission.

Leo swallowed.

'I have had to deal with so much treason today. I really thought you were not like this, Leo. You have greatly disappointed me. Shall we see what your failure has done?' He held out his hand without taking his eyes from Leo. What looked like a small, round coin was in his palm. Leo recognised those ridges. Gerdie played with it so much, how could he not? Oh, Angels. How did he get that? Gerdie would never part with it willingly. Was she...?

He didn't let himself finish the thought.

'Walton tells me you found the sceptre,' Seki said, and Leo thought he saw a brief flash of fear in the conqueror's eyes, something he had never, ever seen before. 'I wondered,' Seki continued, 'if you would ever find it, Leo. I must say, I'm impressed that you did. I thought you were too cowardly to ever even try. Unfortunately for you, Hadrian is loyal to *me*.' He rose from the floor, stretching to his impressive height. He was almost seven feet tall—Leo barely saw him upright; it was a shock to be reminded of Seki's physical strength. Leo felt his own begin to drain. He would endure more than a whipping for this. A bead of sweat rolled down his temple.

Seki waved a hand vaguely. 'Put him in a cell. I will deal with him later,' he said, then strode toward the entrance doors to the palace.

'It has been too long since I saw destruction,' he said as he walked, and Leo felt the trembling vibration each step made. 'Only chaos. It is not enough, sometimes. It is not my *true* purpose.'

The remaining Actions shared uncertain glances, but it was Walton who spoke, clearing his throat before he did so.

'Ah, Your Highness?' he asked, sounding as unsure as Leo had ever heard him. In fact, all the Actions looked frightened in the presence of their conqueror. 'The automatons are for the continents' borders, to protect us. Would you not rather we transport them to the coast first?'

Seki didn't waver; he kept walking until Leo was sure he wasn't going to answer. He stopped just before he reached the entrance doors and turned back to look at them. His fingers lifted to flick in the air, and even though Leo had seen the movement hundreds of times before, there was something about this time that filled him with dread.

Seki lowered his hands and shrugged his shoulders. 'I lied,' he said, and opened the palace doors, blinding Leo and the Actions with the brilliance of the rising sun.

The Actions were stunned, hardly moving as Seki disappeared through the doors.

Gerdie had been right; the automatons were weapons of destruction, not sentinels of protection. Now that Seki had the key, there was no stopping him from letting his creations loose on the world.

'What should we do?' one Action asked, unable to keep the fear from his voice.

'He can't be serious, can he?'

'You saw the blueprints,' another replied. 'You've seen the automatons up close. Those things can do some serious damage.'

'The conqueror has always been...' another began.

Walton sighed, rubbing a hand over his face. 'Unstable? You would be right. I knew something like this was coming, but... Go with him. I have someone at the Core to deal with first.'

'What about Catell, sir?'

Walton shot a glance at Leo, looking irritated that he was there; an annoying tag-along.

Leo lowered his eyes, unable to hold his gaze any longer. Something by the captain's feet caught his attention. Something small and round and slightly smoke stained, peeking out from the bag by the captain's feet.

The M.O.R.T.

Leo's heart soared at the sight of the little bot before it quickly sank. He rejoiced at the familiarity, but realised that if the M.O.R.T. was here, then so was Gerdie.

'Put him in the cells,' Walton said. 'I'll deal with him later.' *If we survive the next few hours* hung unspoken in the air.

Leo's upper arm was seized by two Actions he recognised as Raines and Fadley, and was half carried, half dragged toward the stairs that led down into the old prison. Leo threw a glance over his shoulder at the M.O.R.T., wondering how he was going to get the little bot to follow, but it had disappeared from beneath Captain Walton's feet. He let himself be taken toward the dark stone steps, heart sinking. Something pricked at his ankle, crawling up his leg. He jerked, and one of the Actions slapped him across the ear. Wincing, ears ringing, Leo let his head fall forward. That's when he saw the M.O.R.T. appear above the waistband of his pants, and the soreness in his head was forgotten.

He hadn't been completely abandoned, after all.

As they descended the steps, a tremendous noise boomed around them, dulled by the stone walls, but enough to make the ground beneath them vibrate and send the lights flickering. Fadley swore under his breath, but he and Raines continued to push Leo forward. Down, down, down. The deeper they went, the more profusely Leo started to sweat. He was soon drenched in it, and the more he smelt his own fear, the louder the old voices became.

Coward. Failure. Weak.

Leo had been in the prison a few times before. It had been the initial favourite punishment of Seki's, until Seki decided a more public punishment was better and had the Core built. The half dozen cells were often empty – the Core was where punishment was usually doled out.

He was thrown into a tiny cell, the floor dirty but dry. A narrow bed with only a pillow and a thin cotton blanket was in one corner, a toilet in the other. He dragged himself to the door and pulled himself up to see through the bars. He opened his mouth – to say what he didn't know – when a familiar sight of orange hair through the door bars opposite, like a beacon in the darkness, distracted him from his argument.

'Gerdie, thank the Angels.'

'Leo?' She rose from the bed and came forward, only her head and shoulders visible through the bars. She didn't look pleased to see him. 'Oh no. What happened? Where's the sceptre?' Her eyes desperately searched his face, finding the answer to her question there. 'You were our last chance, Leo, you're not supposed to be here!'

He reeled back, words stinging like a whip lash. Not just because she wasn't pleased to see him safe, but because she was right. Without the sceptre, there was no way of weakening Seki.

'Where's Fell?' he asked.

'Gone.' Her voice was hollow.

He waited for her to say more, because she always did, but

she fell silent. It broke Leo's heart; he'd never heard Gerdie speak a single word and leave it at that.

Another explosion from above vibrated through the stone.

'How did he die?' he asked quietly.

Gerdie sniffed. 'I'm... not sure if he did. I really hope he didn't.'

'What do you mean? What happened to him?'

She sighed. 'He's a comet. The comet up in the sky right now, to be specific.'

'Um,' he said faintly.

Gerdie finished explaining, hands gesticulating wildly as she spoke. She glanced Leo's way every so often as if checking to see if he was still following. He was, but only just.

As impossible as the concept sounded – it made sense to him. Fell had seemed so out of place on Treshane, as if everything about it was new and wonderful to him. And Seki... well, Seki had always seemed more than human to Leo; he'd always seemed like an unstoppable force, consuming everything he encountered. That sounded like the Death Comet.

Leo let his head fall against the metal door, where it gave a ringing *thunk*.

'So, what happens now?' he asked dully.

'I don't know about you,' Gerdie replied, 'but I get to visit the Core soon.'

Tears sprang to his eyes so fast it surprised him, his body reacting faster to this news than his mind. After everything that had happened, after all he'd been through, this last bit of information was just too much to take in. The tears were burning hot on his cheeks. The Core meant torture at best. Death, at worst.

'Gerdie...' he croaked.

'Oh, it's all right.' She did sound all right, almost like her usual self, just dimmed slightly, like a battery wearing down.

They were quiet for a moment. Gerdie stared at something

on the ground of her cell while Leo searched what he could see of her face. He asked, 'Are you scared?'

'Yeah,' she said nonchalantly. 'A little. But maybe I get to see my dad again, you know?' She smiled, trying to be strong even then, and his heart broke again to see it. 'And meet the Angels. It can't be that bad.'

'If you tell yourself something enough,' he said, 'it eventually becomes true.'

'Exactly.' She smiled, then ducked her head and disappeared from the bars.

He hopped to the bed and lay on top of the cool sheets. Something hard and round dug into his back, and he sat up again. The M.O.R.T. rolled onto the bed, its mismatched screws looking like a pair of eyes gazing up at him. A small thrill went through him, and he hopped back to the door to try and squeeze M.O.R.T. through the bars to offer to Gerdie. But her cell was open, and Captain Walton was attaching a pair of shackle bots to her wrists. Leo watched in horror as Walton led her away.

His mind screamed at him to say something, anything, but he remained frozen. As they passed, she whispered, 'See you later, comet crater.'

He couldn't respond, and then she was gone, the prison door clanging shut behind them. He lowered his gaze to the little bot in his palm. She was without her invention, and he realised that after a year of her insisting that he was enough as he was, he had never told her the same thing.

Nineteen

Walton dragged her back through the tourist entrance of the Core, passing walls decorated with old pictures of the Core's development and information plaques. He shoved her into an elevator, then they were climbing up and up. The back of the elevator was made of glass, and Gerdie watched with growing trepidation as the Core slowly revealed itself in their ascent. It was smaller than she thought, a stone cylinder about five meters wide. There were viewing platforms scattered around, at various levels, blocked with a railing to prevent anyone falling in, with more little information signs set up for tourists.

Her breathing quickened, all the stories she'd heard about the Core suddenly rushing to her mind. *All sorts of horrors happen in there after the doors close to the public... People say you hear screaming all through the night in New Londinium... Bubbles of lava sometimes splash tourists in the face, imagine what happens to people there for punishment?*

The elevator slowed, then stopped. As the doors slid open, the heat hit her like a fist, taking her breath away, sweat springing to the surface of her skin. A metal platform circled a gaping pit, so deep Gerdie couldn't see the bottom, but the stone walls glowed with orange heat. Closed doors followed the curve of the platform, her stomach turned to see them; she couldn't imagine what was behind those doors, what kind of torture devices the conqueror had. The Core was quiet but for a faint bubbling, and she almost hated how empty it was, how private this felt. It made her feel small, like she was so unworthy, such a little nothing, that no one even cared if she died.

Walton pulled her out of the elevator and along the edge, following the metal as it curved around the pit. He stopped her at a plank that jutted out over the gaping mouth of the Core. Dad used to tell her stories about pirates on Earth, and how they used to make their victims walk the plank and into the deep waters beneath their ship.

She swallowed.

A small switchboard nearby blinked at her, but she didn't have time to try and read the words beneath the buttons before Walton seized her upper arm against and forced her toward the edge. She struggled, panic seizing her, but once she was on the plank she had no choice but to hold still, otherwise she would lose her balance and fall. The heat rising from the Core clung to her skin, sticky and oppressive, ten times worse than being in a Trunk. Once her feet were firmly on the plank, Walton unlocked her cuffs, pulled them from her wrists, and stepped back.

Even though she really didn't want to, she looked down. It wasn't actually Bellona's core, but she'd believe it if it was. The pit was so deep—the lava at the bottom a small speck of orange—so deep her stomach turned, and her feet prickled.

Walton hovered his hand over the switchboard and said, 'Hail Seki.'

'Wait –'

He pushed a button, and the plank disappeared.

Gerdie screamed. Her stomach evaporated, the hot wind

blowing her hair back. The fall was too long, she had too much time to think, and the fiery orange below grew bigger and bigger, like the mouth of some great beast opening, ready to swallow her whole. She waved her arms, pinwheeling them until her body rotated, and now she was watching the platform shrink. At least she wouldn't know when death was coming, but she closed her eyes anyway. It was getting hotter and hotter, an open flame on her back, then she felt something cold. At first, she thought it was her own body succumbing to death a little early, but something bright burned her eyelids. She opened them, surrounded by white. It... calmed her, somehow, like she knew that it would all be okay. Ah, she was dead, then. Her body felt weightless – but she still felt it. Should you still feel your body when you're dead?

The white light dissipated, and the stone wall of the Core faded into view, falling away as she rose above it. She glanced around. The white light was leaving a trail of light behind it, almost like a tail, almost like...

A comet.

'Fell?' she asked.

The whiteness shimmered, and she thought she could just make out his face above her, feel arms at her back and beneath her knees as he lifted her to safety.

'Fell!' she exclaimed. 'You're okay! You're back!'

He flew them all the way to the top of the Core and dropped her on the platform. As soon as her feet were on the ground, her knees buckled, adrenaline taking hold. Fell had just saved her life. She'd just escaped death.

Alley-oop, indeed.

Fell materialised into the boy she knew, and happiness made her lightheaded; she clapped her hands to her mouth, but a squeal still slipped through. He looked better than when she'd last seen him; she hadn't realised how sick he'd gotten until she saw this *before* picture again. She threw her arms around his neck, embracing his coldness, her heart full to bursting at seeing him again. Fell's arms wrapped around her in return. She closed her eyes and smiled.

Her friend was back.

She pulled away. 'Are you feeling better?'

'Yes,' he replied. 'Much better, but it won't last forever. If I'm going to go after Seki, it must be now.'

'It might already be too late. Seki has his army ready to go, and he has Leo's sceptre as well.'

'It is never too late.' He extended his arms, waiting for permission.

Gerdie nodded, allowing Fell to scoop her up, and the world fell away in a blur of white. She felt weightless and dizzy again as Fell zoomed them away. They stopped a few seconds later in what had to be one of the palace's rooms: grand stone columns in every corner, a large stained-glass window depicting some kind of scene she couldn't quite make out, and marble floors inlaid with dirty gold. Gerdie ran to the nearest window and stood on the tips of her toes to peer through the glass.

Destruction was outside.

One automaton, huge and alive, was knocking down buildings and shooting flames. In the distance, she could just make out the other automatons, marching away. They would probably be going to Rendip, and Mallincroft, and countless other innocent towns who had no idea what was coming.

She only needed to get to one.

According to the blueprints, the automatons worked as a hive mind; the key only needed to be inserted into one, and all of them would come to life – Graphensilk was powerful enough to charge all the automatons from a single source. Take the key out, and all would fall back to sleep. *Simple*, she thought faintly. Even getting near one would be dangerous, let alone having to try and climb it without it noticing and try to shake her off, assuming they had some kind of defense mechanism.

Fell tugged at her sleeve, and she turned away from the window. His face was grave.

'What is it?' she whispered.

'It is time,' he said. 'For me to confront Seki. To stop him.'

'How will you find him?' she asked quietly.

'It will not be hard. He wants me, he'll be looking for me. He thinks he can take my power.'

'And can he?'

'Yes.'

He didn't say it with bitterness or regret. It was just a fact. Still, it made Gerdie's stomach lurch.

'Seki has the ability to absorb my power and make it his own. But I won't let that happen.'

She wanted to believe him, but if just being in Seki's city was enough to drain him of energy, what would happen if he was close enough to touch? Gerdie shook the thought away and hugged Fell one last time. As she pulled away, she whispered, 'Be careful.'

He nodded once, then ran from the room. Gerdie gave a last glance at the automaton before hurrying after him.

i kNoW You hAVE reTuRNed
BuT It Is tOo lAte
MY rEiGN of destrUCtiOn bEgINs AGAin

TWENTY

As Gerdie disappeared out the prison door, Leo broke down. He curled up on the small hard bed, tears flowing down his cheeks and quickly dampening the pillow. Air was too limited, he couldn't get enough of it, gasping as sobs racked his body.

When the tears finally stopped, a state of numbness crept through his limbs. He didn't think he could move even if he wanted to. All he could think about was Gerdie... His only friend, gone.

He must have exhausted himself to sleep because the next thing he knew, something woke him. He sat up, straining his eyes in the dark. A muffled boom shook the walls of his cell, making every nerve in his body prickle with tension. Once things quietened again, he realised that wasn't what had woken him. A shadow moved through the bars of the cell door and Leo froze. Had Seki ordered someone to slip in and kill him in the night? Get rid of him quickly and easily, with no one else around to know he was gone?

Softly and slowly, as if whoever it was didn't want to be heard, the lock clicked, and the door swung silently inward. The figure slipped inside the cell, closing the door behind them without locking it again.

Leo's heart pounded in his ears. He grabbed the pillow and hoisted it to his shoulder, ready to swing – it wasn't much by way of a weapon, but it was all he had. The door wasn't locked now, if he could just hop out and close it behind him, locking the intruder inside...

He braced himself as the figure came closer, bringing the scent of sweat and, faintly, soap. The figure was a familiar bony shape.

The pillow loosened in Leo's fingers for an instant before he quickly tightened his grip again. 'What are you doing here?' he hissed.

Hadrian stopped, as if surprised to find Leo awake. He moved slowly, like he was approaching a wild animal, lowering himself onto the end of the bed. Leo could just make out his raised hands. He obviously meant no harm, but Leo kept hold of the pillow.

'Leo, I...' The words came out as a croak. Hadrian cleared his throat and tried again. 'I just wanted to say I'm sorry. I'm so sorry.'

Leo lowered the pillow, replacing it behind him. 'You got what you wanted. What are you doing here? Rubbing it in?'

'No. I –' There was a scratching sound as Hadrian scrubbed his hands through his hair. 'I needed to talk to you. To see you.' He lowered his hands, reaching into his pocket. With a *click*, a lighter flared between them.

The sudden glow made Leo's eyes burn, along with the lingering gumminess of old tears, but the sting was soon forgotten as he saw Hadrian's face. The flickering orange light threw the already sharp angles of his face into relief, the deep bags under his eyes, the downward curve of his mouth.

Hadrian looked awful, and Leo didn't know why he should care, his heart ached at the misery written over Hadrian's face, and longed to throw his arms around him.

When Hadrian didn't speak right away, keeping his eyes downcast, Leo asked, even though he didn't want to know the answer: 'What's going on with the automatons?'

Hadrian glanced up at him, looking surprised that he had asked. 'Seki started them.'

As if to prove his words, another muffled *boom* sounded from outside. The wall light fixtures shook, and there were murmurs from the other prisoners. Leo's mouth went dry. That was it, then. It was all over.

Hadrian twisted his hands in his lap.

'Why did you do it?'

Hadrian's hands stilled, but he kept his eyes lowered. 'You'll hate me.'

'You already put me in a prison cell,' Leo said. 'You said you wanted to talk, so talk.'

Hadrian sighed. 'Fifteen years ago, a comet crashed on Treshane. Took human form.'

Another one? It made Leo's head spin, wondering how many comets were wandering around Treshane in human form.

'My mother found him and took him in. They had a lot in common, if you can believe it. A human and a ball of... energy, I guess. Ice and rock. They fell in love, had plans to conserve what remained of nature, and restore what they could.'

'Was this...' Leo paused, hardly believing what he was about to ask.

Hadrian saved him the trouble. 'The comet was my dad, yeah.'

Leo opened his mouth without knowing what he was going to say. It seemed impossible. But he had been exposed to many impossible things lately. 'So, you...'

Hadrian shuffled back on the bed so that he could lean against the wall. Leo watched him, trying to see him in a different light, searching for traces of... what? Star? Space? Hadrian was already something extraordinary to Leo, despite everything he'd done.

'It's why I get those bouts of sickness. It's not... natural, what I am. My body can't handle it. I feel it inside me, trying to get out.' He swallowed. 'I was so, so angry when I found out. Like, more angry than usual. Mum didn't tell me the truth about me until dad died. Seki found out about him, about how he was a different kind of energy to Seki. Someone harmonious and good, and therefore a threat to Seki's reign.' Hadrian swallowed. 'That's why he had Dad killed.'

Leo moved to sit beside him, shoulder to shoulder, his back against the cold of the stone cell. 'Then what made you join him?'

'I didn't mean to at first.' Hadrian's hand twitched against his thigh. 'I had plans of joining the resistance. I wanted revenge on Seki, I wanted answers, I wanted –' He cut himself off with a sigh. 'I didn't know what I wanted. All I knew is that I'd felt different from everyone else my whole life. I still do. And I needed to leave. I was so angry with Mum for not telling me the truth. I blamed her for what happened to Dad.'

'It wasn't her fault,' Leo said quietly.

'I know that,' Hadrian snapped.

'Why did you want the sceptre?'

He heard Hadrian swallow. 'There's something you don't know about the sceptre.'

'What do you mean?'

Hadrian turned his head toward Leo. His eyes were just a gleam in the darkness. 'Didn't you ever wonder what it meant to have the sceptre restored and Seki destroyed?'

Of course he had thought about it. It didn't seem enough to just get his hands on the sceptre and physically return it to its rightful place. It also didn't sound like Seki to give up the throne so easily if Leo was to show him he had the sceptre.

'The sceptre is also a sword, forged from Melia root. It can destroy a comet in human form. Draw it out from the inside.'

'Oh...' Leo breathed. His mother had taught him about Melia, a type of rare tree native to Bellona. Mother had always said its roots held magic and power, but he thought she'd meant in the way all nature holds magic. He shifted uncomfortably, feeling stupid that Hadrian knew this when he didn't. What must he think of Leo, who was supposed to be the rightful wielder and didn't even know what it was made of?

It dawned on him. 'That's why you wanted it? To destroy the comet inside you? Won't that... kill you?'

'I... don't know,' Hadrian admitted. 'But I have to try. I can't live like this anymore, Leo.' His voice cracked. 'I can't.'

'It's okay,' Leo said, even though it wasn't, even though the world was literally falling apart outside, and his friend just admitted he was half-comet and possibly dying. Another rumble made the wall shake behind him. He rubbed hard at his face as more booms echoed from outside, taking his frustration out on himself. He needed to feel pain, it was what he deserved. That was his kingdom out there, his family's sacred duty, and it was being destroyed. All he could do was wait until the prison collapsed, killing him –

No. He wouldn't think like that anymore. Not while there was still a chance to stop Seki.

'I have to get out of here, Hadrian,' he whispered.

'I know. That's why I'm here. I brought you this.' He pulled a club-like thing onto his lap.

A prosthetic. Leo's heart lightened, just a touch.

'Thank you,' he said. As he pulled it on and tightened the straps he asked, 'And the sceptre?'

'I have it,' Hadrian said. 'It's hidden. At mine.'

Leo got up from the bed. Leaving behind the warmth of Hadrian, the solidness of the wall at his back, felt like leaving a cocoon he might have stayed in forever. He had to break out of that cocoon. He was the heir; his time had come to prove it. He stood up, made a final adjustment to the prosthetic, and straightened his shoulders.

'Take me to it,' he said.

As they slipped out of the cell, Leo quietly asked, 'Were there any Actions on duty when you came down?'

'No,' replied Hadrian. 'Once Seki powered up the machines, they scattered.'

'Okay, so we –'

'That you, son?' said a hoarse familiar voice.

'Luca?' Leo asked incredulously. He peered through the bars of the cell the voice had come from, and a dozen pairs of eyes shone back at him. The rounded-up Cats from the old mine.

He turned to Hadrian with a nod at the keys. 'Can you let them out?'

The keys jingled as Hadrian stepped forward, sliding one into the lock.

As soon as the door was opened, a single figure charged and headed straight for Hadrian. There wasn't enough time to react before the figure raised his fist and punched Hadrian in the jaw. As the rest of the Cats leapt forward, Leo recognised who it was: Emmett. Luca slapped a hand on Emmett's shoulder, raising his other hand in Hadrian's direction as if to stop him from coming closer, but there was no danger; Hadrian stayed against the wall where he had stumbled, holding a hand to his jaw. It was the first time Leo had ever seen him *not* fight back.

'It's alright,' he panted. 'I deserved that.'

'Too right, you did,' Emmett snarled, straining under Luca's grip. 'I knew you were a bloody traitor, and I was right. You destroyed our home!'

'We don't have time for this right now,' Leo said, and he saw Luca nod at him in approval. 'Seki has started his automaton army.'

The Cats murmured among themselves. Another boom shook the ceiling, and a few gasps rippled through them.

'It's hopeless, then,' someone said glumly. 'We'll never be able to stop an army like that. It's impossible.'

'Yeah,' Leo agreed. 'It's impossible. But that doesn't mean we're not going to try.'

A few heads raised, their gazes intent. Leo swallowed as the attention turned completely on him, but he continued. 'We must fight. We can't just hide here while our country is destroyed. That's not an option. I'm as scared as you are. I've been scared for most of my life, but I don't want to be anymore. You've been fighting for a long time, mostly on my behalf. I appreciate that. I'm asking you to fight for just a little bit longer.'

The Cats' expressions turned hopeful, even with more explosions shaking the walls, and it strengthened Leo's voice as he said, 'Seki has taken enough from us already.' He gestured to his prosthetic, shared by so many others. 'I used to think this made me different, made me weaker. But now I see that it unites us.'

The Cats yelled their approval and agreement, and he even caught a 'Hear, hear!'

'There is hope. We have the sceptre,' Leo said with a glance at Hadrian.

'This is what we've always wanted, Cats,' Luca said, stepping forward to stand by Leo's side. 'A chance to come out of the shadows, to strike one final time without our faces hidden. Let's show Seki that he can take our homes, our friends, our bodies, but he can't take our spirit.'

The Cats roared, and Leo's skin prickled with anticipation at what they were about to do. He had no time to second guess anything, though, because Luca led the charge out of the prison. Leo went to follow when someone tugged at his sleeve. A boy of about twelve gazed up at him with round eyes, mouth hanging open.

'Are you really the prince?'

Leo glanced around, but no one was hanging back for the boy. 'Um... yes.'

'Wow,' the boy breathed, with absolutely no sense of urgency. 'You're going to be able to do so many great things. I wish I could be like you.'

'W-what?'

The little boy ran off to join the rest of the Cats, leaving Leo stunned. There was no taunt in the boy's eyes. What he said was true. Was Leo someone that others envied? His own head, for years, had been filled with *I wish I was more like Gerdie, I wish I was more like my parents*. Heck, he'd even wished he was more like a fictional character from *Earth Ever After*. It never occurred to him that one day someone would be thinking those thoughts about *him*. If that boy knew what Leo's life had been like up until this moment, would he still wish for it? He realised, like a torch illuminating a dark room, that comparisons were pointless, a waste of time. Everyone was given only one life. And it was up to you to make the best of it.

AhhHhHHh, TherE yoU aRe
noT as WEAk As i ThoUghT
nO maTtER
i WiLL dEStrOy YOu noW
tHis pLAnEt IS MINe
i HAVe WorkEd ToO haRD

so hard, perhaps
that you've used up all your power
this planet deserves more than you

aND wHo Do YOu tHINk yoU aRe, liTtLE oNE?
Did tHe sO-CalLeD grEAt COmeTs sEnD You?

yes, they did
and i will fight for this planet

I Am DonE
TalKIng

Carnage met them when they poured out of the palace and into the car park. The automatons, switched on and alive, the ground shaking beneath Leo's feet. Their movements were slow, like they were still getting used to their new heavy bodies. It was one thing to see them stationary, but watching them move, weapons come to life, was the most terrifying thing he'd ever seen. He faltered, fear freezing his limbs. A streak of red brought him back: Gerdie, streaming across the concrete towards the nearest automaton. *Alive.* Relief made his knees weak, his head light. She was followed by an older woman who seemed familiar... With a jolt, Leo recognised Hadrian's mother, Ada Hatch, hot on Gerdie's heels. *What the heck happened?* He didn't have time to wonder, but whatever it was, he was glad it happened. A tugging on his arm made him tear his eyes away.

'Come on,' Hadrian said. 'It's this way.'

'Wait, what about the Cats?'

'Don't worry about us, son,' Luca said. 'We'll slow them down as best we can.'

'Guns are through there, to the left.' Hadrian pointed to a small shed to one side. 'It's unlocked. Seki loves the idea of weapons for the taking.'

'Luca,' Leo said, 'take what you can, do what you can. Maybe those things can be hacked to pieces. Just keep them busy until I can get back.'

'You got it,' Luca said, and he led the charge to the weapons shed.

Leo followed Hadrian around the other side of the palace. The automatons were moving east, so the area of the city behind the palace was untouched. For now.

There was a row of townhouses not unlike what Leo lived in with Peller, only these ones were much newer and in better condition. Even now, Leo couldn't help but feel bitter about the state of the quarry suburbs houses. Hadrian leapt up the front steps of one, white-bricked with brass lanterns on either side of the glossy black door, and went inside, Leo close behind.

The interior was a different story to the neat exterior.

The front door opened onto a small room with no furniture. Small holes, the size of a fist, made for hostile decoration at random intervals along the walls. A makeshift bed was set up in one corner, made up of dirty coats and a few stained cushions. A kitchen was through an open door to one side, the counters stained, and he assumed the bathroom was behind the other door.

'This is where you live?'

'Yeah,' Hadrian said, shoulder heaving as he pulled a locked metal box out from under the coats. 'Seki gave it to me after I ran away from home.'

Leo completed his slow revolution, taking in the corner of the ceiling that was leaking into a bucket, the stacks of canned vegetables with a piece of cardboard balanced on top, serving as a table.

'Hadrian...'

'Yeah, I know,' he said shortly, sliding a key into the lock. 'It's fine, okay? I made my choice.'

Leo knelt beside him as Hadrian lifted the lid of the metal box, revealing the sceptre inside. Leo's heart constricted as if the sceptre had reached out and plunged itself into his chest. It looked ethereal in this grey, squalid space. Gold wand shining like it had only just been made, prongs twisting together to meet at the top, creating a decorative nest for the large blue-green gem.

'How did you get it from Seki?' Leo breathed.

'He was too distracted by the automatons,' Hadrian said. 'He hid it in his room, just not very well.' He lifted it from the box and turned to Leo, hesitating before Leo could take it.

'What if...' Hadrian said, slow and quiet. 'What if we just...go?'

Go to the palace with the sceptre... wasn't that the idea? Yet Hadrian's grip remained tight on the sceptre, making Leo's fingers twitch with unease. At Leo's quizzical expression, Hadrian continued, 'Let's just leave. Go far away while we still can, just you and me in a brand-new world.'

'A brand-new world?' Leo repeated, with vehemence that surprised even himself. Anger erupted inside him, flaring like a lit match. Realisation cut him through—he was tired of running away. From fleeing Courtoff and the automaton, to abandoning his responsibility to his family. *No more.*

'And where would we go?' Leo said harshly. 'You think Seki will stop at Treshane? He'll destroy *everything* he can, whether it's this planet or another one. Look at Earth. Look at Mars. Stay, or run away, do whatever you want, but I'm finishing this, and I'm finishing it now.'

He got to his feet and grabbed the sceptre from Hadrian's unresisting hands. Hadrian's wide hazel eyes swam with a hurt Leo knew well. He gazed up at Leo, pleading for...what?

Understanding? Forgiveness? This is how Leo must have looked back in the outskirts of Balthasar, when Gerdie was leaving with Fell and inviting him, in vain, to go with her.

I don't understand why you're so reluctant to make change happen sometimes.

Leo finished her words as he made for the door. 'We could do this, you know. And I will, even if you won't.'

Hadrian remained rooted to the ground, but Leo didn't have time to wait for his answer. He gripped the sceptre with both hands, the metal cool against his palms, closing the door behind him as he walked out.

TWENTY-ONE

The courtyard was in chaos; people screaming and running like disturbed ants, the ground shaking like an earthquake, and the grinding metal of the automatons' joints made Gerdie's teeth hurt – she felt it more than she heard it. The air rippled with the heat of their fire-blasters, several homes already blazing. She hoped no one had been inside. She glanced behind her for Ada, but Ada had already disappeared in the confusion.

Gerdie frantically scanned the closest automatons, tripping over debris as she moved around for a better look. Even in her panic, she couldn't help but be impressed by the automatons, but it was strange knowing that her father helped to invent them, and no one could deny he had been good at what he did.

She slid behind a mound of loose bricks as another tremor shook the ground, trying to catch her breath. The automatons were slow, but their sheer height meant they covered a lot of ground quickly. A bright flash of light shot from the palace and took to the sky, a comet's trail streaming behind it. Gerdie watched as it circled around one of the palace towers. It was followed by a second ball of light, this one the red of copper in the setting sun. Could a ball of light be too heavy? This one certainly looked it; it wobbled and dipped, moving sluggishly like a car sputtering out of petrol.

Fell appeared light, airy, and natural. The same effect that the plants and trees had. Seki looked dirty and sick, reminding her of the factories, of those fat lazy flies you could never seem to swat. Nature and machines.

Harmony and chaos.

Even as much as he struggled to catch Fell in the air, she knew better than to underestimate Conqueror Seki, especially as, albeit smaller version of, the Death Comet. *Please, Fell. Be enough to take him down.*

A whining sound drew her attention – an automaton had turned in her direction, and glinting in the sunrise was the reddish-gold of her coin in the middle of its chest. Hardly believing her luck, she jumped over the fallen pile of bricks and ran for the automaton.

Gunshots sounded and Gerdie ducked, thinking Actions had recognised her. As she whirled around, the Cats streamed toward her and the automaton. They seemed unafraid to be so close to its massive feet that could squash them and not even notice until it was cleaning the bottoms of them later. With its covering of Kolimant, the automaton was immune to their bullets. The only way to stop it was to take out the key. She spotted Luca, a large gun hoisted on his shoulder, aimed high. Bullets *ping ping*ed off the automaton.

'Luca!' she shouted.

He lowered the gun and peered around, weathered face breaking into a grin as he recognised her.

'It won't work!' she yelled over the din. She waved a hand at the other Cats, each with weapons. 'Tell them to stop shooting at that one and let me handle it. Help the people in the city!'

He nodded his understanding, then called out to the others. Bullets stopped ricocheting off the automaton. The automaton had bent to pick up a particularly large piece of glass from a shattered palace window, and Gerdie quickened her pace, seeing her chance. Her lungs burned at the effort, but she didn't dare stop. She was so close.

The automaton was already starting to rise, lifting the arms she'd wanted to jump on. They would take her close to the middle of the automaton's chest, where the coin would be.

Just... don't think about it too much.

She took a deep breath and sprinted.

Grooves along the automaton's metal arms made for easy gripping, but it took all her strength to hoist her lower body up after her. Her finger pinched between a gap, and she wrenched it free with a gasp, eyes watering. The arm she clung to fired off a shot, and the force of it knocked her into the air, her whole body vibrating. She hit the ground and rolled, coming to a stop on her back. The impact of the shot boomed somewhere to her right. When she opened her eyes, two large balls of light circled each other, one glowing a soft white and yellow as it zoomed gracefully around, dodging the attacks of the other: an angry red light, its edges looking sharp and scratchy as it moved erratically this way and that. With a burst of energy that surprised her, the red light shot forward and knocked the white to the ground. Red fell on top of it, swallowing the white entirely.

No. No, Fell! Before she could move, the white light pulsed blindingly bright, pushing the red back, and they were both zooming through the air again.

Gerdie pushed herself gingerly to her feet, pain shooting through her shoulder and down her arm. She waited for the wave of dizziness to pass. The automaton turned its attention toward a line of shops, but had not gotten far yet. She had to move.

Jogging through the pain in her arm, she made for the automaton again, and this time, she wouldn't fall.

DId tHAt huRt, Little OnE?

no.

ARE you SuRe? it'S a LONG way tO fall

*you are crumpled and crooked
a boulder beaten by too many waves
a rock chipped by its tumble down the mountain.*

tHAt'S a Lie. I am sTrong. i aM POweR

then what use have you of me?

*YoU Have poweR, littLe one. I can Feel iT. LET Me takE it
FrOM yOu anD I MigHt lET yoU liVe.*

The automaton was constantly moving, heavy and measured. Destructive and strong, yes, but slow.

She couldn't wait for an opportunity like lowered arms again; she darted forward, skidding to a stop when a massive foot came down, making her stumble. The other foot was already rising, *run, run, run,* and she was on the automaton's foot.

When it lifted beneath her, her stomach disappeared, left behind on ground which was now about ten feet away, her hair pushed back from her face. When the foot came back down, it jolted her so much, her teeth clacked together. She soon found a rhythm, climbing in time with the automaton's steps. Her movements were measured even though adrenaline was screaming at her to move faster and that there wasn't time for her to take any care. This might be her only chance. She didn't have time to take risks. As she reached the automaton's hip and adjusted her grip so that her fingers wouldn't be crushed as it moved, a horrible smell reached her nostrils.

Gas.

Great. Thoughts of the automaton suddenly exploding flooded her brain and she picked up her pace despite the burn in her shoulder and limbs. *Think of the key, think of the key.* She imagined her hand reaching for it, because if you tell yourself something enough eventually it will become true.

Gerdie reached just under the automaton's chest, clinging to grooves in its stomach. Hot air singed her back as fire blasted from one of the arms.

Gleaming in the middle of the chest was her coin. Her heart skipped a beat to see it, so familiar. Dad. Home. Amongst this chaos.

Her heart pounded as she stretched out her hand, wrapping her fingers around the coin, it shifted under her grip, loosening –

The automaton made a sudden move, and she slipped, stomach dropping to somewhere near her feet. Sweat streamed down her face, stinging her eyes. She just managed to hold on, righted herself, ready to reach again for the coin, when the automaton moved again, and she was sliding down the arm without a way to stop herself. If she only had the M.O.R.T. with her, she could throw him, have him bridge that distance and remove the key.

But she didn't have the M.O.R.T., she only had herself, and it was going to have to be enough.

You are enough. You are enough.

She only had one shot. Gerdie planted her feet in the

automaton's elbow joint and launched herself onto its chest. She hooked her fingers under the key again and it slid free.

Then she was falling.

She hit the ground on her back, hard, and it knocked the breath out of her. She couldn't breathe, her body seized up – fighting for air, but the automaton's foot was coming down toward her, her swimming vision making the bottom of it look wobbly. It didn't matter that she couldn't breathe, that she might have broken her back: this was how she would die, squashed to death by a giant's metal foot. That weird wheezing sound was coming from her own mouth. Forcing air into her lungs, but she still couldn't make herself move. All she could do was watch that metal foot loom toward her. She squeezed her eyes shut. She didn't want to see her own death approaching.

Gerdie kept them closed, waiting. It took a very long time to be squashed. The foot should have come down by now. She opened one eye, just a crack. The foot had stopped, hovering just above her. She opened her other eye. Her lungs burned and she sucked in a ragged breath, lungs complaining even though they only had this one job.

The automaton was frozen. She waited, heart pounding, but it didn't move. Gerdie had done it. A quick glance around proved the others had stopped as well. She pushed herself to sit up. Something warm tickled her nose and she rubbed a finger beneath it, her skin coming away slick with blood.

An explosion startled her, and she tilted her head back, bloody nose forgotten. A burning ball of light hovered above, darkening the sky as if it sucked up all other light, roiling like an angry storm cloud. The ball of light separated into two, and one came crashing down with a force that shook buildings and vibrated Gerdie's skull, which didn't help her dizziness. Another blinding flash of light, and when she could look again, Seki was there, in gigantic, terrifying human form, breathing hard and surrounded by debris. The second ball of light floated to the ground, graceful as a feather, and Fell materialised. His white-blond hair was messy, and his cheeks were slightly flushed, but he looked okay. He barely took a step when a yell made her turn.

Hadrian Hatch ran at Seki, a golden sword raised above his head. With his wide hazel eyes crazed and teeth bared, he looked nothing like the gentle boy Gerdie met in the underground mine. He just about reached Seki when he swung the sword down, ready to jab forward and into Seki's heart. Although Seki was injured and tired, he was still strong. His hand shot up before Hadrian could pierce his chest, gripping the boy's wrist so hard he was able to lift Hadrian from the ground. Seki's other hand made a fist and buried itself in Hadrian's stomach, sending him flying backwards like he'd been hit by a train. He'd dropped the sword at Seki's feet, and Seki scooped it up, walking purposefully toward Hadrian.

Fell took a step. 'Seki, no!'

Hadrian scrambled backward, unable to get his feet under him enough to stand. Gerdie could see what was about to happen, playing out like a movie she might have seen before, but she was powerless to stop it.

'Foolish boy,' Seki said, resting the tip of the sword on Hadrian's heaving chest, finally stilling him. 'I gave you everything. Everything you wanted in your pathetic existence.'

'You gave me nothing,' Hadrian snarled, 'but self-doubt, and the belief that I was something unnatural. You –'

He never finished his sentence.

Seki pressed the blade to Hadrian's chest, and it went through him, smoother than silk. The blade, where it wasn't covered in blood, looked like it was glowing, catching the sun with surprising brightness, setting Hadrian's chest aglow as well. He made a horrible, horrible sound that made Gerdie's own skin prickle. Blood bloomed around the blade, seeping fast across his shirt, so fast, too fast. Hadrian made a final awful, choked sound, eyes fluttering closed.

Seki pulled the sword free, and Hadrian's body spasmed as the movement jerked his body, like a doll discarded by a child. A small moan escaped his lips.

Seki dropped the sword. It clattered on the stone and into Hadrian's pooling blood; he turned to Fell.

'*Hadrian!*'

Leo sprinted into view, dropping by Hadrian's side, hands fluttering around his body like the moths that followed Fell.

'*NO!*' Another heart-wrenching cry burst out. Ada shot out of nowhere, dropping to her knees beside Hadrian. She pulled his head onto her lap, her tears falling fast as she stroked Hadrian's face, his hair, his shoulders.

Gerdie got shakily to her feet and ran over as well. Hadrian was still alive, his breathing rapid and shallow.

'Leo, what's going on?' Gerdie asked, her voice trembling. 'What was he talking about? He knows Seki?'

'This is the sceptre,' Leo said through his tears, waving a hand feebly toward the gold sword, still lying on the stones beside them. 'It's meant to burn out the comet inside a human. Hadrian has comet in him, too, but I think the sword was too strong, and oh, Angels. It didn't work.' His voice broke. 'It didn't work.' Then, quietly as if to himself, 'He was too human.'

'No,' Hadrian whispered, his breathing wet and ragged. He met Ada's eyes. 'It... did work. I am still... free.'

He closed his eyes, his hand turning limp in Leo's.

Ada let out a wail that pierced Gerdie's heart like a knife, dropping her forehead onto Hadrian's. Leo seemed to fold in on himself, sinking into the ground like his bones had disappeared and she feared he would melt away. Suddenly, like molten steel being tempered, his body hardened, his hands began to shake, and when he raised his head, there was only hatred in his eyes.

The terror that squeezed her heart was stronger than any she'd felt from the automatons. She'd seen fear, gentleness, curiosity in those beautiful eyes. She'd seen sadness and uncertainty.

Never hate.

Leo picked up the sword and raised it, either unaware or not caring that it was slick with Hadrian's blood, and charged at Seki with a roar. Gerdie leaped to her feet – he had to be stopped, Seki would kill him, and she couldn't lose Leo, not like this...

Seki must have heard him, but he didn't turn around, and somehow that was more terrifying. He was planning something, it seemed, waiting for something.

As Leo neared, Seki raised his hand. Gerdie screamed Leo's name and Fell lunged forward. A ball of light burst from his hand and hit Seki in the chest. It only made Seki stumble, but it was enough of a distraction for Leo to reach Seki and plunge the blade into his stomach.

Leo used both hands to push the sword into Seki's massive bulk, his arms trembling with the effort. They stared into each other's eyes, Seki's bulging, and it was so intense she felt like she should look away lest she burned. Seki's stomach around the blade began to glow, as it had with Hadrian, the same red light as his comet-form. The blade glowed that colour too, as it drew out Seki's celestial power like a magnet.

Seki's skin turned grey, and he seemed to be shrinking, shriveling as the sword took the life from him. She saw Leo's lips move, speaking words too low for anyone but Seki to hear.

Seki was nothing but a husk, an empty bellows, the sword glowing with all his power, his malice, his cruelty, his chaos. Leo pulled the sword free, but Seki was already dead. He crumpled to the ground as Leo stumbled back.

The world was quiet.

A roar of cheers erupted from the Cats, exploding like a blocked machine. They rushed over, swamping Leo in shouts, laughing, claps on the back until he disappeared under the swarm. A smile tugged at the corner of Gerdie's mouth, but she couldn't let it out, not with Ada and Hadrian behind her.

Someone sidled quietly up beside her, and when she turned to him, tears filled her eyes, tears of exhaustion, of relief, of happiness. She threw her arms around Fell, ignoring the pain that shot through her side at the movement, pressing her face into his cold neck. His arms wrapped around her with surprising strength, but after watching him as a ball of light for the past hour she was glad to have him solid again.

'What happens now?' she whispered.

'To Bellona?'

'To you.'

'Seki is gone,' he said. 'I have completed my purpose. There is nothing left for me here.'

She pulled back to look into his bright blue eyes. 'Really? Nothing?'

He gave her a sad smile. 'This is not my world.'

'You could make it your world.'

Fell shook his head, raising his eyes to the sky like he couldn't help himself. He looked older, suddenly, like he'd aged five years since the day she found him on the ground at Odds and Ends – had it only been a week ago? Maybe it wasn't him who had changed. Maybe it was her. She could finally see him for what he was – stardust and magic and infinity.

His eyes lowered and caught something over her shoulder, and he stepped back with a smile. Gerdie turned and was immediately scooped into Leo's hug.

She squeezed him back and whispered, 'I'm proud of you.'

'I couldn't have done it without you,' he said, pulling back. 'Any of it.'

'Pshaw,' she said, and went to lightly punch his shoulder when her arm seared with pain again, tears springing to her eyes. 'Ow.'

Leo snapped to attention. 'You need that arm taken care of, it looks dislocated. The Cats have already started to treat the injured or take people to the hospital. Luca's over there,' he said, pointing. 'Will you be okay? I should...' He trailed off, glancing behind Gerdie.

She nodded, and Leo strode off.

Gerdie made to start forward, then paused. 'Fell?' she asked, and her voice sounded small. She wasn't ready to say goodbye just yet.

He smiled and came to her side, his nod seeming to say, *Just for a little while.*

TWENTY-TWO

So much of New Londinium was destroyed: buildings reduced to nothing but rubble or piles of ash. Two oxygen turbines had been knocked down by cannons from the automatons, the green and brown of their blades lying still.

Those who had escaped their homes and businesses slowly emerged once the world had quietened, and now they gathered in the ruined courtyard and spilled out onto the street, some looking scared, others joyful that Seki's chaotic reign was over at last. A few awkwardly started making piles of brick and rubble, unsure of what to do next. Gerdie included, since her shoulder was patched up quickly and she was desperate to do *something*, fingers twirling in her lap. But Leo wanted everyone to eat first.

The palace staff were all too happy to follow Leo's instructions. Gerdie, Leo, Fell, Ada, the Cats, and a few others Gerdie didn't recognise packed into the hall, eating with their fingers and sitting on the ground because there weren't nearly enough seats. Seki didn't entertain much. It was a bit like being amongst the community in the quarry, but on a much larger scale. Proof that Seki had been the one keeping them apart. Now that he was gone, Treshane was whole again.

Gerdie and Leo took their plates into a corner and Fell followed. Apart from the awed glances in their direction, and the occasional person coming over to shake Leo's hand, they were left alone.

'This food is delicious,' Gerdie said. The fruits and vegetables on her plate were fresh, grown from the greenhouses in New Londinium, which had thankfully survived the automatons' attacks. 'My plate is like a rainbow. I've never even *seen* this green one before. I don't know what it's called but I like it. Leo, have you tried it?'

Leo was staring at his plate and didn't look up until Gerdie repeated his name.

'Hm? Oh, sorry.'

Gerdie lowered her fork. 'You okay?'

'Yeah,' he said, but his voice was gruff, like he had something stuck in his throat.

'I've been meaning to ask...What did you say to him?'

'To who?'

'To Seki. When you...when...I saw you say something to him.'

He gave her a grim smile. 'I told him "this is for my family".'

'They would be so proud of you, Leo.'

'Thanks.' He put down his plate, food still untouched, and turned to Fell. 'What will you do now, Fell?'

Gerdie's stomach did a back flip; she didn't want to talk about that. She'd almost hoped that if no one mentioned Fell leaving, then Fell would forget it was something he wanted to do.

'I will be returning to the Merten Cloud,' he said serenely. 'Home. I believe Treshane is in good hands now.'

Leo smiled, and this time the look in his eyes matched. 'Thank you. For everything.'

Fell inclined his head, then his eyes found Gerdie's. Shining in the blue, like a miniature galaxy, a myriad of emotions.

The food she had been enjoying just moments ago suddenly tasted bitter in her mouth. 'Right now?'

'I have to go,' he said gently, and got to his feet, leaving no more room for argument.

A warm hand touched her shoulder. 'Gerdie...' Leo said gently. 'You know he doesn't belong here.'

Gerdie pushed her plate to one side and stood up. With a glance at Leo, who nodded in encouragement, she followed Fell out of the hall and into the courtyard. The sun had disappeared below the horizon, the sky awash with pink and blue. It was quiet but for the gentle *whoosh whoosh* of the blades of a still standing oxygen turbine. They stood on the front steps of the palace, the sky open above them.

'I am happy that you were the one to find me. I am happy that you are my friend.'

Gerdie launched herself at him, clutching him tightly as if she could keep him from leaving by sheer strength alone. 'None of this would have happened without you, Fell,' she said. 'You saved us all.'

'No,' he murmured against her shoulder. 'You are brave and strong. A new world has been created because of you.'

Pressure built behind her eyes, and her words were thick when she said, 'I won't forget you.'

'I will never forget you,' he replied. Then, with a quirk of his lips, added, 'Because I am immortal.'

A hysterical laugh bubbled up her throat. 'Wow, I suppose that's true. I guess that means I'll be kind of immortal, huh? That's a really nice thought. As long as there's memory, we all live forever, right?'

'I do not think your story will be forgotten,' said Fell.

He stepped gently out of her arms. His skin started to glow, a blue-white light.

'Wait – What will the moths do without you?'

He gently came apart in little orbs, drifting up to the sky like bubbles, but she still caught his faint smile. 'It is not only creatures with wings who are meant to fly.'

A sob wrenched free from her chest. 'See you later, comet crater.'

Fell was translucent now, lighting the evening around her with his glow. Gerdie kept her eyes on his face, on his small, comforting smile. His voice was almost noiseless as he said, 'In a while, engine dial.'

Then he was gone.

'Goodbye,' she whispered.

The day of Leo's coronation dawned bright and clear a week later, which seemed like a very good omen. Gerdie was filled with such nervous excitement it was as if *she* were the one getting coronated. The promise of food and celebration and all that was one thing, but mostly she was excited because seeing Leo was guaranteed: she'd barely laid eyes on him over the past few days. He would disappear for hours at a time, seeing to this and that during the clean-up of the city. Once everything settled down, she hoped he would have a proper chance to rest and mourn Hadrian.

Gerdie was right at the front of the hall for the ceremony at Leo's request, and she bounced in her seat as the throne room slowly filled with people, swiveling this way and that to scan the other excited faces. She spotted Bryan and Carter Musgrave, the brothers from the quarry who always gave Leo a hard time. They looked sulky, but when she caught Bryan's eye, he gave her a grudging nod, and she returned it. *They'd travelled a long way to be here*, she realised, *to show support for a boy they supposedly didn't respect.* She smiled smugly. Leo had earned their respect. She hoped no one would disrespect him again.

Ada, sitting beside her, placed a warm hand on her knee, and Gerdie spun back around to face her. She'd let Gerdie brush her grey hair this morning and plait it into a long braid down her back. This felt like a brave first step for Ada, whose eyes were still rimmed with red. Gerdie covered Ada's hand with hers and squeezed. They'd been sharing a room in the palace for the past week. Those nights when Ada held her close felt like she had a mother again, and she'd realised that Ada had always been something like that to her. She wanted to be there for Ada, too, now that Hadrian was gone. They might have gained back their country, but they had lost so much in between.

Gerdie's fingers automatically dug into the pocket of her new overalls. The day after Seki was overthrown and Leo started moving into the palace, he found the royal accounts, and while he didn't tell Gerdie exactly how much *ki* Seki was sitting on, she guessed by the dazed look on his face that it was *a lot*. Even the amount he'd given Gerdie for new clothes and food – an advance on her first paycheck, he said – was enough to make her jaw drop. Leo also said he'd be changing the currency from *ki* back to dollars: the currency pre-Seki's reign.

Gerdie's coin wasn't in the pocket, though. Even with Seki gone and the automatons empty shells, it was too risky to have the powerful Graphensilk coin lying around, especially when other inventors knew by now of its existence. She'd thrown it into the Core rather than have it fall into the wrong hands again.

An emerald green carpet lined the aisle between chairs, leading up to the throne at the front of the room, which was flanked by marble pillars, gleaming, freshly polished, in the setting sun. The room was blissfully free from Actions. They were all currently in jail, awaiting retribution.

A hush settled over the room as Leo appeared in the entrance.

He'd been fitted with a new prosthetic, an elaborate twisting of silver with a thick sturdy foot. It was beautiful, and Gerdie marveled at it as he came down the aisle; it wasn't until the leg was level with her that she came to her senses and snapped her eyes upward. Leo was smiling at her, looking amused, but the corners of his mouth wobbled slightly. Nervous, of course. She beamed at him; he was here anyway. Just last week he probably wouldn't have been. She wasn't the only one who had changed.

He came to a stop at the foot of the raised platform that the throne rested on. Luca stood waiting, his dark hair brushed back, face clean-shaven. Leo had appointed him prime minister, replacing Thomas Badbey, who'd had plans to retire. Though Gerdie already knew Luca was a great leader, apparently, he'd known Leo's parents when they were alive, and Luca's family had worked in the palace for generations, his great-grandfather killed alongside Leo's great-grandfather, the king at the time, when Seki threw his coup.

Leo knelt on a cushion, and Luca began a heart-warming speech about how the reign of terror and chaos was over, a new era had begun, and read some official questions about Leo accepting this new responsibility. Leo agreed to everything, repeated the vows to Treshane; that he would work to better the future of the planet and put its inhabitants first. His affirmative voice reached every corner of the huge room. When he'd said everything that needed to be said, he rose and faced the hushed room, and Luca lowered a thin gold crown on his head and placed the glowing sceptre in his hands. Gerdie shivered a little to see it.

'King Leo Catell,' Luca boomed, and the room erupted into cheers and clapping.

Leo nodded in acknowledgement; his smile awkward at the attention but his gaze unwavering. Gerdie raised her hands above her head as she clapped until her palms stung.

'My first act as king,' he said to the crowd once the cheering had finally died down, 'is to appoint Gertrude Sailor as Treshane's chief inventor.'

Gerdie's insides swooped as the crowd clapped and cheered. She stared at Leo in disbelief, and he laughed and beckoned her forward. She did so on shaky legs, her stomach turning flips – that was *a lot* of people. She wanted to keep her eyes downcast, as she noticed a few people in the front rows looking at her birthmark, but despite the stares, everyone was smiling *at her*.

Leo continued, 'It was Gerdie who stopped Seki's automaton army from destroying the entire planet. She has so many amazing ideas on how to make the factories safer places to work, and with her help, Treshane will become a fairer place to live. Besides,' he added, as the cheering died down again, 'we might as well put the parts from the automatons to good use.'

Gerdie beamed at him, mind already turning over all the ways she could use those parts. As she cast a last, embarrassed glance out over the sea of faces, she spotted Mr. Tulk, Mr. Jameson, Mr. Groz, and Mr. Lee from the Inventors' Guild toward the back of the room. They were glaring, sullen, in every direction but hers. Gerdie raised her chin. Finally, they would understand.

She thanked Leo and sank back into her seat next to Ada, cheeks flaming, but unable to wipe the smile from her face. Leo spoke for a little while longer, mostly on further clean-up and rebuilding plans, as well as pardons for the Cats and anyone else that had been considered an enemy to Seki.

Then the party began.

The massive entertaining hall – boarded up during Seki's time – had been cleaned and refurnished even under such short notice, and now boasted long tables creaking under the weight of food platters, with a band set up in one corner playing music that thumped in time with Gerdie's heart, a space in front of them cleared for dancing. Gerdie danced – well, she jumped around a lot – and even managed to drag Leo onto the floor despite his many, *many* protests.

Hours into the night, hot from dancing and breathless from laughing, Gerdie staggered outside and into the cool night air. The heavy palace doors slowly closed behind her, and the revelry inside became a muffled hum. She sat in the middle of the courtyard among the remaining debris and rubble, glad for a moment to catch her breath and her thoughts.

Something tickled her hand, and she lifted it to see. A moth, crossing the back of her wrist on its tiny, delicate feet. Gerdie smiled at it, raising her face to the sky, to where the first of the evening stars were appearing. One twinkling light flashed, brief and bright, almost as if it were winking at her.

Acknowledgments

Made of Steam and Stardust was written on the unceded lands of the Wurundjeri and Noongar peoples, and I pay my respects to their Elders, past, present, and emerging.

I started writing this novel in 2018, so I have a lot of people to thank. It wasn't until I started writing these acknowledgements that I realised how truly blessed I am to be surrounded by so many amazing people. If you've been involved in my writing journey in any way: thank you.

First and foremost, thank you Stag Beetle Books. I wouldn't be writing these acknowledgements without you. Thank you for saying yes and making a dream come true. Secondly, thank *you*, reader, for picking up this book. It means the world to me, and I hope you enjoyed reading it as much as I enjoyed writing it.

Thank you to the Australian Society of Authors; winning the 2021 Award Mentorship for this novel remains a highlight of my career, and your support and expertise has been invaluable. Thank you, Kate Ryan, for being an excellent mentor.

Speaking of mentors, a huge thank you to Sasha Wasley and the 2023 Path to Published group. Your kind words on this novel made me giggle and blush every week and your support kept me going even when it felt hopeless.

Part of this book was written in the UK while on semester exchange and so many of my experiences there are seeped deep into the novel. Thank you to Lancaster University, especially Ines Gregori Labarta and the other students in the Creative

Writing Workshop module; your early feedback helped shape the beginning of the novel into what it is today.

Charlotte and Maddie, you were the best university friends and travel buddies. I will never forget our time spent together and all the writing chats (and thank you for letting me borrow your middle names).

Sarah and Shaun, you are one the best parts of my life. Thank you for everything (including letting me borrow your last names).

I've been lucky enough to work around books for the past few years, which means I'm surrounded by colleagues who *get it*. Thanks to the Robinsons Bookshop crew, especially Amy, Stuart, and Erica. The very first words of this novel were written on a lunch break with your excited faces watching. Thank you to the ladies of The Literature Centre, who were always so supportive, understanding, and put up with a lot of my yapping. Megan, who started as a work buddy and is now one of my closest friends, thank you for feeling like a personal cheerleader in anything I do.

Bridie, for being my best and most supportive friend for longest. Bek, because I know she would be so proud if she saw me now, and influences my work more than anyone will ever know.

Writing communities have been my everything, so thank you to everyone involved in the #LoveOzYA, YA for WA, The YA Room, and WA writing communities, in person or online.

HM Waugh, for being one of my first contacts in the WA writing community, for helping me tighten the first chapter, and just generally being so supportive of this novel.

To the team at Just Write for Kids and their annual Pitch It! Competition; placing third with the pitch for this book in 2020 helped me to think I was on to something, and the feedback from Kate Gordon was so kind and helpful. Thank you for your all your hard work.

Thank you, Nicola, for being such a wonderful and warm member of the Australian YA book community. Your early enthusiasm kept me going.

Scribendi, for some early draft feedback.

Tamara, for being the most wonderful friend and mentor. Your passionate support for this project helped get it here now, and I'm so grateful. Thank you, Louise and Chenée for your support and friendship, too.

Thank you Jes Layton for bringing my characters to life with your beautiful illustrations.

To my loving family, thank you for all your support, even though this journey has been extremely long. Alex, thank you for everything and I'm sorry about my use of the word 'turbine'.

Sian, Chiara, Abbi, Laura, and Deni, thank you for your support and friendship from the other side of the world.

Julie and Jill, from the other *other* side of the world. You're the best writing friends anyone could ask for. Where would I be without you?

And thank you to the rest of my magical online family. If it weren't for you, I'd still be wondering how to get onto the platform.

From the Publisher

Thank you so much for reading Made of Steam and Stardust!

We hope you enjoyed the journey and characters as much as we loved bringing them to you. We'd love for you to leave a review on Amazon and Goodreads while the story is fresh in your mind. Reviews are writing fuel for authors and help their books get into the hands of other hungry readers. If you're a big fan of speculative young adult and middle grade fiction, we invite you to join our street team. Get copies of our books in advance, early access to covers, and other freebies!

Stag Beetle Books
www.stagbeetlebooks.com

9 7 9 8 8 8 9 1 7 0 4 9 5